I0733389

CAPTIVATING MAGIC

The Thorne Witches Book 14

T.M. CROMER

To CJ:
Thanks for all those late-night sprinting sessions. You got me through this project quicker than I'd have done it on my own.

To Monica:
Thanks for always being ready with your editing pen despite my tardiness.

To my beta readers Deb, Lissa, Shannon, and Mark:
You've helped me pull another rabbit out of the hat.

To my Buy Me A Coffee supporters:
Thank you for your continued love and donations. This one is for you!

*L*aszlo Thorne sipped his cappuccino and, with careful precision, placed the mug back on the matching saucer. His bored gaze traveled over the occupants of the coffeehouse with no clear target until a petite, dark-haired woman stepped through the door and captured his attention.

Although vastly different in looks from his sister Liz, the woman possessed the same efficient movement and no-nonsense expression. Not necessarily beautiful, hers was an arresting visage. Heart-shaped with eyes too large for her face. Sun-kissed skin—or perhaps a bit flushed from an exciting experience before she entered the shop—was set off by the close-cropped riot of espresso-colored curls.

Ebba James.

Her name was similar in sound to the famous Etta James, but Ebba didn't possess a lick of talent. In fact, her horrendous singing voice could peel the paint from walls and deafen the already hard of hearing. She was also a giant pain in the ass. A persistent one, at that. This was why Lo found himself sitting there, waiting for her to approach so he could continue with his already jam-packed day.

When she spotted him, a broad smile transformed her face, and Lo sucked in a breath. Therein lay her true beauty. The genuine smile that nearly split her face in half, the pulsing yellow aura, and the barely hidden yearning in her dark chocolate eyes.

Yearning for him.

The sleeping beast inside him woke from a long nap, and an insidious thought crept in. He was no longer a married man, and if Ebba was willing to settle for a few weeks of steamy sex that wouldn't leave her heart bruised when he walked away, they might have some fun.

A foot from the table, she jerked to a stop and stared. "Wow."

Uncertain why she'd expressed surprise, he glanced behind him, then back at her.

"Just wow," she mumbled again, almost to herself.

Realization dawned, and Lo grinned. His desire must be as apparent to Ebba as hers was to him. It wasn't something she was used to receiving from him. Whenever they'd met in the past, he was coolly polite, never allowing himself to look at her as anything but his sister's pesky friend. If he had, his jealous ex, Charlotte, would've lost her shit and clawed the poor woman's eyeballs from her head.

"Ebba."

"Laszlo."

"Call me Lo like everyone else. We both know it's a mouthful."

Her already large eyes flew wide, and color surged into her cheeks. Dear Ebba's mind plunged right into the gutter. The urge to tease her was acute, but he resisted. They needed to get down to business.

Drawing out a chair, he waved a hand. "Have a seat and tell me why you need the services of a paranormal liaison."

"Can I order tea first?" Ebba gestured toward the barista.

"I took the liberty of ordering it for you. And here it is, right on time."

Before he finished speaking, one of the café staff laid a tray with a teapot and two teacups in the center of the table.

"Yorkshire Gold?"

"Yes, Ebba. Yorkshire Gold," he said with exaggerated patience. "Now, can we move this along? I don't have all damned day."

A frown drew her near-black brows together in the middle of her forehead. "You could be nicer, ya know."

"This *is* me being nice. Sit."

"Dick."

Leaning to push her chair forward, he placed his lips next to her exposed ear. "Can't keep your mind from going there, huh?"

"I—"

She was saved from a reply when Laszlo's older brother Wilder stepped up to the table. The warm smile he cast Ebba got under Lo's skin, though he couldn't precisely say why.

"Ebba. It's great to see you again."

"Wilder. I thought you were jet-setting around the world?"

Stark pain came and went in Wilder's eyes, and his expression tightened. "Yeah, well, I'm home for the foreseeable future." He glanced at Lo, and a silent communication traveled between them—one of abject sympathy on Laszlo's part and icy disdain on Wilder's.

Having lost his love during a climbing trip, Wilder had returned a broken man. Miserable and tortured because his magic had failed him when he needed it the most. The timing had coincided with an enemy's attack on the entire Thorne family, resulting in a collective loss of power. A rebuff from

Wilder came when Laszlo couldn't call up Abbie's ghost and give his brother the peace he so desperately craved.

It was only recently that Wilder had begun venturing out for coffee or the occasional social interaction. Whenever their family tried to rally around him and show their support, he rejected their overtures, unprepared to discuss in detail what happened on that mountain.

"Well, I need to get back. Work and all," Wilder said before striding away just short of a run. His demons were always nipping at his heels.

"What happened with your brother, Lo?" Ebba asked, her gaze locked on Wilder's retreating back.

"I'd have thought Liz would've told you."

"No. She keeps family stuff private."

It occurred to him that she might not know his family possessed magical abilities, and it left him scrambling. Covering his disconcertion with another long drink of his cappuccino, he mentally ran through his memories and their previous interactions. They all equated to the same thing.

Ebba didn't know what they were. Liz had never revealed they were a family of powerful witches.

Shit.

"The basics are that my brother and his girlfriend were on a climbing trip, and her rope broke, sending her plummeting down the mountain. They never found her body, though not for lack of trying."

"Ohmygod! Poor Wilder! Poor Abigail!" Tears brimmed in Ebba's large eyes. "I met her once and remember thinking they were so perfect together."

"Yeah." Lo shook off the horror of the incident as best he could. Still, as one who could actually see and speak to ghosts, he found it difficult to dismiss the fact that Wilder's girlfriend had never attempted to make contact after passing away. Loved ones *always* sought to connect.

"Have you… uh, well, done your psychic thing for him?"

He narrowed his eyes. "What exactly do you think you know about me and what I do, Ebba?"

"With your success rate and by all the positive Google reviews, I thought you were able to, you know, talk to the dead."

Fuck!

"All the positive Google reviews?" he asked, dread weighing down his heart.

She nodded. "There's all sorts of testimonials in favor of your work."

"I see."

Outside, he maintained a calm façade, but on the inside, he was a bubbling cauldron of panic. Over the years, he'd kept what he could do under wraps as much as possible, yet somehow, news of his ability had leaked to the internet. More and more people would be seeking him out soon.

"Am I wrong, Lo?"

"Not really, but it's not as basic as people believe."

"How so?"

Hoping to ease his irritation, he rubbed the back of his neck and glanced around the coffeehouse. Gauging the distance between tables and exactly how much could be overheard, he decided a conversation muffler was necessary for what he needed to tell her.

"*Sonus distorquere,*" he murmured.

"What?"

"It's Latin, and I'm distorting our conversation so others can't hear us."

"*Oh*-kayyyy." Ebba laughed.

He answered her amused look with an unblinking stare.

Her eyes widened. "You're serious. You think you can distort conversations?"

"I don't *think*, Ebba. I *know*."

"You're *not* a wizard, Harry," she teased, altering the famous quote. When he didn't crack a smile, she repeated it. Slower, as if talking to a patient in a mental ward.

His irritation ratcheted up, and he curbed the desire to snap at her. Never before had he revealed what he was, but if he'd given any consideration to the matter prior to that moment, he'd have done it differently. Offered her proof of some sort.

"No. I'm a warlock, or perhaps you might've heard the term male witch."

Her expression turned incredulous, and she eased sideways in her chair. Lo was positive she wasn't aware of her instinctive move, but he'd been expecting it.

"You're trying to prank me, right?" The wobble in her tone revealed her nervousness, but also a tiny bit of hurt. Any annoyance he'd felt fled in the face of her deeper emotions.

"No, ma'am, I'm not." He clasped her hand and held tight when she tried to draw it back. "Magic exists in everyday life, and I'm not talking about Wiccan practitioners or Paganism. I'm talking actual magic—manifestations, conjurings, spells."

"You're cracked in the head!"

He suppressed a satisfied smirk as he waited. Any second, she'd realize her overly loud exclamation had never reached the ears of those around them.

She frowned.

His brows shot up, and he couldn't prevent his smug smile.

With new eyes, she studied their surroundings. Opening her mouth, Ebba screamed loud enough to give him tinnitus for life and have would-be heroes charging to her rescue.

If they could hear her.

No one responded.

"They can't hear me? None of them?" Her vocal tremble was telling.

"Ebba. Take a deep breath and remember who I am. Who

my sister is. You've known our family your entire life, and we've never sought to harm you or anyone else," he said soothingly.

Her gaze snapped to his, and a smidgeon of anxiety eased from her face. Her frown deepened as she looked down at their joined hands. "Will you let go of me, please?"

"I will if you promise to hear me out and not run away."

"I promise," she agreed, but her hands shook, and Lo had only minutes to convince her she was safe.

EBBA DIDN'T KNOW WHAT THE HELL TO THINK. HER bloodcurdling scream was thrasher movie-worthy and the sort that brought people running or, at the very least, turned heads. She'd been ready with the excuse that she'd seen the tarantula of all spiders or a mutant mouse, should anyone question it.

But no one had responded! No one!

And now, here she was, trapped in a soundproof bubble with the man of her dreams. Or the guy who used to be the man of her dreams. She hadn't figured on the fact he was a warlock, witch, wizard, mage, or whatever the fuck he called himself in this situation.

Their gazes locked, and she saw intelligence, confidence, and perhaps a little wariness regarding her behavior in his amber eyes. That slightest vulnerability encouraged her to stay instead of sprinting out of there like an Olympian going for gold. Also, she didn't run, so there was that.

"Why hide what you are from friends?" she asked.

"Did you see your reaction?" he countered in a dry-as-dirt tone with one dark-brown brow raised halfway up his forehead in a cocky, questioning way.

The point was conceded with a nod. "Fair. Why reveal it to me now?"

"Instinct," he replied succinctly. "Something is telling me to trust you. To let you inside."

A tad more anxiety eased, and she squeezed his hand. "Thank you. I guess."

His sudden grin stole the air from her lungs. Only Laszlo Thorne possessed the ability to make her forget to breathe. Never anyone else, as hard as she'd searched for *the one* throughout her thirty-six years. Why? She couldn't say. Certainly he was handsome, but not drop-dead gorgeous like other family members. The Thornes had enviable genetics.

"It's not a bad thing, Ebba."

She was sure they were thinking about two different *things*. His devastating effect on her system was *absolutely* bad, but she appreciated his trust.

"Probably not. What do you do with your… What do you call them?… Abilities? Powers?"

"Abilities. Gifts." He shrugged a shoulder and sat back after releasing her. "To answer your question, whatever needs to be done. Liz works for Thorne Industries, and they collect magical artifacts to keep items out of the clutches of those who would abuse the power."

"World domination. If I were a witch, I'd go for it."

He laughed, and a warm glow sparked inside her. Whenever she could make Lo crack a smile, she considered it a win. When he was still married, he'd been considerably more uptight, but then again, that bitch-ass ex-wife of his made anyone's humor sour.

"I use my particular set of skills to help people get rid of the spirits haunting them."

"So you said you weren't psychic. Can witches be psychic?"

Expression decidedly grim, his gaze locked unseeingly on an object outside the storefront window. "Some. Eventually, they go insane. They can't tolerate the combination of visions and magic. It becomes difficult to tell the difference between real and imagined, and they get lost in their minds." He was grim. "Psychic witches usually have their powers bound at an early age or, at the very least, on the verge of madness. The havoc they can cause is immeasurable."

"That's horrible!" Could he be hiding the fact he was one to avoid having his power bound? His hunted expression said it was probable. What went into binding magic, and was it painful? Ebba desperately wanted to ask but held back, sensing it wasn't the place or time. She gathered the courage to touch his wrist. "Who do you know that's got that ability, Lo? Your reaction seems deeply personal."

Staring down at her hand as if it held all the answers of the Universe, he placed his over hers and absently caressed her knuckles with his thumb. "My cousin, Mackenzie. But so far, she's managed it well."

"*Mack?* Mack is psychic? *And* a witch?"

It shouldn't have surprised her after discovering the truth today, but never would she have guessed one of her two best friends was psychic or that they'd both been lying to her for their entire lives.

And wasn't that the rub?

Ebba had trusted the Thornes, but they'd never trusted her in return.

"Yes, she is." Weaving his fingers with hers, he shook her hand to get her attention. "I'm sorry if you feel betrayed, Ebba. It's a secret that can't get out, and we guard it fiercely."

"I'm not going to say I'm not hurt. But why tell me now when you couldn't be bothered to before?"

Lifting their joined hands, he brushed his lips across the skin of her inner wrist and met her gaze with a frank one of his own. "Because we're going to be lovers."

2

*"*B*ecause we're going to be lovers."*

Ebba felt like the biggest coward on the planet for running, but that's precisely what she did. When Laszlo went all seductive and turned all that panty-dampening charm her way, she bolted. Why? She couldn't say. The panic-inducing desire to run had consumed her until she was left with no choice.

Maybe it was the fear of her fantasy life meeting reality. What was the sage saying about never meeting one's idols? What if he turned out to be a dud in bed or, worse, his personality sucked? What if she'd built him up in her mind to be this amazing guy, but he was really an asshole? What did she truly know about the Thornes? Clearly, only what they'd wanted her to.

An echoing pop had sounded the instant she cleared the coffeehouse door, and it belatedly occurred to her that not only hadn't the patrons of the place heard Laszlo and her, but she hadn't heard them, either. All sound returned the instant she left. Traffic noise suddenly seemed thunderous and everywhere, disconcerting her after the relative quiet. It was worrisome anyone could wield such power, and it gave Ebba pause. Should she avoid the Thornes from here on out? How did she escape the awkwardness of being a dupe for twenty-plus years?

Curled up in her bed and hiding under the covers as if she expected Laszlo to blow the hinges off her barricaded door and storm the castle, so to speak, Ebba released a miserable groan. Sure, the half of her forever crushing on him was all for decisive action on his part. But the other half, the one that didn't know how to process what the hell she'd learned or if she should seek therapy for what might be a psychotic break, was happy to hide out by herself in her sanctuary from the outside world.

"What's *wrong* with you?" she asked herself aloud.

Jars rattled on a nearby shelf.

Okay, so she wasn't alone, alone, and it was in no way a sanctuary with the pain-in-the-ass ghost haunting her.

"Go away, you fucking asshole!" she hollered, losing her temper for the first time since her invisible roommate had appeared several months ago.

The temperature dropped by a good twenty degrees, and her comfortable space became unbearably frigid. The moisture caused by her ragged breaths met the cold air, creating small, misty clouds with every exhale. Lights flickered like in an early episode of *Supernatural,* and if she had rock salt, she'd have made a protective circle around herself. A glance around showed no iron in the immediate vicinity. Dean was always handy with a poker.

She didn't have any knowledge regarding ghosts, but with certainty, she shouldn't have pissed off her resident spook. Based on recent experiences, things were about to get dicey. They always did whenever she accidentally annoyed the spirit haunting her.

It had been five months since her accident. Five months since the death of her then-current guyfriend, Spencer. That timeframe coincided with the manifestation and her periodic blackouts. She wavered back and forth between believing the apparition was real and a figment of her imagination.

Was it possible her brain was scrambled, or had Spencer refused to cross over? If so, why? They'd only gone out on a handful of occasions, and there hadn't been enough time to fall into feelings. The guy had bored her to sleep during their one and only picnic. Granted, she'd worked a double at her mother's new bakery that day because Mom had been short-staffed. Still, it was a dastardly dull dinner date.

But what else could the constant haunting be? *Who* else?

"Why didn't I remember to ask Lo?" she muttered. After all, that had been her primary reason for seeking him out. Or so she told herself. Sure, the ink on his divorce papers was finally dry, but that hadn't played into her visit.

More dishes rattled, and she drew the covers closer around her neck.

"I don't know what you want." She whimpered like the total coward she was, eyes squeezed shut.

An answering breeze swept the hair back from her chilled skin like the softest caress. The next instant, the covers were swept away. Apparently, Ebba wasn't allowed to wallow in misery, and no reprieve from the chaos and cacophony was to be had tonight. One by one, self-help and empowerment books fell from the shelves to litter the floor.

"Funny," she muttered, not finding it humorous in the least.

Banging sounded on the front door, and seizing the opportunity to escape, she bolted across the room. Maybe if she could get out of the apartment, the entity would calm the hell down. But before she made good her escape, a vase crashed to the floor, sprinkling shards of glass in her path. Barefoot, she skidded to a halt. If she sprinted the last five feet to freedom, she'd cut the hell out of her bare soles.

"Why can't you just go away?" she shouted in her frustration, not even wincing at the begging in her voice. She was fed up by the countless sleepless nights due to the icy feel of fingers stroking her hair. Her ghost had an obsession, and she was it.

Laszlo's muffled voice was apologetic from the other side of the wooden panel. "Of course. I'm sorry to bother you, Ebba. I was just checking—"

"*Lo?* Lo, I—"

She screamed as her body was thrown sideways into the wall.

Then again when the door flew back on its hinges.

Arms raised for battle, wearing an intensely dark and frightening look on his handsome face, Laszlo blasted his way inside. There was no other word for it. He summed up the situation with a single glance and rushed to Ebba's aid.

"Back off," he warned as he scooped her off the floor.

It took her a few confusing seconds to realize he wasn't speaking to her.

"You see it?" she whispered.

"I do," he replied grimly.

"Thank God I'm not going crazy."

He snorted but never glanced down, and his steely-eyed stare was focused on something or someone she couldn't see. "If you are, I am."

"Can you, uh, talk to them, too?"

"Sure, and so can you. The difference is I can hear the reply."

Ebba gaped at him, noting the challenging expression he cast her eerie entity. What must it be like to see and speak to things beyond the normal? For that matter, what did it feel like to blow the door off its hinges without the need for mortal tools?

"Can you ask whoever it is to go away and leave me alone?"

He hesitated, and the frown between his slashing brows deepened to trench-like depths. "There's a problem with that request, Ebba."

The sound of his too-solemn tone woke butterflies in her belly, and not the good kind. "What? What problem?"

"The spirit on the other side of the room… Yeah, it's *you*, Sweet."

Her heart stuttered and stalled like a standard transmission shifting from first gear to second with a novice working the clutch. The vigorous thudding hurt her chest.

"*What? How can that be?*" she croaked.

And what about Spencer? She had to remember to ask him when things weren't so fucking terrifying.

"Don't know for certain, but I'd recognize that stubborn expression anywhere." A half smile curled his lips, but quickly dropped away. "We'll get it sorted, but I need to contact a friend first."

"Oh, yeah. Sure. Okay."

What the fuck else could she say, anyway? Something like, *"Oh, yeah, and while you're phoning a friend Who-Wants-To-Be-A-Millionaire style, why don't you call a shrink for me?"*

Laszlo's mind was reeling as he stared at Ebba's ghostly form across the room. So far, she refused to speak, glaring between them as if she were furious he'd come to the rescue.

Perhaps she was.

Ebba was independent. Had been since they were children and her parents left her to her own devices. Her entire child-hood was their generation's version of a latchkey kid. The loneliness radiating off her had prompted Liz to take Ebba under her wing and bring her home. But it was Ebba's engaging personality and can-do determination that had gained the Thornes' respect.

"Listen, I'm going to lift you onto the counter, and I want to examine your ribs. Then we'll clean the glass from your feet. Is that all right with you?" he asked her spirit self.

"Yes—oh!" Eyes wide, the corporeal Ebba in his arms blinked. "You weren't talking to me."

If the situation weren't so serious, he'd have laughed at her confusion. As it was, a split soul was exceedingly dangerous. Lo had to find a way to rectify the matter—and soon. Because if the soul was fractured, as hers appeared to be, other evil entities could make her body their plaything. And *that* he wouldn't let happen.

As he shifted her against his chest, a white-hot ball of energy whizzed past and halted behind him. He hated to keep his back to the salty spirit, but he had to trust neither Ebba would hurt him.

"Seems your ghostly self is keeping watch to make sure I don't do anything untoward," he said dryly as he set her on the counter.

"Or maybe she's mad you haven't yet," Ebba quipped, and then she blushed to the roots of her hair. "Fucking A! I don't know why I said that."

He grinned. "Maybe she's your filter."

Wide-eyed, she nodded. "That seems reasonable enough."

Staring at him as she was, with those large brown eyes eating him up, her mouth slightly agape, and a becoming flush, Ebba caused his pulse to race. The hammering in his chest felt different from anything he was used to and was uncomfortable in a way he didn't like.

The wonder fell from her as she shook her head and looked away. He could only assume he had unknowingly scowled. Charlotte was always bitching at him for his involuntary expressions, saying things like he could frighten small children.

"Did I, um… did I scare you with…" He swirled a finger around his face and tried to suppress his frown.

Ebba's head whipped up, and her brows crashed together. "What? No! How… why would you think that?"

Shrugging one shoulder, he turned. His confidence had taken a hit when she ran from the coffee shop. There he'd been, attempting to be all flirty and suave, and she'd bolted like a greyhound out of the gate, chasing the mechanical rabbit.

Her hand shot out, gripped his, and tugged him back around. "Lo? What's this all about? You can't honestly believe you scare women, right? You're the nicest guy I know."

"I thought my suggestion at the café and magically breaking down your door might've turned you off."

Ebba sandwiched her lower lip between her straight, white teeth, and her eyes flared wider.

He held his breath as he awaited her response. Why did he have to bring either of those things up? Did he have a tumor, or had he grown terminally stupid in the last half hour?

Her small snort preceded a giggling fit, and she released his hand to press her fingertips to her mouth. Tilting his head, he smiled and fought the urge to laugh with her, though he didn't know what she found so amusing.

When she had her humor under control, she shook her head. "Okay, first, your statement at the café didn't scare me. Not in the way you think, anyway."

"What other way could there be?" His brows met.

"I'll circle back to that. Second, the magical rescue was hot as hell and greatly appreciated. I mean, I don't know what the hell to do about that busted doorknob tonight, but it was worth the cost of a locksmith to see you in action."

Lazslo laughed. "I'll fix the door before I go. I promise there will be no out-of-pocket expenses for any of my rescues."

"Whew." She swiped a hand along her brow and grinned, but her expression froze in abject horror as her gaze locked on something behind him. "Niall!"

"Niall?"

Lo glanced over his shoulder and noticed a burly stranger with a vase raised over his head. His reaction was immediate. Pivoting, he bent sideways and shot his foot into the other man's midriff, then followed it up by knocking the impromptu weapon from his meaty fist and clipping his jaw. The guy shook like an angry bear and rose to his full height as if Lo's defensive tactics were a mere annoyance.

"Niall, no! He's a friend!" Ebba cried as she launched herself off the counter.

Remembering the broken glass and vase shards, Lazslo caught her around the waist and swung her to safety. Unfortunately for him, Niall, Ebba's grizzly-bear-sized friend, took exception and shoved Lo before he could turn around.

His head became closely acquainted with her entertainment cabinet, and it was lights out.

3

"*Lazslo!*" Ebba's heart stopped and resumed again at an abnormally fast rate. So fast, the lights around her flickered and dots appeared before her eyes. Could one stroke out from fear alone?

Blood pooled from the gash on his forehead, and she dropped to the floor beside him—mindful of the shattered vase shards he'd tried to protect her from. Whipping off her shirt, she pressed it to the wound and prayed to God he hadn't sustained brain damage. That horrific, soul-shriveling thud when his head had connected with the corner of the entertainment center wasn't a sound she was likely to forget.

"Niall, please hand me my phone." She fought against a suffocating panic and pasted on an encouraging smile. Her neighbor's brother had been intent on helping her, that much she gleaned. Possessed of a panda bear's temperament, Niall wouldn't seek out trouble, but if he'd happened to overhear Lo crash through her door, he might've assumed she was in danger.

"Is he your friend, Miss Ebba?"

The uncertainty in his deep voice was painful to hear.

"Yes. He is. Will you hand me my phone so I can call an ambulance? The bleeding is too much for me to stop on my own."

After rushing to the side table she pointed to, Niall returned with her cellphone. "I'm sorry, Miss Ebba. I didn't mean to hurt him. Will I get in trouble? Will the police take me away now?"

"No, Niall. I'll let them know it was all an accident and Lo stumbled, okay? Please, give me the phone."

Worry and confusion tightened his craggy features, and his ordinarily wide, smiling mouth was pulled down at the corners.

She wiggled her fingers in an impatient gesture. Infusing command in her voice, she said, *"Now, Niall."*

After punching in the number, she placed the device on Lazslo's chest and lifted the corner of the material to peek at his wound. The blood flow showed no signs of stopping or even slowing, and the ringing through the speaker was overly loud.

"For fuck's sake! It's an emergency line! What the hell is taking so long?" she muttered.

"Must be a busy afternoon," Lo murmured, eyes still closed. "Hang up, Ebba. I'm fine."

Although she did as he requested, she shook her head. "You're not. I can't stop the blood." Inside, she cringed at how whiny her tone sounded. She'd never been horrible in a crisis, but since the accident, her ability to stomach blood had drastically diminished.

"I promise you it looks worse than it is." His lids lifted, but before he could meet her eyes, his locked on her chest. "Did I miss all the fun? What happened while I was out? Were you practicing to become a stripper? I'm totally down for that."

Having forgotten her topless state, she scowled. Thank

goodness she was wearing a full-support bra. Had it been her demi-cup, she'd be dead from humiliation.

"They're called exotic dancers, and will you focus?" she growled.

"Oh, I'm focusing, all right," he assured her. A wicked grin curled his mouth as he closed his eyes. "I'll be recalling this in my dreams."

She fought a smile and lost. Who didn't love attention from a secret childhood crush after twenty-odd years?

"I really think we need to call an ambulance, Lo. This looks bad."

"Call Liz."

Ebba recoiled and glanced at the phone's screen with indecision. For their entire friendship, her best friend had lied to her. Facing her at a time when the betrayal was still fresh would only lead to accusations and arguments. She wasn't prepared to sweep it all under the rug and pretend it had never happened.

When she registered the sensation of being watched, she looked at Lo, only to find him observing her. The concern on his face wasn't misplaced, but her behavior was silly when he was the injured party. Firming her resolve, she lifted the device, prepared to do what she could to see him healed.

His hand stayed her.

"Use my phone and call my cousin Alastair if that makes you feel better. He's skilled at healing, and he can also help us with your other... uh, issue," he said after casting Niall the side eye.

The subtle hint registered. They needed Niall gone, not just because he shouldn't be there when another witch arrived to heal Lo, which she assumed was possible, but because her resident spook could start throwing items around in a fit of rage at any moment.

Ebba hadn't had time to wrap her mind around Lo's claim

that hers was the spirit haunting the place. What the hell did any of that truly mean anyway? With a minute shake of her head, she urged Niall to return to his place, citing she didn't want him to get into trouble when the police showed up with the doctor.

"Doctor?" Lo murmured as Niall hightailed it toward the lopsided door.

"In my mind, your cousin is a witch doctor. What else would you call someone who heals witches?"

His chuckle stole the chill from her bones, and although she wanted to join in the amusement, she refrained.

"Al will get a laugh from that one." He reached up and brushed the curls from her eyes. "I'm sorry we didn't tell you sooner, Ebba. It had to be hurtful to find out the way you did."

A mere shrug was her attempt at hiding her discomfort and upset. Of all the people in the world who she believed would never lie to her, Liz was her number one and Mack was her number two. Lo didn't necessarily rank since they'd only been friends in passing. To discover the opposite was devastating, but she didn't want to discuss it while he needed help.

After shifting the device to capture Lo's face and unlock the screen, she scrolled through his contacts until she found the one she sought. "Alastair Thorne? He's the only one with that first name."

"That's him."

When the man on the other end of the line answered, her eyes about rolled back in her head from the pleasure his deep, cultured voice caused. He could make millions operating a sex hotline. Before she could stop herself, she said as much. Laszlo sputtered his indignation at the same time Alastair barked out a laugh. Oddly, it was the rusty sound, as if he rarely released his humor, that snapped her back to reality.

"Oh, uh, sorry." The skin of her face felt like it had been

seared by the noon-day sun for five days running. "Yeah, Lo is hurt and wanted me to call you, Mr. Thorne."

"Please send me the address and a picture of your apartment, my dear."

Confused but willing, she did as requested. Before she'd finished speaking, a blond-haired man, who appeared to be in his mid-to-late forties, was standing in her living room. There was no time to appreciate his chiseled features or Old Hollywood flare. Her mind was still trying to process how he'd materialized from thin air.

"What the actual fuck?"

For someone who rarely swore, her exclamations that day were as emphatic as it got.

LASZLO SPUTTERED A LAUGH. HIS HEAD ACHED LIKE A BITCH, BUT Ebba's mind had to be scrambled at this point, especially if she was reduced to swearing. Although she tended to be freer with those close to her, she usually retained the small niceties and refused to utter expletives around those she wasn't acquainted with. At least until she encountered a trying situation like the one they were currently dealing with. Between learning of the Thorne family's magical status and that her soul had split, likely from her recent accident, she was experiencing information overload. There were exceptions to her extreme-situation swearing rule—calling him a "dick" had been one. She couldn't hang with the Thornes and not pick up a *few* bad habits.

"What happened?" Alastair's forbidding tone jerked Lo from his musing.

"I tripped."

His cousin's blond brows shot upward, and disbelief was heavy in his tone when he said, *"You?"*

Stifling another laugh, Lo nodded and immediately regretted it when his pain transitioned from throbbing to migraine intensity. Hissing in a breath, he gripped his head between his hands.

Ebba released a distressed meep and returned to apply pressure to his wound.

"Who helped you along on this *trip?*" Al asked dryly, making a point not to glance at the scantily clad Ebba's chest.

"A mountain of a man, but he's been dealt with." Lo sucked in a breath as he eased to a sitting position, wishing like hell he hadn't, as sharp, shooting pain pierced his temple. Ignoring Alastair's penetrating gaze, he said, "Go ahead and get that look of promised retribution off your face, cuz. There will be no revenge today."

"How about tomorrow?" asked another voice he didn't recognize.

Leaning slightly sideways, Laszlo sought the source behind Alastair's pristine-suited form. The man was big, much bigger than Lo's six-foot frame, and possessed a shoulder-length mane of white-blond hair. His eyes were an icy blue but, oddly, contained a wealth of warmth, as evidenced by the crinkles beside those disconcerting peepers.

"Thanks for the backup, Castor, but I believe your services won't be needed after all." An engaging grin threatened to transform Alastair's visage to friendly instead of imposing.

Castor's gaze swept Ebba's form, and an unidentifiable look flashed in his eyes before a spark of interest flared to life. "Speak for yourself, Al. The lady has a mind and tongue of her own. I'm dearly hoping she's in dire need of my *services,*" he said with a roguish grin.

Irritated by the man's high-handed attitude, Laszlo tapped Ebba's sagging jaw shut and growled, "You're catching flies." Lowering his voice, he added, "And you might want to put on a shirt, Sweet."

"Nonsense." She swatted his hand and scowled but never took her shining eyes from Castor. How had she gone from flashing cow eyes at *him* to watching another man like a starving puppy eyeing a burger? "This covers more than my bikini, and I have company."

"You're a fickle woman, Ebba James," he accused, hiding his grin when she responded with a breathy laugh and a pat on his cheek.

"Fickle? Please tell me you're not spoken for, love," Castor replied in her stead. Placing a hand over his heart, he pasted on a woe-is-me expression. "I'll never recover from the blow."

"Read the room, Alex," Alastair said wryly.

"I thought I was. She seems as enamored with me as I am with her."

Laszlo took exception to Castor's statement. "She's not enamored. Likely, she's never seen a baboon up close and personal."

The wide grin and laughing eyes Ebba turned on Lo were all the reward he needed. "Hush, you big baby. Even with your new head wound, you're still as gorgeous as ever."

"Right." Alastair leaned forward and eased back the edge of the wadded shirt. "About that, I can fix you right up, son."

Holding up a hand to pause his cousin, Laszlo met Ebba's curious stare. "For my sanity, please put on a shirt. I'm not sure your furniture can take the soaking from the drool pouring out of that guy's mouth." The quick shift of his head in Castor's direction was a mistake, and Lo sucked in another breath. He'd be lucky he didn't end up with brain damage after all was said and done.

"Be right back." Ebba patted his shoulder and jumped to her feet. As she hurried toward her bedroom, Castor shifted to watch her luscious moneymaker swish from side to side.

"Jesus, she's something."

"I suppose we should get one thing straight, buddy." Lo's tone was pure steel. "Ebba's not a good-time girl, and if you don't keep your smarmy comments to yourself, I'll rip your tongue from your head."

The bastard had the nerve to laugh, and Alastair looked equally amused.

"Try me," Lo growled.

"Is now a good time to tell him what I can do, Al?" Castor asked, crossing his arms over his burly chest.

Alastair's dark-blond brows drew together as he examined Lo's head injury. "He's a Traveler, my boy. If he wants your girl, he'll alter time to before you were sweet on each other and take her for himself."

"He'd have to go back to when I was a teenager," Ebba's spirit piped in from her perch on the counter behind the men. "One glimpse of those abs at Liz's pool party, and I was done for."

A slow smile curled his mouth, and he closed his eyes against the sweet victory he felt. "Good to know."

Only she knew he was speaking to her and not Alastair.

Assuming Laszlo was in good hands with another Thorne witch, Ebba took a few extra minutes to wash the blood from her hands. Despite all the teasing, the sight of him injured had triggered her. She'd always viewed him as so alive and strong. Of course, Lo had no way of knowing, but Spencer had been similarly injured, only he'd never recovered from his head wound.

After nearly scrubbing herself raw, Ebba inspected her hands and nails to assure herself not a trace of blood remained. She splashed frigid water on her hot face, hoping to cool herself down. Yes, she was overstimulated by recent events, but these random feverish moments had started well before today.

At strange periods throughout the day, her flesh felt too tight for her body, and her muscles would cramp. One would assume the injuries she sustained in the wreck had created lingering physical maladies. Still, it didn't explain why her core temperature would spike and feel like the Chernobyl reactor in the hours prior to the nuclear disaster.

Ebba dried her face and sank onto the mattress's edge as

she recalled her recent accident. If what Lo had said was true, she was haunting herself, and the spirit riding her back wasn't Spencer's. How was that possible? For the most part, she felt normal. Sure, there were a few memory gaps, but she'd retained the ability to function and work. If the spirit had left her body, wouldn't she be dead or in a coma?

And what about Spencer? Had he moved on after his eventual death? Should she ask Laszlo if he could find out?

"Ebba?"

His worried voice penetrated her chaotic thoughts, and when she shifted to face the door, she gasped. His wound was completely healed, and his clothes were returned to their standard pristine condition. No evidence of Niall's attack remained.

"How is that possible?" she croaked. "Am I losing my mind?"

Lo sent a frowning glance down at his shirt before shaking his head and joining her on the bed. "No, you're not losing it. It's witchcraft."

"Witchcraft," she repeated, feeling inane and out of her depth. Was she dreaming? Had she never woken up after her car hit the tree? Perhaps she was in limbo, where oddball things were passed off as the norm.

Cupping her face, he caressed her jawline with his thumb. "Are you okay? You seemed to be fine earlier, but now you look pale."

"I was recalling my accident." She drew back to avoid his touch. "And Spencer."

"I remember Liz saying he didn't make it. I'm sorry, Ebba."

Unexpected tears burned her lids as she closed them against the sympathy he displayed. "Don't. Don't be nice about it. It was all my fault."

"Accidents aren't anyone's fault," he countered gently.

When she lifted her lids, it was to see tenderness reflected in his eyes. "We fought that night. I wanted to apply the brakes on our relationship, but he… he…"

"Because you were driving and wanted to end your relationship, you think somehow *you* caused your jeep to hit a tree?" His voice was thick with skepticism. "Unless you purposely aimed for it, you're not at fault."

"That's the thing. I think I did."

He sucked in sharply and stared at her. His compassion changed to utter shock.

Lord, how damning her comment sounded!

"I wasn't trying to end things that way," she rushed to add. "I just wanted to scare him. Make him think I was crazy so he'd get the message and take a hike."

"There are better ways to get rid of someone," Castor said from the doorway, but he appeared unperturbed by her confession. "I could teach you a few."

"Ironic, since he's one of those who won't get the message and take a hike," Lo muttered.

"Are you saying crazy doesn't work to scare men off?" Ebba released an incredulous snort.

Castor's grin flashed. "Not when they look like you. Men welcome your kind of crazy, love."

Under his direct stare, she grew warm and considered splashing more cold water on her face. Anything to cool off from the excess of attention being shown her. Who knew this much testosterone in one room could fire her up quicker than an engine at the beginning of a NASCAR race?

Speaking of cars…

She met Laszlo's watchful gaze. "Do spirits linger at the site of their death? Would Spencer be in the vicinity of that tree?"

"Sometimes that happens. They're more likely to go where they were the most comfortable or where there's unfinished business, like in your case."

"Her case?" Castor straightened from the doorway where

he lounged, his entire demeanor changing to one of concern as he strode across the room. "You're being haunted?"

Lo surged to his feet and stepped between them. "Settle down, tiger. I'm on it."

Icy blue eyes narrowed as they swept the length of him and summed him up. With a shrug of dismissal for Laszlo, Castor shifted to go around him, but came up short when Lo side-stepped in his way, anticipating the move.

"Close enough. Neither of us knows you."

A mocking smile curled the other man's mouth. "I'm one of your cousin's oldest friends, boyo. Alastair doesn't grant affection lightly, and that should tell you everything you need to know about me."

Acknowledging Castor's challenge with a grimace, Lo's shoulders eased from their tense position. Ebba breathed a sigh of relief. Why was he being so protective of her? It wasn't because of her split-spirit issue, right?

"Your living room has been restored to its former glory," Alastair said, poking his head into the room. His sapphire gaze met hers and displayed a wealth of understanding and kindness. "Why don't we adjourn there to discuss what's happening?"

Could the man sense her overwrought hormones? She didn't dare ask. The answer was likely too embarrassing for her to live another moment longer.

Lo gestured for Castor to precede them from the room, but when she'd have followed, he halted her with a hand on her arm. "When we're through here, I'll see what I can discover about Spencer. See if he's moved on."

The immense gratitude she experienced caused her to fling herself at him. She was somewhat shocked when he was quick to anticipate her move and return her embrace.

"Thank you, Lo."

"You're welcome, Ebba."

For the longest moment, he held her, and all felt right with her world. As if she was experiencing a sense of wellness and a homecoming of sorts. And because the feeling was so foreign from anything she'd known, she drew away, giving him a tight smile but not meeting his eyes.

"We should go," she said in a low voice.

He simply nodded and guided her toward the door.

WHEN THEY WERE ALL COMFORTABLE, LASZLO LAUNCHED INTO the tale of two spirits and how potential splits happened. In Ebba's case, he surmised a near-death experience.

Castor initially showed disbelief, then transitioned to fascination, while Alastair expressed deep concern for Ebba. As an empath, his cousin tended to feel things stronger than most, though it wasn't well-known. His badass reputation kept people at a distance, fearful of his darker side. And rightfully so. As the Thorne Patriarch and favorite of the Goddess, he possessed untold gifts. Lo doubted if their family knew the full extent of the man's abilities. Other, more powerful beings existed, but they gave Al the respect he was due, mainly because he was as crafty as they came. If a clever plan was required, one need only call Alastair.

But if his cousin was worried about Ebba, it was likely she was suppressing signs of her anxiety, and he was picking up on it. Perhaps she was unconvinced or in denial. Eventually, however, she'd need to get on board with his plan to fuse her fractured soul and body back together.

"Is it possible to have the soul split off completely?" Castor asked, for once not over the top with his abundant sexuality.

"The journals I've read would indicate yes, but it would leave an uncaring, ruthless individual in its place. I'm not convinced it happens that way," Lo replied. When his answer created a trio of frowning faces, he continued. "The body needs the spark of a spirit to live. If the soul leaves the body, nothing remains but a husk."

"But wouldn't that relate to what you've read? Isn't the personality shift the same thing?" Ebba asked.

Lo considered the question, then shrugged. "Technically, I suppose so. If one's body were healthy enough, they could survive without a soul. I'm inclined to believe you need both, though."

"Actually, I've dealt with split souls in the past. I can assure you, when that happens, the physical body does indeed house an uncaring and ruthless individual, as Laszlo suggested," Alastair said, climbing to his feet to cross to the kitchen. With a backward glance and half smile for Ebba, he nodded to the coffeemaker. "Do you mind?"

"Oh! No! Not at all." When she would've jumped up, Laszlo placed a restraining hand on her thigh. "Wait for it."

It took less than a minute for Alastair to place four mugs on a tray and conjure the coffee to fill them. Lo laughed at her astonished expression as a bottle of aged Glenfiddich appeared in the center of the tray.

She shifted wide eyes to him. "Can you do that, too?"

"Yes."

Next, she turned her wondrous gaze on Castor. "And you?"

His smile was pure wicked delight. "Would you like me to show you what I can do, dear Ebba?"

"Ye—"

"No, she would not!" Lo stated succinctly, dropping an arm across her shoulders. The probability was high that he'd just reacted as Castor intended he should, but he'd be damned if the man didn't get under his skin with his model good looks and jackal-like grin. Though, if Laszlo was inclined to be generous, he might say it was wolfish or devilish. Yet he wasn't so inclined and was one hundred percent prepared to view his new rival in an unfavorable light.

Satisfaction shone in Castor's eyes as he watched them, and Lo was left to wonder if the man was trying to manipulate the situation in some unexpected way. If so, why? Was his intent to have Lo lay claim to Ebba? The man hadn't met either of them before that day, so what was in it for him?

Yet as Ebba watched Castor, a frown drawing her brows together on her lovely visage, she appeared confused. Was it possible she was on the same wavelength and recognized the oddity of Castor's behavior? Later, when they were alone, he'd ask her.

He looked at Ebba's detached spirit lingering atop the kitchen island. Her hands gripped the counter on either side of her hips, and she swung her dangling legs as if bored. When she noticed his attention on her, she nodded toward Castor.

"He was there that day."

"What?"

His emphatic shout, seemingly from nowhere, startled the returning Alastair enough to have mugs and decanter clinking as he steadied the tray.

"Jaysus, boy! You almost gave the old man a heart attack," Castor chortled. "I thought I'd never see the day."

"Stuff it, Alex," Al growled, dividing his displeasure between Castor and Lo equally. "What was so all-fired important you needed to shout, son?"

Ignoring him to glare at Castor, Laszlo surged to his feet. "Why didn't you tell us you were there when Ebba had her accident?"

5

*L*aszlo's truth bomb caused shock, or something like it, to arrest the expressions of those around him.

Ebba, the last to recover, shifted to stare at Castor. "You were there? Why don't I remember you?"

"You were barely conscious, love, and then you weren't. I'd be surprised if you *did* remember me."

"But…" She shook her head. "How? Where did you come from?"

Dipping his head toward Alastair, he said, "Those woods border his estate."

"That doesn't explain why you were there," Lo stated in a hard voice. "Or why you didn't say something before."

"Calm down, Raging Ralph, and I'll tell you." Castor didn't quite roll his eyes, but his annoyed vibe was a living thing.

Spirit Ebba laughed from her seat behind him, but other than giving her a narrow-eyed glare, Lo didn't respond to her pointed amusement.

"Today, junior," he growled at Castor.

Ignoring him, the other man met Alastair's curious gaze.

"You remember, Al. It was about five or six months ago now. What started out as an evening run turned into a rescue mission. I told you about the accident I'd witnessed that night when I returned."

Alastair's sapphire eyes turned solemn as they shifted to Ebba. "I do remember, and I'm sorry for your trials, Ms. James."

When Lo would've bombarded Castor with questions, the other man held up a hand. "Like I said, I was out for a run. As I rounded a bend on the path, I heard tires squeal and the vehicle impact against the tree. The second I realized what happened, I rushed to help."

"What did you do?" she asked.

"I could instantly see you were mortal, but you weren't breathing. Normally, I'd let nature take its course, but I was caught by your loveliness and an overwhelming urgency to help you."

"That was me egging him on," Spirit Ebba said when Castor paused to smile at her physical self. "I had the oddest feeling I shouldn't move on."

Other than to send her an acknowledging nod, Lo didn't reply.

"Why wouldn't you help someone if you could?" Ebba asked, confusion clouding her eyes and her mouth dipping at the corners.

Call him petty, but Laszlo loved that she'd consider it a mark against Castor that he wasn't inclined to help a person, regardless of status. Remaining quiet, he gave the other man enough room to hang himself.

"The Goddess. The Fates." Castor shrugged and sent her a considering look. Seeing she didn't understand his simple explanation, he elaborated. "As mortals, people follow their faith, whether that be the Almighty God from the Bible, Allah, Hindu Gods and Goddesses, or the like. If atheist, they don't feel the need to be accountable to anyone but themselves. But as magical beings, we are subjected to a different set of rules."

"And ye harm none, do what ye will," Alastair said.

"I don't know what that means." Ebba glanced at Lo for an answer, and warmth spread through his chest that she trusted him enough to seek his counsel.

Lacing his fingers through hers, he said, "Do what you will as long as you don't hurt another. It's a witch's creed. We're brought up to respect and value life, but we're also taught not to displease the Fates, Gods, or Goddesses. It has repercussions if we do."

"Why would they be displeased if you save a… mortal?" She grimaced as she said it, likely still trying to wrap her mind around what she'd learned today.

"The Fates might have other plans for you or whomever you were with at that moment. By saving you, Castor may have put a target on his back," Alastair said with a reproachful glance at his friend. The cheeky bastard simply grinned.

"So it's why you left Spencer to die?" she snapped at Castor.

Compassion filled his visage, and he shook his head. "No, love. I stabilized him, too, before calling for an ambulance. However, like I said, you weren't breathing, so you were the number-one priority. By the time I revived you, the ambulance had arrived and taken your friend away."

A good amount of her anger died away, but she still squeezed Lo's hand as if it were a lifeline.

"Thank you," she said. "I should be more grateful, especially since you'll likely get in trouble on my behalf."

"I haven't been called to task yet, but despite the severity of any punishment meted out, I'd do it again," Castor assured her warmly. "You could pay me back by having dinner with me."

"Not gonna happen," Lo replied on her behalf.

"You really should let the lady speak for herself, boyo. No one likes to be told what to do."

With dread, he shot Ebba a look of apology. "As much as I hate to admit it, he's right. I'm sorry."

"Let it be known she's speaking for herself." Her shining eyes locked with Lo's a second before she turned to Castor. "And she's saying, thank you, but no."

A small smile played around her mouth, and Lo had the sudden urge to kiss her until they were both mindless. Unfortunately, it wasn't the time. They had company and the split-soul issue to take care of first.

"I can't say I'm not brokenhearted." Castor placed a hand on his chest in the vicinity of said destroyed organ. "But far be it from me to come between lovers."

"Oh!" She recoiled, and her expression resembled an owl with its perpetual startled appearance. "We're not—I don't—we... Tell him, Lo."

"We're not lovers," he dutifully replied. "Just old friends who intend to become lovers," he added.

A flush darkened her cheeks, and in her flustered state, her hands flitted about as if they had a mind of their own. "You have to stop saying that!"

"Why? It's true, isn't it?"

"No!"

Inside, he winced, but he maintained his careless grin. The pretense was killing him, but he'd be damned if he reacted to the egg on his face in front of the playboy.

Ebba clasped his hand again and stretched to kiss his cheek. "I'm sorry. But I need more time."

"I'm an idiot," her spirit self muttered. "My brains went by way of my soul, and nothing's left in that empty-headed shell of mine."

Meeting her gaze across the short distance, Lo bit the inside of his cheek to keep from laughing. He desperately wanted to reply, but the others would buy him a one-way ticket for the loony bin.

"Get me back into that body, and we'll definitely discuss this further," she added.

Ebba barely suppressed the urge to hit her forehead with the heel of her hand. Why in the world was she putting on the brakes with Laszlo when she'd been infatuated with him forever and a day? Maybe because her earlier worries weren't alleviated yet?

Perhaps.

Truthfully, she doubted he'd be a dud in bed. He was considerate and caring. Kind, too. Added to the mix was his unfailing honesty. Or at least it should've been added to the list of things in the pro column. But the one con, as she saw it, wasn't his magic; it was the fact his family, the people she'd claimed as hers a long time ago and who she thought had claimed her, had lied to her for years. For her entire relationship with them, in fact.

Her phone rang, and she welcomed the opportunity to distance herself from the men.

Liz.

As soon as she saw the caller ID, she rejected the incoming call and placed it face down. For whatever reasons she couldn't discern, she was less inclined to forgive Liz than Laszlo. Although, in fairness, she should be angry with him as well as the rest of the Thornes for their secret. Why couldn't she be trusted? What was it about her that screamed, "Lie to me?"

Spencer hadn't had a problem with that. They'd only gone on a handful of dates when she discovered the man was a pathological liar. When she called him on his bullshit, he—

A sharp, stabbing pain behind her eyes derailed her thought, and she sucked in a breath, pressing her fingertips to her brow bones.

Laszlo was there in an instant.

"What's wrong?" Concern was heavy in his voice, and in an unexplainable way, his attentiveness bothered her.

"I'm fine," she snapped, backing away and drawing the notice of the other men. With a tight smile, she entered the kitchen and poured herself a glass of water. With her back to the men, she slowly sipped her drink, trying to gather her thoughts.

"Ebba, what's going on?"

"I'm fine, Laszlo. Give me a minute."

Why was she irritated with him? It didn't make sense unless it was residual anger over the lies the Thornes had told her.

But had they truly lied?

Or was it simply a matter of omitting the truth?

She snorted. Yeah, Spencer was great at that.

Another blinding pain struck behind her eyes, and she closed them, concentrating on breathing and not throwing up.

The spontaneous headaches had been happening to her since the accident, and she assumed it was a side effect of injuring herself. But maybe it was something more. Maybe Castor could help her figure it out.

When she turned around, he was in a deep discussion with Alastair. Laszlo hadn't returned to the living room but lingered at the bar with his head cocked in the slightest of manners as if he were listening to a different conversation. His amber-colored eyes weren't focused on anything in particular that she could tell.

The sudden need to escape the oppressive atmosphere made her skin clammy, and Ebba wished she had their effortless ability to teleport away. What she wouldn't give for a magical power like that!

After setting her glass on the counter, she smoothed her shirt down her stomach and hips, then returned to the couch, doing her damndest not to interrupt the men debating the merits of saving mortals.

"Oh, give over, Al," Castor said with a snort and a wink at Ebba. "Tell me you wouldn't have saved her."

Alastair straightened his tie before tugging his shirtsleeves and aligning his cuff links with the seams of his suit jacket.

Ebba frowned, realizing he'd never mussed his suit in the entire time he'd been at her apartment. No blood from Laszlo's wound or wrinkle to be had. It was as if he'd stepped from a photo shoot for a men's style magazine straight into her living room. How was that possible?

She met his sparkling sapphire gaze and noted his unholy gleam of amusement. It occurred to her that he enjoyed sparring with his friend. When he faced Castor, she studied his features. It seemed all Thorne men possessed strong jawlines, bodies to die for, and bright eyes regardless of color.

Was it a reflection of their magic?

She'd have to ask Lo later.

As if thinking about him recalled him to her side, he joined their small group and sank down on the cushion beside her. This time he was careful to keep a respectable distance, as if in deference to her earlier waspishness.

Relief swept through her, and she frowned at the conflicting feeling. Prior to five months ago, she'd have given anything for Lo to look at her with desire. To hold her hand and treat her with great care. Hell, *anything* to be noticed by him! But the second he'd suggested they become lovers, she was running scared.

Why?

What was with this conflict between what she always wanted and what she was now receiving from him?

"The question is, what do we do?"

Alastair's voice caught her attention.

"Do?" she asked.

"About fusing your soul back into your body, child."

Ebba balked at the word fusing. "Sounds painful. How

about we shelve this discussion for another time? Thanks for coming out, fellas."

Discordant and awkward, she sprung up like a Jack-in-the-box, knocking her knees against the coffee table and rattling the dishes. With a spastic wave, she rushed for her bedroom and locked herself in.

Under no circumstances was she prepared to be fused!

6

"What do you suppose got into her?" Castor said with a light laugh.

"Hmm. That's a great question." Alastair sent a considering glance toward the bedroom door. "Her emotions were ricocheting about."

"It's highly unusual behavior from her," Laszlo replied, scrubbing his hands over his face. "If I had to guess, she's overwhelmed by everything we've revealed."

With a shake of his head, Alastair expressed what he was thinking. "The girl showed admirable resilience and strength during the earlier incident. But it was as if she shut her emotions behind a sturdy steel door and locked everyone out."

"Hence the overwhelmed part," Lo replied dryly.

Over the years, Laszlo's natural-born humor had taken a backseat to his wife's dour personality until he rarely cracked a smile. As someone who strove to ensure his family was happy as well as healthy, Alastair found it difficult to bite his tongue. The one time he did take the younger man aside to discuss the sorrowful state of his marriage, he was told in no uncertain terms to mind his own business.

Despite the Thornes' "only love once" blessing—or curse, depending on who one was mated with—Alastair was damned if he'd allow a family member's suffering to continue. Buying off Charlotte was easy. The woman ate, breathed, and shit money. If an item wasn't diamond-encrusted, she'd turn up her nose and dismiss it. Her money-hungry personality wouldn't allow her to forego his offer of one million per year for life. A life that wouldn't be long, according to Isis.

Interestingly, for a man in love, Laszlo hadn't objected to her leaving and seemed profoundly relieved. His cousin's lack of caring cemented Alastair's certainty he'd done the right thing.

The new development with Ebba interested him on many levels. But the main one consisted of Laszlo coming to life whenever she was in his general vicinity. His gaze would follow her, and the depressing gray his aura had developed throughout his marriage would disappear. His cousin hadn't woken to the truth yet, but he loved the girl. Ebba, not Charlotte, was Laszlo's true soulmate.

The problem, as Alastair saw it, was the woman's reticence. The push and pull of her emotions fluctuated as if she were suppressing them on purpose—*or somebody else was.*

"Tell me about this boyfriend of hers who died," he said to Laszlo. "What do you know of him?"

"Not much. I'd heard in passing from Liz that Ebba was seeing someone, but I didn't know who." Laszlo's mouth turned down at the corners, and a strong wave of annoyance rolled off him as if the idea of Ebba dating another bothered him.

Good.

The information worked in Alastair's favor. Now, if he could keep Castor from mucking things up, he'd have these two kids together in no time. His wife, Rorie, would get a kick out of him dusting off his matchmaking hat and likely insist on helping.

"What has you thinking so hard, Al?" Castor asked him with a knowing sparkle. "I recognize that look, but I'd like it confirmed."

"Worry about your own affairs, Alexander."

"Oh! It must be serious if you're using my full name."

"Sod off." That expletive was the closest he could produce without calling down locusts on their small town, though there were many times a stronger sentiment would've been nice.

Castor laughed, and Alastair was hard-pressed not to join in. They had been friends for over half a century, and their children were joined in marriage, making them family forever. Around mid-thirties, the aging process for magical beings slows to a crawl, and Castor appeared little older than his son, Quentin. Of course, Alex took advantage of his good looks and used them to their fullest in his quest to seduce the entire female population. The exceptions were the Thorne women. The unspoken rule was they were off-limits. He'd be sure to add Ebba James to the list.

"If you're concocting a scheme, and here I have no doubt you are, Al, I'd like to be privy to the details," Laszlo said with a determined look. "I've known Ebba since we were children, and I'm determined nothing's happening to her on my watch."

"Isn't he darling?" Castor taunted, folding his hand over his heart and batting his lashes. "It's like he's in love or something."

None of them saw the melamine flower vase until it struck his forehead. Silk rose buds littered the sofa around them, and the sheer shock on Castor's face sent Alastair off in peals of laughter. Tears streamed from the corners of his eyes, and he held his ribs as he struggled to draw a breath.

Laszlo chortled his glee. "Well done, Spirit Ebba!"

The apartment lights flickered in what Alastair could only assume was her acknowledgment of Lo's praise.

"I guess I should've warned you. She has a vicious temper and hates to be mocked," Lo told Castor, adding a tsk-tsk to the mix.

Color crept up his friend's neck, and Alastair placed a restraining hand on his arm. "Let it go, Alex. You started it."

"Yeah, well, I've got somewhere to be. Have fun with the haunting harridan."

In a blink, he was gone.

"Was it something I said?" Lo's dancing amber eyes proved his question was far from innocent.

Grinning, Alastair conjured two whisky tumblers and poured them each a dram of his favorite scotch. After handing one off, he tapped his glass to his cousin's. "Well done. Now, let's get down to business."

As her headache dissipated, Ebba eased into a sitting position and hugged a pillow. Why was she resistant to Laszlo's help in resolving her split-soul issue? She was the one who'd sought him out to take care of the problem. Yet once she'd discovered who was haunting her, she shut that shit down faster than a knife fight in a phone booth.

The logical side of her acknowledged she had a serious situation on her hands, but there was a niggling voice inside her brain urging caution. Whenever she tried to make strides toward resolving things, she received a massive migraine for her troubles.

A knock sounded on the bedroom door.

"Come in."

No sooner had the words left her mouth than Lo turned the knob and peered into the room. "How are you feeling?"

He made no move to venture forward, and she couldn't blame him for being gun-shy. Her earlier snottiness had confused her as much as it must've confused him.

"Better." Offering up a smile, she gestured him closer. Once he'd seated himself sideways on the mattress, with one leg tucked under him and facing her, she nodded toward the living room. "Are the others still here?"

"No. Your ghostly self heaped abuse on Castor's head for being a dick, and he left in a huff. Alastair wanted to consult with his son, Nash, at Thorne Industries. Maybe see what they could find in the family book."

"Family book?"

"Grimoire. It's where we store the spells passed down through history."

"Those exist?" When he nodded, Ebba shook her head in wonderment. "I've watched witchy shows and movies, and I've always loved the idea of a spellbook. But I've never considered the reality of one existing before."

"Would you like a little history?"

His willingness to share surprised her. Perhaps it shouldn't have, considering he'd revealed what his family could do, but she didn't think he'd be as open as he was.

After she nodded and scooted to the side for him to get comfortable beside her, Lo launched into the tale of the Goddess Isis.

"Six original families were gifted with abilities. We're from her direct line, while others descend from different gods or goddesses. Over time, some married mortals and diluted their power, but—"

"Wait! Are you saying if you marry someone who doesn't possess magic, you lose some of yours? That's bogus!"

He laughed. "No. I'm saying that any children from a non-magical union might not be as powerful as I am or my ancestors before me. They *may* be, but the likelihood is great that they won't."

"Oh. I thought it was some witch supremacy bullshit like you had to keep the lines pure," she grumbled.

He expressed great amusement, and his amber-colored irises appeared lighter than earlier.

Ebba frowned as she stared into his face. "Your coloring is a tad different than your family. Why is that?"

Lifting his arm, Laszlo rolled up his sleeve and casually examined his olive-toned skin with an unconcerned air. "It's probably a throwback to my Egyptian ancestors. Or maybe an illicit affair somewhere in the family tree, resulting in a child born on the wrong side of the sheets."

"You joke, but wouldn't it *dilute* your power?"

His grin was quicksilver, causing her heart to flutter. "Not if both parties possessed equal abilities."

"Good point." With a bump of her shoulder against his, she said, "Tell me about the other families. Would I know any of them?"

"I'm not sure. We're not so different from anyone else, with one small exception. We work, fall in love, marry, and produce children just like the next person."

"Liz and I met in middle school. I still can't believe she never accidentally revealed what she was." She'd be inclined to teach mean girls lessons in kindness. Although, looking back, she couldn't recall anyone being particularly awful, so perhaps Liz had.

Knots formed in Ebba's stomach whenever she thought about the colossal secret her best friend had hidden.

"Ebba, it isn't that my sister didn't trust you. She, like the rest of us, was under strict orders not to reveal what we are to mortals. Remember what Castor said about consequences?"

Frowning, she nodded slowly.

"Throughout history, when one of my kind believed they

could trust another with the truth, bad things happened. Our most recent past consisted of the Witches War, where those who feared us tried to wipe us out."

"*What?* Who would do that?" The knot in her belly expanded and squeezed her heart. The ghastly images of Lo or Liz being hurt because of some stupid war plagued her mind. "How recent?"

"The war was about twenty years ago, but the last of the Désorcelers Society wasn't disbanded until a year or so ago. They were hellbent on destroying all witches, and the Thornes in particular. We couldn't use our real names whenever we traveled for fear of repercussions."

Seen in that particular light, she could understand why the Thornes had remained mute about what they could do. The burning sense of betrayal wasn't as fierce, though it still lingered.

"Liz had to know I could be trusted, though, right?" She gazed up at him, silently urging him to take her side. "How can you be friends with someone for close to thirty years and still think they'd stab you in the back?"

"Do you consider us friends, Ebba?"

"Of course!"

"But you're not angry with me?"

"I might be. A little," she admitted. "But it's different with you, Lo. We aren't close. Not like Liz and I."

A shutter came down, and his features settled into a neutral mask as he nodded. "True enough. Anyway, you should call her. She's texted me twelve times to check on you. She'll be beating on—"

Pounding came from the other room, and a wry smile curled his mouth.

"Do I know my sister or what?"

"How do you know it's—"

"Ebba?" Liz called as she hammered her fist on the entry

door. "Ebba James, you'd better open this door and stop avoiding me right this minute!"

Lo's brows shot up. "You were saying?"

"I—"

Liz entered with a bang as the handle slammed into the living room wall. She didn't bother to be quiet as she stomped into Ebba's bedroom followed by her husband, Rafe Xuereb.

"What the fuck, Ebba? You can't be bothered to answer your phone or return a text?" Hurt and worry shone in her friend's amber-colored eyes so like Lo's. They were darker than usual, and it wasn't the first time Ebba noticed the changing irises. Now, she had to wonder if it was related to a witch's mood, because Lo's had altered a minute ago, too, when she said they weren't close.

She sucked in a breath and whipped her head around to stare at him. Was it possible he was upset by her comment? Nerves like live wires, she studied him as he studied her, and she experienced a driving need to know what he was thinking. Just as she was opening her mouth to ask, the piercing pain from earlier returned, wringing a cry from her.

Laszlo cradled her face between his large palms. "Breathe, Sweet. In and out, slowly for the count of four."

Trailing fingers over her brow, he spoke gibberish, or if the words meant something, she couldn't make it out. But the warmth from his fingertips as they traveled across her forehead caused a tingle in her extremities and her heart to hammer harder than before. He lowered her to the mattress, careful to position a pillow under her aching head. His presence both soothed her and triggered a cloying, claustrophobic reaction inside.

Wedging her arms between them, she shoved at his chest. "Get off me! Get off me!"

"Ebba, Sweet, I'm not on you. I'm not touching you in any

way except for my fingers on your forehead. Hear my voice. Hear my words."

Frowning, she tried her damndest to do as instructed, but the clawing need to get him away from her increased. She screamed, long and loud enough to bring Niall running, should he be inclined. In an instant, Lo was off the bed and across the room to stand beside the slack-jawed Xuerebs. Once again, excruciating pain jackhammered into her brain, causing her to cry out.

Laszlo stepped forward only to be stopped by Liz and Rafe.

Allowing darkness to take her, she closed her eyes and welcomed the relief of oblivion.

7

"Something's wrong with her, Liz. I can't stand by and do nothing," Laszlo growled.

"Shut up and look at her. Really *look*, Lo."

He followed his sister's pointing finger. A ripple started under Ebba's smooth skin as if a parasite traveled beneath the surface, and a gray haze filled the air around her, clouding her aura and causing her standard glow to dull.

Until that exact moment, whenever he witnessed her shine waver, he'd assumed it was from the memory of the accident and Spencer's death. Now he knew differently. She was under a psychic attack!

"Ebba! Get in here!" he shouted, calling her spirit self.

Liz and Rafe stared at him like he'd lost his ever-loving mind.

"Yeah, you missed that part, but I don't have the time to explain." To the ghostly Ebba, he said, "Start talking. What the hell is going on? No bullshit."

With a grimace, she floated to the bed to watch herself.

"I'm not sure, but if I had to guess, I'd say my body is

50

possessed." The large doe-like eyes she turned on him held sorrow. "Whatever it is, it's hurting my physical self. I've been trying to chase it away, but it's stealthy, hiding out and feeding negative thoughts. Making it seem like they're my own."

"When did this start?"

"I can't recall with any certainty. The days fade in and out. But the first time I remember something being off was when I appeared in a hospital room about twelve hours after my body was admitted. Liz was talking to me, her, er, my body. Fucking hell, this is confusing." With a shake of her dark curls, she focused on his sister. "She said I wasn't allowed to move on because she wouldn't know what to do without me. I've been fighting to get back into my body ever since."

Consternation drew his brows together, and he nodded slowly before facing Liz. Facts needed to be verified, but first he wanted to know what she had done to secure Ebba's spirit to this plane.

"Liz, I need you to think back to the day of Ebba's accident when she was admitted to the hospital and you spoke to her."

"How did you…? Never mind. I can guess." Waving her hand, she dismissed her previous question and asked, "What specifically do you want to know?"

"Did you use magic to tie her to this plane?" Her sharp inhale was followed by a coughing fit, and it was all the answer he needed. "Okay, that's a no. But her spirit is present, and she said you called to her. What exactly did you say?"

Frowning, she glanced at the bed, likely trying to recall the words she'd uttered in her worry and grief. "I told her she couldn't leave me, and I wouldn't know what to do without her."

Her gaze was stark with remembered fear. "Ebba was so fragile, lying there, Lo, and the doctors weren't confident she would pull through. But I remember, in those early hours, it was like she wasn't there. Like her body was a shell of itself."

"It's all right, *qalbi*." Rafe wrapped an arm around his wife and kissed her temple. "She'll be well soon. We'll make it so."

A charming mix of Maltese and French, Rafe was a woman's wet dream. In addition to his dark good looks, he had the whole ex-spy thing going for him, lending him an air of mystery. But he only had eyes for Liz, and she for him. After a holiday fling and a four-year separation, they ran into each other again. Rafe took his mission to make her the happiest woman alive seriously, and from what Laszlo could tell, his brother-in-law was succeeding. He'd promise her the world and do his damnedest to fulfill that promise.

"I love him for her," Spirit Ebba said, releasing a hearty sigh. "They are true soulmates."

"Yes," Lo agreed, letting the others assume he was responding to Rafe's comment.

What was it like to find your one true love? Castor and Alastair had busted his balls earlier, but he wasn't in love with Ebba, as they suspected. He didn't have the capacity to love fully. Charlotte had seen to that. Perhaps it was for the best that Ebba had rejected him. If he did anything as stupid as seducing her, there would be no way she emerged unscathed. Her heart was too open and giving. If they became involved on more than a friendship level, she'd end up in a world of hurt.

He ignored his cynical internal voice, laughing its fool head off.

Heaving a weary sigh, he approached the bed. All he wanted was to curl up beside her and take a nap. Maybe cuddle her in the process. He smiled at the lovely picture she made, but it quickly morphed into a scowl as another ripple passed beneath her skin.

"I'm going to eradicate you," he promised the other entity haunting her.

Lo wasn't prepared for it to strike back, and the forceful

shove sent him into the nightstand. The corner impacted his hip.

Sonofabitch!

"What the hell?" Liz ducked as objects began to fly, and Rafe bent to protect her from the debris.

A shard of glass caught Lo just below the eye, and he swore under his breath. "Go! Get out!"

Two more figurines crashed into his shoulder and head as he ushered Liz and Rafe from the bedroom and slammed the door.

"We've got a serious problem," he told them.

EBBA WAS SUFFOCATING, OR AT LEAST IT FELT LIKE IT. THE weight on her chest made breathing a struggle, and with each inhalation, the pressure grew. Her skin felt too tight for her body, and it itched as if fleas were biting her torso. The desire to scratch was strong, but her extremities wouldn't move.

"They think you're crazy, Ebba," the voice inside her mind taunted, and the sneering sound made her stomach ache. "You have to get out of here. Escape."

Escape.

Escape.

Escape.

The word drummed through her head without relief, allowing no other thought but to do as instructed. The instant the pressure on her chest subsided, she jumped up and ran for the window. After she inched it open, she glanced down.

"Two stories isn't high," the voice assured her. "Lower your body over the edge and hang on with your hands. Let your feet dangle as far as you can, then let go."

She nodded, but doubts assailed her. Twenty feet was a long way to fall.

"Ebba."

Lo's voice was calm, but there was an edge of urgency.

"Don't look at him. Jump," the voice inside demanded. "Do it, Ebba, or they'll lock you up. Do you want to be locked up for being crazy?"

The room turned cold, and her quick, panting breaths produced visible puffs of air. Fighting the urge to face Lo, she rubbed her arms against the chill and wished the decision to jump wouldn't risk a broken ankle or two.

"Ebba, Sweet, listen to me, not whatever is urging you to go out that window." Lo eased closer, and she rebelled against the phantom voice to glance at him. The confidence in his eyes and the hesitant smile screamed trustworthy. *He* knew she wasn't crazy. Hadn't he already said he saw the ghost?

When he was less than five feet away, the drumming started in her mind.

Escape.

Escape.

Escape.

She swung a leg over the ledge. Anything to ease the relentless noise in her head.

"Ebba, please don't. I can't help you if you jump," Laszlo said, taking another step closer.

And she *did* need his help, didn't she? Wasn't that why she'd gone to see him in the first place?

Then he was there. His solid hands were warm on the freezing skin of her arms, hauling her back into the room as the window slid shut behind her without the aid of human contact. The lock was engaged for good measure.

"For what it's worth, your spirit self didn't think jumping was wise either," Lo assured her, wrapping her in a bear hug. Tangling his fingers through her short hair, he eased her head back, and she met his worried gaze. "Whatever that other voice says, don't listen to it. *Ever.* It doesn't have your best interests at heart and only wants to retain control of your body. Do you understand?"

"It's so loud in my head," she croaked. "It's screaming and swearing, warning me to stay away from you. I've never heard it before, but I think it's always been there."

"It's because whoever's in there is going to get their sorry ass ejected, and they know it."

Instantaneous rage overcame her, and she shoved his chest. When he didn't budge, she curled her fingers into claws and aimed for his face. As if he'd anticipated the move, Lo captured her wrists in an instant.

"Your days are numbered, fucker," he muttered.

Helpless tears welled, and Ebba blinked to clear her vision.

Concern for her was evident in his eyes, but his grip didn't ease. "We'll get this sorted, Sweet Ebba. I promise."

"Help me, Lo," she cried. "Please."

"I intend to."

"Don't put me away. It says you will. Don't lock me in an institution."

"Never!"

His fierce promise eased the panic building within, and for the moment, she was able to suppress the voice. The strength drained from her, and she sagged against him when the fatigue made it too difficult to stay awake.

8

"I'm going to pulverize that fucker when it's out of me," Spirit Ebba snarled.

Laszlo snorted as he cuddled her sleeping physical self. He'd always admired her feistiness and can-do drive, but her ghostly form revealed her personality in a whole new light. One he appreciated the hell out of.

"Don't think I won't!" she ranted.

"I believe you would if you could. But the ultimate goal is to eject the interloper and put you back where you belong at that exact moment. It's likely you won't exist in the same place and time."

"Dammit!" As she stomped back and forth at the end of the bed, casting them worried glances, the curtains flew and tchotchkes rattled on the dresser.

"Temper, Sweet," Lo warned. "Save your energy for the transition. We're going to attempt it soon."

"Right," she muttered.

Liz entered with Rafe on her heels. "How is she?"

"How does it look?" Spirit Ebba snapped. "Like she's been possessed and unable to take advantage of a hot dude—oh, uh!"

If a ghost could blush, she would've. As it was, the look she cast him was decidedly uncomfortable.

Lo grinned.

"By your fool smile, I'm assuming she's doing better," Liz said, dropping to the edge of the bed and stroking Ebba's dark curls.

"She's not, but her spirit's retained her snark."

Liz laughed. "That's why we love our girl."

Love. It was the second time someone had bandied the word about him today. The cynical side of him laughed. Supposedly, Thornes only loved once, and he'd screwed that up royally with Charlotte. Or rather, she did. Her jealousy and accusations drove him mad until he couldn't take another minute of the fighting. All because of his frequent quests to help others exorcise their ghosts. In the end, it had required a spell from Alastair for her to find him repellent and to sign the divorce papers to end their misery.

He prayed to the Goddess that Charlotte was happy now and could move on to have a loving relationship with someone else. Just not him. Whatever he'd once felt for her was nothing more than ash in his mouth. The proverbial bad taste transferred to his current mood, leaving him uncomfortable while holding Ebba. Easing her away, Laszlo sat up and covered her with a blanket.

"Whoever is possessing her isn't going to make it easy to take her body back. It had her convinced to jump out the window," he said.

"What?!"

Liz's shock was mirrored by Rafe, and they shared a horrified glance before turning their attention back to Lo.

"She could've been killed!"

"Doubtful." Lo snorted. "It's only two stories, but she

could've definitely been hurt. Still, it's not something we can't heal if it comes down to it."

"That healing thing is badass," Spirit Ebba said from her dresser perch.

He laughed. "It is."

"What is what?" Liz frowned.

"I wasn't speaking to you."

"Oh. *Oh!* You mean Ebba's spirit is here? *Now?* It didn't register properly before."

He nodded toward the dresser and grinned as Liz and Rafe squinted, hoping for a glimpse. With disappointment pulling her mouth down, his sister harrumphed her displeasure.

"What's our game plan? Do I call Spring to see what spell she thinks would work, or should we raid the Thorne Industries vault for artifacts—Wait!" She had a lightbulb-went-off moment. "Nash had something similar happen with Ryanne. They swapped her soul for her sister's—"

Laszlo shook his head. "I remember Nash telling me about it, but this situation isn't the same as his mate's. Ebba's not in stasis. This is more of a possession than a soul swap."

"Right. Okay. What about Alastair? Surely he's come across this before?"

"Already spoke to him. He's checking to see what Nash and Spring might know." He hated to leave Ebba, but he had his own source to suss out. "Can you stay with her and make sure the entity haunting her doesn't harm her in any way? I have to talk to Clutch."

McClutchin "Clutch" Adams was a long-time friend and colleague. He and Lo had met in the early days of their ghost-seeking careers. If anyone knew about possession and exorcism, it was the ex-priest turned hunter.

"Sure. We'll keep her safe."

"Please hurry, Lo," Spirit Ebba urged. "This was the closest he's gotten to harming her."

Lo nodded, but before he'd taken two steps, he froze and spun back. "He?"

"Spencer," she said condescendingly, making it sound like he should've figured it out long before that moment.

"You don't think that was a bit of crucial information you might've told me before now?"

"I didn't know. But now that I do, it's obvious. What other spirit was I around recently? The timing was right for it to be him." She shrugged. "And based on the fucking eye-blinding light he's trying hard to hide, I'd say he's one of you."

"Wait, *what*?"

"Lo?" Liz appeared anxious as she waited for his conversation to play out with Spirit Ebba. "What's going on?"

He glared at his sister. "Did you know she was dating a witch?"

"No! How could I?"

"You never met the man?"

"She said they weren't serious. As far as I knew, they'd only gone out a few times, and she said she was planning to end it. There wasn't time to meet him."

Somewhat pacified, he nodded. Still, the idea of Ebba dating another witch felt, well, for lack of a better word, icky. "It's possible this will be trickier than expected if he has magic on his side."

"I agree. You call Clutch, and I'll seek out Nash. I remember an item from our inventory that could work to capture—"

"No more saying anything aloud," he warned. "I have the feeling he has a way of hearing us." Addressing Rafe, he said, "I'll need you to guard her, man. Can you do that while we're gone?"

"With my life," his brother-in-law assured him, hand over heart and head bowed.

Liz snorted. "Don't get extreme, babe. You need to be around for many years to come, if only to keep me happy."

"I live for your happiness, *qalbi*."

The twinkle in Rafe's eye added to Lo's building uncomfortableness.

"Yeah, okay. I'm out, but I'll be back soon."

"Why can't you just call Clutch?" Liz asked belatedly.

"He shorts out electronics. Something to do with energy frequency and his ability to attract spirits." Fascination flared to life in her eyes, and when she opened her mouth to speak, Lo shook his head. "No time, sis, but you can annoy him with questions when you see him again."

Picturing Clutch's apartment, Laszlo drew his power around him like a cloak and sent a thread across the distance as a feeler. When he detected no movement, he began the teleport into his friend's living room above the antiques-and-oddities shop he owned and operated.

EBBA GRIPPED LASZLO'S ARM, MEANING TO ASK HIM A QUESTION prior to his leaving, but in the next second, she was out of her apartment and squarely in another.

"Ebba!"

A sense of vertigo swept through her consciousness, causing her to sway, and she once again latched onto Lo, if only to prevent the room from spinning.

"What were you thinking?" Anger caused his voice to deepen, and the rough quality sent a chill through her. Or it would've had she been corporeal. Still, she had a sense of self. As if she *did* possess a physical form but her body didn't seem to fit, and the skin of that non-real body felt thin, as if it would take nothing to peel off her muscle and bone.

"I don't feel well," she admitted right before her knees buckled.

Lo dove to help before they both remembered she didn't have a physical self in her current state.

"It's dangerous for you to be away from your body, Ebba."

"I didn't intend to leave. Hell, I didn't think I *could* leave." She pressed her fingers to her temples. "I've been stuck in that fucking apartment for months."

"Stuck?" His frown was dangerous and dark, similar to when he first burst through her door. "What do you mean stuck? You should be able to go anywhere your body goes."

"No. If I touch the knob to the outside or even a window, it burns me."

A door clicked shut behind her, and Lo's gaze swept the newcomer before focusing on her again.

"Burns? How exactly?" the man she assumed was Clutch asked, joining them.

"You can see me?" When he nodded, she became oddly emotional. Gratitude flooded her entire being, and she had a massive urge to throw herself into the man's strong arms.

She took stock of his person, too overcome to speak. Standing about six-three, he was dark-skinned and possessed a smoothly shaved head. His midnight-colored eyes glowed with an appreciative light, and when he grinned at her speechlessness, straight white teeth greeted her.

"You're gorgeous," she blurted.

"Excuse me?" Lo choked on a laugh.

"Oh, I... um, he..." She cleared her throat. "His build. He's pretty much perfect."

"Yeah, I get that a lot," Clutch said with a deep belly laugh. His was the voice of a soulful blues musician, and the pleasurable raspy sound added to his appeal.

"I bet you do," she mumbled, unable to take her gaze from his thick biceps and heavenly shoulders.

Lo's fingers materialized in front of her, and he snapped them a few times to gain her attention.

"Ebba! Stop eyeing him like a tenderloin at a steak-lovers' convention and focus on the subject at hand."

Clutch's grin widened. "He's just jealous I'm hotter than he is. Eye-fuck me all you want, girl. I live for these moments."

She laughed. How could she not when the man was so down-to-earth and funny?

"As if," Lo muttered. His surly attitude and Clutch's throaty chuckle caused her to laugh harder.

"I bet the sight of you two together has caused many a woman to check with her cardiologist." Pleased her comment had Laszlo fighting a smile, she winked in his direction. "But now I understand why you never brought him around while we were younger."

"Yes, he only seeks me out when he needs something." Clutch's warm gaze traveled the length of her and back before he shook his head. "Too bad he saw you first, Ebba girl."

"Oh, we aren't a thing," she assured him. "He's—"

"He's interested, so hands off," Laszlo growled with a glare for his friend.

"Careful, Lo. You're beginning to sound like your ex." A sardonic smile curled Clutch's generous mouth. "That girl was pure evil."

"She wasn't," he denied.

"That's why it required a spell to get rid of her, right?"

Ebba looked at Lo with new eyes. "It did?"

His discomfort with the conversation was seen in the tensing of his shoulders and the micro grimace before he changed the subject.

"We have a problem, Clutch, and I'm hoping you can help."

The man got right down to business. "Possession?"

"Yes, but he's magical. What tricks do you have in that book of yours to extract him?"

"It's not as simple as whipping out a voodoo doll, my man. It's more nuanced with witches and warlocks. You know that."

"But you've come across this before, right?"

As the two men conversed, they strode across the room to

an altar-like area filled with what appeared to be antique relics. In the center was a black leather-bound book, roughly twenty by twelve inches. The exposed edges of the pages were wavy and darker than regular paper, as if they were aged parchment. Ebba had only ever seen the like in museums.

A wave of dizziness struck her, along with a bitter cold.

"Uh, guys?" she called weakly. "I don't feel so well."

As one, they spun toward her. Clutch's reaction was mild, and his features barely registered a problem. Laszlo's eyes flared wide, and he rushed in her direction, only to be halted by his friend's hand on his arm.

"Don't move, Lo," he ordered in a low tone. "Not an inch. That's Death you're staring down, and she don't play."

Ebba froze.

Death?

Like, what the fuck? How was Death an actual entity? Yeah, she'd seen *Meet Joe Black*, but that was fiction, right?

"McClutchin Adams and Laszlo Thorne." The names were spoken in a tone as cold as the ice in Ebba's veins. Or what would be in her veins if she were whole. "You've been very naughty boys. *Again.*"

9

*F**uck.*

Laszlo wished he could swear aloud, but he took his cue from Clutch and froze.

For now.

But if it came down to a bargain with Death for Ebba's soul, he'd do it in a heartbeat. He wouldn't have a choice. There was no way he'd let her go in the prime of her life. Not when none of this was her fault. He met Ebba's terrified gaze and willed her to remain calm.

Death sauntered forward, capturing his attention and catching him off guard when her black cloak dissolved in a swirling mist. He'd never seen her in the flesh before, but he had a better idea of Clutch's obsession with her.

The blonde was centerfold material in her red leather catsuit and gold, two-thousand-dollar Rene Caovilla heels. Her proportions were the perfect hourglass, and with every step, her hips tempted the Saints. Neither Clutch nor Lo were saints, so the struggle to not be hypnotized by her movement was real.

Ebba's eyes narrowed as if she guessed his thoughts, or perhaps it was the sweat beading on his brow that concerned her. Either way, a smidgeon of her fear receded the longer she stared at him.

"You ogled Clutch. All's fair in love and war, Sweet," he murmured.

Death's perfectly coiffed head whipped around to glare at Ebba.

"In the most respectful way possible," she squeaked, edging closer to Lo and pointing at him. "We're together."

Clutch nearly busted a gut laughing. The three who didn't find it as amusing all stared in shock as he doubled over.

"Start talking, lover, or the lost soul comes with me," Death warned with her hands on shapely hips.

Sobering, Clutch strode to her and cupped her neck. "Don't be jealous, girl. You know I don't cheat."

"There's no cheating Death," she reminded them all. Her comment served to drive home the seriousness of the situation. If they couldn't talk their way out of this and didn't find a way to help Ebba, Death would come for her.

Her icy blue eyes lit on Laszlo. "Speak."

"Ebba was in a car accident some months ago. A Traveler bound her to this plane, hoping to save her. In doing so, it opened her body up, and a warlock hitchhiked a ride when he should've crossed over. We recently discovered this and now need to eject his sorry ass. We arrived here less than ten minutes ago, hoping Clutch had a spell we could use."

She studied him through narrowed eyes, weighing the truth, then shifted her head to Ebba. "What's your full name?"

"Ebba James."

A scroll materialized in thin air, and the cylinders holding it worked in unison as the parchment unrolled and rolled faster than imaginable. It was impossible for them to read, but Death scanned every line until the magical scroll stopped moving. Light backlit the name etched into the paper, causing it to glow and pulse.

Ebba James.

The date was written in Roman numerals, making it difficult to decipher or calculate.

"You were supposed to die five months ago, Ebba James. I will take you now and be done with this mess."

"No!" Lo stepped forward, blocking her from Death's apathetic gaze. "Respectfully," he added with a gulp, fighting against the threatening panic. Yes, he answered to Isis, but Death would always find a way. "This isn't her fault, but Spencer can't be left inside her body."

"Who is this body-stealing Spencer?"

Ebba sidestepped Lo and approached the blonde. "His name is Spencer Barlowe. He's an insurance broker from Greenville."

Lo frowned. "Really? You went out with an insurance broker? *Dude!* No wonder you were bored."

Both women scowled in his direction, and he mimed zipping his lip. Behind Death's back, Clutch grinned like a damned fool, earning himself her elbow to his ribs.

"Behave, McClutchin," she ordered.

"Your wish is my command, Queen."

She rolled her eyes but warmed considerably after his endearment.

"You're into necrophilia?" she asked Lo. When he sputtered his indignation, her brows arched, and her mouth curled in a mocking smile. "Surely you and Ms. James weren't cheating on poor Spencer Barlowe while they were an item, yes?"

"Of course not!" he and Ebba denied in stereo.

"That means you—what's the term, McClutchin—hooked up?" At his nod, she continued. "That means you hooked up after her demise, i.e., you are into the deceased."

"We haven't hooked up," Lo ground out, sure his molars couldn't take the pressure of his frustration much longer.

"Then you lied, Ms. James," Death stated in a frigid tone, turning chilly eyes on Ebba. "You're not 'together' as you claim."

Looking terrified, Ebba cast him a beseeching look, and he wanted nothing more than to hold her.

"It's okay, Sweet. It'll be okay."

"You can't promise things of that nature, Laszlo Thorne," Death countered. "Despite your gifts, you aren't in charge of who stays and goes. *I* am."

Easing closer to Ebba, he nodded. "Understood, but if you could find it in your heart to—"

"You have forty-eight hours to deliver the runaway souls of Ebba James and Spencer Barlowe to me. Here at McClutchin's dwelling. Don't be late." With a wave of her hand, she rolled the scroll, vanishing it in a poof of smoke. She sauntered toward Clutch's bedroom. Stopping at the entrance, she cast a coquettish look toward his friend. "Are you coming, lover?"

"Yes, ma'am!" Clutch said with a grin that didn't reach his eyes. "Let me show them out, Queen, and I'll attend to your every need."

"You'd better."

Clutch sobered when she disappeared through the doorway. "Look, man. I won't make any promises, but I can talk to her, maybe change her mind, okay?" After crossing to his spellbook, he opened it about a third of the way, then flipped a few pages to find what he was searching for. "Here it is. I think this one could work." He tore the page from its binding and handed it to Lo along with a baseball-sized sphere and a clay figure without any discernible features.

"I know I said it wasn't a matter of Voodoo dolls, but it's all I've got in a pinch. Use the doll to draw out ol' Spencer, then shove him into this holding globe. Hopefully, it will keep him, but don't count on it. Death understands a captured spirit is as good as a free one." He gave Ebba a regretful look. "I'm sorry, girl. You'd have given Lo a run for his money, alright."

"You sound like it's a done deal," she croaked.

He shared a long look with Laszlo, and they both understood what he left unspoken. By the time either of them was called and Death showed her ravishing self, it was a done deal.

"She rarely changes her mind. But I'll try," Clutch said.

With a quick hug for Lo, he rushed away.

Silence hung in the air between Ebba and Laszlo after his departure.

"He looks like he can show her a good time. Maybe there's a chance," she said.

The desire to laugh battled with his urge to throw the mother of all tantrums. To keep both reactions at bay, Lo merely nodded.

"How do we get home?" she asked.

"We aren't going straight back," he said as an idea occurred to him. "We're going to pay a Goddess a visit."

"I DON'T UNDERSTAND," EBBA SAID FOR WHAT SEEMED LIKE THE hundredth time after they arrived in the clearing by Thorne Manor.

"You will in due time, Sweet. Can you cut me a break here? My head feels like it's about to explode." The tension was killing him, and Lo didn't want her to catch on to how worried he was about her future or lack thereof. Although he'd never met Death in person, he knew she didn't play when it came to mortal souls. His only hope was Isis. Which was why he was waiting on sacred ground after texting Alastair to meet him here.

He glanced at his watch.

What the hell was taking him so long? His cousin was prompter than prompt. Al's motto was along the lines of "Arrive early. If you're on time, you're late."

"Why do you keep looking at your watch, Lo? I'm sure your hot cousin will be here any minute. We didn't give him much by way of notice, you know."

He stopped pacing to glare at her, seated on the altar and swinging her shapely, petite legs. "What the hell is with your infatuation with all the men you meet today?"

"I was seeing if you were paying attention."

Her grin disarmed him, and Lo was enchanted by her arresting face. That damned smile was beginning to do strange things to his insides. It was more than his desire to spend endless steamy nights together. It had become a physical need to see her face light up when she looked at him.

He scowled harder when she sighed and launched herself off her stone perch. As she sauntered to him, she trailed her gaze over his visage, pausing on his lips before meeting his eyes.

"You have to face facts, Lo. I have." Her mouth twisted into a sad half smile. "You might be unable to save me, and that's okay."

"No! I—"

Pressing her finger to his lips, she shook her head. Her touch was more a slight vibration than physical restraint, but it was enough to quiet him.

"Just promise me you'll get Spencer out of my body and send that fucker to hell, where he belongs."

His eyes burned, and he had to blink to clear his vision. The gathering moisture on his lashes created a kaleidoscope of greenery. He wanted to tell her he would save her, promise her a long life, but the rules were different for her kind, and Castor had fucked them by binding her to this plane. She'd be lucky if the Powers That Be allowed her to reincarnate on the next go-around.

As if Ebba read his mind, she cocked her head and asked, "What did Death mean when she called Spencer and me 'runaway souls,' Lo?"

"They're spirits who avoid moving on to the afterlife. They become outlaws of a sort."

Her troubled expression conveyed what he was feeling.

"I'm going to do my best to help you, Ebba. Believe it."

"But if you can't, I need you to be at peace with it."

"I'm not sure that's possible," he replied through a tight throat. His voice was gravelly, as if he'd repeatedly downed flaming Blue Blazer cocktails and burned the lining of his esophagus.

The urge to hold her overcame him. The frustration attached to that inability was making his skin feel too tight and driving him mad. Oddly, he suspected he needed the comfort more than her. Acceptance came freely to those closer to true death. Not the living.

"I'm not prepared to lose you just yet, Ebba James," he said hoarsely.

Her smile was luminescent, and her soul glowed with her pleasure. The tug of her inner beauty was strong, as was his desire to bask in her warmth.

"You're not losing anyone, son."

He spun to acknowledge his solemn-faced cousin's comment. "Death came for her, Al. I don't know what to do." Lifting his hands, he showed the page, the globe, and the voodoo doll. "Clutch only had these to offer, but I thought if we could call Isis and explain what Castor did…" The desperation in Laszlo's voice was cringeworthy.

"She's family to you and Liz, and that makes her an honorary Thorne. We'll do what we can," Alastair promised.

10

If she lived to be a hundred, Ebba would never forget the following ceremony and the resulting appearance of the Goddess Isis in the clearing.

Castor arrived not long after Alastair, and Ebba was left to assume he'd called his friend prior to showing up. After Castor and Laszlo shared a look of mutual dislike, the three men set about "casting" a circle.

The process consisted of wreathing salt around the altar and placing white pillar candles in a pentagram shape inside the mineral barrier. The wicks flared to life with a mere wave of Alastair's hand, causing Ebba to doubt her sanity. Surely this was all a bizarre dream, or someone had slipped her 'shrooms and she was tripping dinosaur balls.

Their first spell was to reveal Ebba's spirit to the group so they could see and hear her, allowing her to participate in the discussion and decision-making. Next came the call for the Goddess.

"Goddess, hear our plea.

71

Assist us in this time of need.
Come, Exalted One, we need thee."

A line of eye-popping white light materialized above the stone slab, growing in size until roughly seven feet tall. The line flared brighter, causing Ebba to shield her face or sear her retinas, and when she felt the pulsing heat die down, she dared to peek.

A petite woman with olive-toned skin and waist-length black hair stepped through what could only be construed as a veil opening between worlds or planes. Ebba didn't know which. The female was dressed in a flowing teal dress loosely gathered below her breasts and held up at the shoulders with jeweled clips. Golden asps were wrapped around each bicep, emphasizing her toned arms. Her features were perfectly symmetrical, and her nose was what every woman who sought a plastic surgeon hoped to achieve. All-knowing eyes were lined with black kohl, adding to her exotic good looks.

She was a living goddess and the most beautiful woman Ebba had ever seen.

Their gazes locked as Isis floated down from the altar and sashayed her way to Alastair.

The men dropped to one knee and bowed, not daring to address the Goddess until she spoke.

"Beloved."

"Exalted One," Alastair replied, smiling at her with devastating charm. "Thank you for gracing us with your presence."

She cast another glance Ebba's way. "Why is this mortal child here, and why is she not showing me the proper respect?"

Panicked, Ebba dropped to her knees and bowed her head.

"Apologies, Exalted One," she gushed.

"Clever girl," Isis murmured, moving to stand above her. "You may rise and tell me why two of my favorite rascals have summoned me."

"That's my fault—" Castor began, only to stop when she held up a hand.

"I didn't ask you, Alexander. I asked this child."

Lo met Ebba's worried gaze and nodded his encouragement.

After climbing to her feet, she lifted her chin and inhaled deeply. Upon the exhalation, she relayed the story to the Goddess, leaving nothing out.

"Death is now demanding Lo—that's Laszlo—deliver both Spencer and me to her within two days," Ebba said in conclusion. Girding her loins for the ask, she gulped down her trepidation. "Can you help us?"

"No."

Laszlo sucked in air so quickly he coughed, capturing Isis's notice.

"Laszlo Thorne. I don't believe we've had the pleasure of meeting in person."

Red-faced from his fit, he shook his head. "No, ma'am."

Kohl-lined eyes narrowed as Isis looked between them.

"Not lovers… *yet*," she murmured. "I'd say mere friends, but your exchanges are filled with heat, and your auras continually shift. There is more to your relationship than it would first appear."

Uncomfortable under the Goddess's regard and unable to meet Lo's gaze, Ebba cast a quick glance at the other men. Castor appeared amused, and Alastair, well, he was positively gloating as if proven correct.

"Exalted One, may I be so bold as to ask why?" Lo redirected everyone's focus to her denial, and Ebba could've kissed him for his timely intervention.

Black brows rose, and Isis's luscious mouth curled ever so slightly. "Being bold is a Thorne trait." She gestured for them all to rise and led the procession to the altar, snuffing candles with nothing more than a wave of her hand as she passed.

"Why bother with all the pomp and ceremony of a protective circle, Alastair? You know it's not needed to summon me."

"Theatrical effect for the young 'uns," he replied with a roguish grin, earning a laugh from Castor and a glare from Laszlo.

Ebba bit her lip to contain her amusement, thoroughly charmed by the older man. Or she *assumed* he was older, but maybe not by much. Ebba's secret obsession was movies from the thirties and forties. Charming actors like Grant, Peck, and Gable elicited a girly sigh whenever they walked on-screen. Alastair Thorne easily fit in with those men with his tailored suits and stylish haircut. His vibe screamed gentleman from a bygone era, yet he appeared to be in his mid-forties at best.

"How old are you?" She winced even as the question cleared her lips.

His brows shot up as Castor clapped him on the shoulder with another hearty laugh.

"Pushing eighty," Laszlo said, grim satisfaction in his expression. "Sorry, Al. She deserves to know that not only are you old enough to be her grandfather, but you're married to boot."

"You should point out Castor has a son her age," Isis added with an air of faux innocence, smiling wide when Castor's mouth clamped shut and a muscle ticked along his jaw. "She's meant for another, Alexander. You shouldn't muddy the waters."

He replied with a stiff nod and an affronted look.

Laszlo's heart sank to his stomach. "Who? Who is she meant for?"

Once again, Isis's brows rose.

He'd surprised himself, so there was no doubt everyone else might be, too. Why the hell couldn't he keep his mouth shut?

"I would think that's obvious," Al replied in a desert-dry tone. "But let's circle back to that, shall we?"

Miserable and feeling particularly foolish, Lo nodded.

"I suspect I know the reason, Exalted One, but for the sake of those who don't, why are you unable to help?" Alastair asked.

"There must be balance in all things. Even Death," she explained with a sympathetic smile for Ebba. "When Alexander bound you to the Earth, he threw off the balance. It must be rectified."

Lo hated her answer. Inasmuch as Castor's impulsive action knocked Ebba's fate off course, it had also bought the Thornes time to help her or, as it looked to be the case in two days, time to say goodbye. "Is there a way to do it without costing Ebba her life?"

"Her life was forfeit the moment her vehicle struck the tree, child." The Goddess stroked a finger along his brow, and a small margin of the anxiety he was experiencing eased. "Death will have her payment."

Ebba's eyes, enormous and tragic, met his, and though her smile was brave, it wobbled.

"No." He shook his head. "No, that can't be the end. Not for her. We're magical beings, for fuck's sake!" Working up to a full steam, he began to pace. "What other sacrifice can we make? Abilities? I'll give mine."

"That's not enough," Isis said with compassion not typically attributed to a deity. They had no real reason to care about the plight of mortals, yet for some unknown reason, she did.

Ebba drifted to him and placed her hand against his chest, over the region of his heart. The pulsing energy warmed him, chasing away the cold from the finality of Isis's answer.

"It's okay, Lo," she said, intent on reassuring *him* when she was the one whose life was over. "You've done all you can."

"No. No. I can't accept this. If she won't help, I'll find

another way, Ebba." He pressed his hand over hers, jerking in shock when the contact felt solid. His should've passed through hers, but the very real sensation of her skin was disconcerting. "Don't give up."

"If anyone can do it, it'll be you." Her faith in him was humbling, but it was the acknowledgment and acceptance of her ultimate demise lurking in the depths of her chocolaty eyes that had his heart skipping beats.

"I need you to believe in me. Don't assume this decision is final," he begged, not caring how desperate he sounded. "We'll reverse it somehow."

She rose on tiptoe and pressed her lips to his. The sweet innocence of their first kiss wasn't lost on him, and the memory would be one he cherished forever.

Wrapping his hand around her neck and marveling at how real she felt, he drew her close to whisper, "I don't intend that to be our last kiss, Ebba James. Remember what I told you at the café. We will be lovers," he promised.

A saucy smile curled her full lips, illuminating her beauty and sparking an answering fire inside him. "When we get back to my apartment and give ol' Spencer the boot so I can have my body back for whatever ti—uh, so I can have my body back, I'll hold you to that, Laszlo Thorne."

"Why do you have this spell and implements in a sacred space?" Isis interrupted, glaring at the objects on the altar. "Do you think to trap me?"

The subtle shift of their group's energy told Lo he'd fucked up. Big time!

Voodoo and Thorne magic weren't meant to blend, and the spells in their family grimoire were as far from the Haitian religion as two worlds could be.

The sensation of his balls shriveling to raisins almost had him unzipping and checking his junk. Never had a man backpedaled so fast in the face of a woman's rage as Laszlo did.

"No, Exalted One! I unthinkingly laid them there when we began casting the circle. The spell is meant to trap Spencer—the soul occupying Ebba's body. I swear."

His adrenaline spiked, and the need to flee from her fury was causing his heart to hammer. Nausea churned his belly, threatening to spew forth. Struggling to keep it down and not shit his pants in the process, he passed the back of his wrist across his upper lip to mop the sweat forming there.

"I meant no harm or disrespect."

Her kohl-lined, amber eyes narrowed with her displeasure, and it belatedly occurred to him where his father's family had obtained their unique looks. Many times while growing up, he and his brothers had been the recipients of a similar stare from Leland Thorne. Or they were until he took off for parts unknown, never to return.

"Is my dad on the other side?" He wasn't sure what had prompted him to ask, other than Leland's resemblance to Isis. Long ago, he'd given up caring about the man who couldn't be bothered to contact his family.

"No. He's not a resident of the Otherworld." Her haughty response was tempered by a grudging kindness, suggesting she understood the endless agony of not knowing.

Endless agony? Where did that ridiculous sentiment come from?

"What of Hell? Would you know if he's a resident there?" Ebba asked the Goddess, somehow sensing his desire to know but also realizing he would never venture to ask.

"I would know. All souls, even mortals such as yourself, come through the waiting room of the Otherworld. Leland Thorne never crossed the veil. As far as I know, he's still living."

Lo's breath whooshed out, and he met Alastair's considering gaze. A discussion was in order, he was sure.

Overhead, the clouds began morphing into different shapes

as they darkened in color. The sky's afternoon light flickered as if transitioning to an eclipse. The air currents picked up, blowing the salt from their protective circle to the winds, and the items flew from the altar, landing a hundred feet to Laszlo's left, far from Isis.

"Calm your emotions, child," she advised him. "Like Alastair, yours are tethered to your power. I imagine you've never been upset enough to cause a tornado, but as an air elemental, you have the potential."

"Lo is doing this?" Ebba glanced around in wonder. "The wind, light, and swaying trees?"

"Indeed." The Goddess sauntered to the stone altar, spread her arms, and used the current he caused to lift herself. When she rotated toward them, her long locks were dancing with the breeze and the skirt of her dress was playing a game of peek-a-boo with her smooth, shapely legs. "My advice is to cherish, not squander, the time you have with your beloved, Laszlo Thorne. Every moment counts while she's with you."

The entry to the veil glowed behind her as she tapped one tapered finger against her pouting lips, the picture of a woman deep in thought. "I suppose it's a good thing you don't have a familiar to amplify your power. This area would be devastated by your brewing storm."

11

"There's a clue in her parting words." Castor nodded toward the sealing veil. It snapped shut with a spark and sizzle behind Isis's grand exit. "She's great with riddles."

"You think she was trying to get a message across?" Ebba asked, fighting a yawn.

Her energy had amped up in the presence of the Goddess, but now that the deity was gone, fatigue was knocking on her door and reminding her she'd been active far too long. Spirits were like the living, and they needed to rest and regenerate. Sleep was as imperative to her as it was to any other.

"Undoubtedly," Alastair replied in his stead. Of Lo, he asked, "Have you ever called forth your familiar?"

"I've never felt the need."

Glancing between them, Ebba wanted to ask what all their discussion of familiars meant, but kept silent. She gleaned the concept from books she'd read and television she'd watched for entertainment. What self-respecting paranormal fan didn't know about the talking cat from *Sabrina the Teenage Witch* or the beautiful cat with a Triquetra symbol on its tag in the series *Charmed*? More recently, birds of prey, like Hedwig from *Harry Potter*, were symbolized as familiars.

Ebba frowned, recalling Liz and Laszlo watching some of those shows and movies with her. Their unexplained hysterical laughter now made a helluva lot of sense.

"What?" he asked, edging closer to wrap an arm around her waist. Or what should've been. His touch never landed, instead sweeping through her, causing a chill.

"Okay, *that* was freaky." She shuddered and sat down, using the stone wall for support. At least the smooth surface still felt solid!

Lo followed, plopping beside her, stretching his legs out, and crossing his ankles. With his hands folded in his lap, he rested his head against the wall and closed his eyes. "Why are you frowning so hard, Ebba?"

"I was thinking about the whole animal-familiar thing and recalled you and Liz laughing at me when we were younger."

"What?" His lids flew open, and he stared at her as if she'd suddenly developed a fat, hairy wart on her nose. "We never laughed at you! How the hell can you—ah!" His lips curled into a smirk. "Your obsession for witch and wizard movies. Got it."

"You're a jerk," she snapped. "You had the perfect opportunity to tell me then, but you and your siblings chose to mock me. Right to my face, I might add, without me ever knowing I was the butt of your jokes."

He sobered. "No, Sweet. We were mocking the show and how much they got wrong."

"Nothing was right?" Her disappointment was keen. She loved the paranormal.

"Some," he admitted with a twinkle. "Wands can be useful tools, and grimoires exist. Only the most talented can cause someone to fly through the air, because it takes a major energy surge to accomplish it. Freezing people can only be done by Travelers or those as powerful as Alastair, but never for long."

As she absorbed everything he'd revealed, along with the indulgent expressions of the other men, Ebba grinned. "That's badass."

"You seemed frightened earlier," he reminded her.

"Not me. Chickenshit Spencer was in charge." Sighing, she crossed her arms. "I wish I'd have known sooner. I'd have loved the extra time to learn all about what you can do."

"I'm happy to answer what I can."

"Time's running out," Alastair reminded them. "We need to get Ebba back to her body and find a way to subvert her ultimate death."

"You still intend to help us?" Lo's voice and face revealed his surprise. For one with such a close-knit family, why did he behave like every kindness was shocking?

Alastair seemed thrown by his disbelief, too. "Of course. Why wouldn't I? We're family, son."

The Adam's apple in Lo's throat bobbed repeatedly as if he were struggling with deeper emotions. Her lack of physical self thwarted Ebba's desire to hold him. Hoping to change the subject and allow him time to recover, she peppered Alastair and Castor with her questions.

"Do vampires exist?"

"I've only met one man who made me believe they could. His name was Lucian. He had an old-world air and an impossible-to-place accent," Castor said with an exaggerated flare of his eyes. "I could sense his power, but he wasn't any type of witch or warlock I'm familiar with."

"Really?" Ebba leaned in. "What happened when you encountered him?"

"Not much. We were both at a fundraising gala in New

York about ten years ago or more. Our eyes met and held across the distance of the ballroom, but I felt his presence from where I stood." Castor shrugged. "There have been very few instances when it felt as if someone walked across my grave. That was one."

"Did you speak to him?"

He chuckled. "No. My companion was eager to, though, and I abandoned her to her pursuits to find other entertainment for the evening."

"What?!" She punched his chest—and missed. "How can you leave a woman with a strange and potentially dangerous man? What's wrong with you?"

"I assure you, Ms. James. Lily was thrilled with the idea and highly capable of caring for herself."

"Lily?" Alastair grinned. "Not Lily Townsend?"

"That's the one."

With an amused snort, he tugged his cuffs. "She likely ate him up and spit him out."

"My thoughts exactly, Al," Castor replied.

Glancing between them, Laszlo joined in the conversation. "What about shifters? Are they real?"

"Shifters?" Castor and Alastair shared a disconcerted glance.

"Like werewolves," Ebba said, nodding in her curiosity. "Do werewolves exist?"

"Not that I'm aware. Al?" Passing the question off to his friend, Castor collected the pillar candles.

"I'm not certain I'd call them werewolves. Not as you'd see at a cinema, anyway. But perhaps the creatures from the Netherworld dimension could technically be classified as shifters."

"Netherworld dimension?" Aware her voice was piercing in her excitement, Ebba moderated her tone to ask, "What are they like?"

"Their snouts are elongated, their teeth able to rip a man—or woman—to shreds, and their saliva is acidic. The Aether created them to guard a child trapped in the Netherworld."

She shook her head, torn between disbelief and wonder. How did these things go on without notice? Were non-magic mortals ignorant of their surroundings twenty-four-seven?

Collecting her wayward thoughts, she tuned in to Alastair, who had continued discussing mythical creatures. "I believe historically, legend has labeled them Cerberus," he concluded.

"Wait, what did I miss? The three-headed beast that guards hell?"

"Yes."

She scoffed. "You're having me on, Mr. Thorne. Pardon my language, but no fucking way!"

"Actually, it's true," Lo said with a short laugh. "Multiple family members saw it when…"

"When?"

"This sounds even more outrageous, but when my cousin Autumn's children accidentally went through a portal to another dimension."

"Ohmygawd! That's possible?" Ebba circled back to the idea she might be tripping on psychedelic mushrooms.

"Yes." Alastair smiled in the face of her incredulousness. "Perhaps one day, in the far distant future, when it's your time to cross over, you'll experience those things."

LASZLO APPRECIATED HIS COUSIN TRYING TO EASE EBBA'S potential fears about what was to come, but the ugly truth was that Lo was in a worse state than her.

"What do you think Isis meant when she mentioned a familiar, Al?"

"They enhance a witch's power to the umpteenth degree. It may be what you require to defeat Death and keep Ebba here."

Could it really be as simple as that? Somehow, Lo doubted it.

"I've listened to your stories in the past, cousin. You've conversed with Isis many times and always came back with a new problem to solve. The two of you delight in finding workarounds." Lo sat up straighter. "That's it, isn't it? She's trying to tell me that anything I do will require additional help."

"That's what I believe, son. She can't outright tell you what to do without breaking cosmic rules or stepping on toes, but she's brilliant when it comes to supplying the tools to do things yourself." Alastair straightened his tie. "We merely need to discover what those tools are."

Ebba yawned, attempting to cover it with her hand. "Fifty dollars says it has to do with a familiar."

"I'd take the bet, but I suspect you're correct," Alastair replied. "I like you, Ms. James. You have the necessary spunk to see this challenge to its conclusion."

"Challenge." Castor chuckled. "You have a way with words, Al." Pausing in front of Ebba and Laszlo, his expression turned solemn. "If I'd have known I was going to cause you this much trouble, love, I'd have found another way to save you."

"I don't understand how you bound her to Earth. What the hell kind of spell did you use? Is it possible to reverse engineer it?" Lo asked, rubbing a hand along his neck to work out the kinks.

"Castor is descended from Zeus. He doesn't require anything but a thought to stop time and create chaos." When the man in question would've objected to Alastair's statement, his cousin shook his head. "It's not meant as an insult to you, Alex. I'm clarifying why this happened. For whatever reason, in the moment, you were compelled to save the girl at any cost. Your supercharged DNA tethered her to the earthly plane in place of her body."

"She was unable to reenter after I healed her," Castor concluded slowly. Swearing, he palmed his forehead. "I'm an idiot!"

"No argument here," Lo muttered.

Ice-blue eyes narrowed on him. "I don't believe comments were invited from the Peanut Gallery."

"And yet you got them anyway. So sad for you, dude. But maybe *think* next time before you randomly throw magic around."

"I'm *thinking* about freezing time and using your face like a piñata. Make you nice and pretty for your new girlfriend here. Interested?" His mouth kicked up on the left side in a chilly smile. "And my *unthinking* act saved her, allowing the time for you to say goodbye. You can thank Zeus for my little gift."

Lo turned salty at the suggestion of saying goodbye to Ebba. "Fuck off."

"Gladly." Castor nodded once to Alastair. "Call or text when you're ready for me to reverse what I did. I'll be waiting." With a tight smile for Ebba, Castor teleported away.

Heat crept up Lo's neck as Ebba and Al focused on him. "Sorry, but that man gets on my last fucking nerve. Like it's his personal mission to piss me off."

"It is," Alastair replied with a short laugh. "He lives to irritate. If you want to drive him insane, don't engage."

Ebba stood and brushed off the seat of her pants. Lo suspected it was out of habit since there was no physical dirt clinging to her ghostly form. "I believe you're the smartest person I've ever met, Mr. Thorne."

"Shh. Don't let word spread. Others will expect things I'm not willing to provide."

"I'll take Ebba home." Laszlo climbed to his feet with all the enthusiasm of a man heading to the gallows. His work hadn't begun, but when it did, things would get rough. "The first order of business is to eject Dipshit Spencer, the rotten pig-fucker. Will you call me if you figure out how a familiar comes into this, Al?"

"Of course. There's one other source I intend to speak to, but I'll be along shortly to work through this problem."

"Thank you."

12

*L*o whisked Ebba home at a mind-boggling speed. When they arrived, she felt out of breath, although she had no physical form for her reaction to be legit. Perhaps it was everything she'd witnessed Laszlo and his family do in the last twenty-four hours, but she never wanted to return to living in the dark about the supernatural.

"I could get used to traveling this way," she said with a laugh. "No airports or long TSA lines. No delays or lost luggage."

"No atmospheric disturbances to prevent a flight from taking off," Liz added with a grin.

"Wait! You can hear me?" With excitement bubbling up, Ebba rushed across the room to join her.

"I can see you, too, but there's a translucent quality to your skin and a pale yellow aura around you."

"Do you suppose it's leftover from the spell you cast in the clearing, Lo?" she asked him.

"Probably." He shrugged, and a part of him seemed distant as if their time with Isis had hardened his heart and resolve.

"We should take advantage of Liz's ability to see you and have the tough conversations."

"Are you okay?"

"No, Ebba, I'm not. And neither are you. Neither will Liz be when this is over if we can't find a way to save you. So how about we do away with all the touchy-feely crap and get to work?"

Recoiling from his building rage, she shared a concerned glance with Liz. Never had Ebba been subjected to his fury in the past, and if asked, she'd have said he was slow to anger.

Liz sprung to her feet and wrapped her arms around his middle the way Ebba had been dying to all her life.

"It's okay, brother-mine. Nothing is going to happen to her," Liz assured him.

"It already has," he snapped, though he embraced her back. "Death showed up looking for her while we were at Clutch's. We have less than forty-eight hours to resolve this situation, or Ebba takes a one-way trip to purgatory. She'll be forced to stay there until the Fates decide where her soul is to go."

"Sounds ominous," Ebba muttered.

Humor lit his amber eyes. "I thought you were the serious one of us, Sweet. When did you become the wise-ass?"

"Floating around the ether, waiting for people to notice your body is housing someone else, will do that to you." She gestured to the bedroom with her thumb. "How do we get rid of that… what did you call him? Pig-fucker?"

Liz choked, likely on her spit. When she finally had her coughing under control, she wiped her eyes and shook her head. "Next time, warn a girl when pig-fucker is coming."

Ebba grinned.

"I want to take a closer look at Clutch's spell," Lo said, heading to Ebba's fridge. After perusing its contents, he withdrew two beers and the makings for a sandwich. He offered one to Liz and then began constructing a hoagie. "He wouldn't have ripped a page from his grimoire if he didn't believe it had value. The voodoo doll is generic and hasn't been used before from what I can tell. There's no residual energy signature, so I can only assume it was recently created from clay."

Ebba nodded. "I watched a show once where the main character shrunk a person and turned them into a clay figurine. They fired the doll in a kiln after leaving it to dry out. Maybe we can do that?"

Both of her friends stared at her like she was the Cerberus that Alastair had assured her was real.

"No? Not something witches can do?"

"You're twisted," Lo said with wonder.

Her stomach turned to a ball of lead, and she hated he saw her as a mental case. Sure, she might be, but—

"I fucking love it," he added with a wide-ass grin. Giving her an approving nod, he looked at Liz. "She's one of us."

"One of you?" Ebba ventured.

"A Thorne." Liz tapped her bottle to her brother's. "We've always thought you were, though. Haven't we, Lo?"

His eyes glowed with an unnamed emotion. One Ebba desperately wanted to explore at length, but the timing was all wrong. It always had been. The initial age gap, his relationship with Charlotte, Ebba's death. The world was conspiring against them. Or, at the very least, against her. In her mind, Laszlo Thorne would live a rich, long life with the woman of his dreams. He'd be happy with his 2.5 kids and eighty-pound lab resting at his feet.

Rafe called Liz away, and after she left the room, Lo cornered Ebba.

"What's wrong?" he asked softly.

"I've always wanted to be part of your family. All of you, Mack included, have made me feel special when I'm far from it. Far from whatever it is all of you are. But you never made me feel I was lacking."

"You're not."

"I've loved you forever, Lo."

He wasn't surprised by her confession, and in fact, he appeared downright uncomfortable she'd said anything at all. Yet Ebba needed to be heard this one and only time. She might not have another chance to reveal what was in her heart.

"I don't expect you to say the same. If you did, I'd know you were lying." She cast him a wry smile. "But I do love you, and another minute I didn't tell you was another one wasted."

"I'm honored."

Ebba snorted. "Yeah, you look like you mean that." Rolling her eyes, she wished she could take a long pull of his beer. How the hell was her throat parched without a physical form? "You're going to hate this next part."

"Don't say it," he warned.

"I have to. You know I do."

"Ebba—"

"When I move on—"

"I don't want to hear this, dammit!"

She touched his arm. "When I move on, I want you to forgive yourself, then forget this entire incident."

"Are you fucking crazy?"

His fury caught Liz's and Rafe's notice, but Ebba waved them off.

"No, Lo. I'm accepting of what's to come. You need to be, too."

"Well, I'm not, so knock it off with this acceptance bullshit."

"No. I want you to promise me you'll do as I requested. You won't beat yourself up for things out of your control."

He shook his head like an enraged bear, prepared to argue.

"Laszlo."

Again, he shook his head.

"Laszlo, look at me. Really look."

The eyes he turned on her were filled with pure torment.

"Tell me, Ebba. What is the point in having my abilities and being able to see spirits if I can't do a fucking thing to save them? Especially the most important one of all. *You*. Huh?"

"Maybe you aren't meant to. Maybe you're only meant to ease our way or the minds of those left behind."

"I'm the one you're leaving behind!"

THEY STARED AT EACH OTHER. SHOCK SENT THEIR JAWS plunging toward their chests. Laszlo was the first to recover and tapped her mouth closed. His confession was in order.

"You're my friend," he said simply. "But more importantly, you're someone I've come to realize I want to know better. In every sense of the word. How can I do that if you cross over?"

"There will be other women, Lo." Her look bordered exasperated. "Liz could make you a list of women she knows who are willing to leave their significant others forever just for a single hour in your bed."

He scoffed.

"Dude. You are so clueless." She shook her head. "Why do you think Charlotte threw hate rays at every female who had the audacity to glance your way?"

"She was a jealous shrew."

"With good reason. Have you taken a gander at the mirror recently?"

Heat crept up his neck. "You're making me uncomfortable, Ebba."

She had the nerve to laugh, and Lo wanted to kiss away her sass. Goddess, did he! Shooting a glance at his sister and brother-in-law, he shoved away his desire with an internal lecture on the impropriety of lusting after a ghost with others present.

"I don't care about any of those women," he said gruffly. "I care about you. About this."

"The accident wasn't your fault. Spencer possessing my body wasn't your fault. Death demanding our runaway souls is not your fault, either." She hammered home every point in a calm, collected way. Though Lo recognized the wisdom of her words, a part of him would never get over being unable to save her, and he didn't know how to convey it to her. It wasn't love, he assured himself. It was guilt for being a useless fucker.

Their silent stare-off ended when his phone rang.

Clutch.

Laszlo rushed to answer. "Hey, man. Were you able to soften her up?"

His friend laughed. "She's not that easily swayed. Have you attempted the spell yet?"

"No. We paid a visit to Isis in the hopes she'd intervene."

"Will she?"

Despair settled over him, and Laszlo gave Clutch the unvarnished truth. "No."

"Ouch."

"Yeah."

"For what it's worth, Lo, I'm sorry."

"Thanks, man." A sigh escaped from his tired soul. "Want to join us to capture Pig-fucker Spencer inside your clay doll?"

"I'd love to, man, but Death is beckoning."

"Not cool."

"No, but funny."

"I'm hanging up now."

But before he could, Clutch said his name. "It doesn't state it in the spell, but when you tie Ebba's body to the bed, use black bindings. Silk or satin might burn less when she writhes to get away."

"Stop it, you're turning me on."

"Shut up. You know what this is for. Also, the clay form should be pressed face down into the bare skin of her chest. The point is to leave no room for escape."

The idea of hurting Ebba in any way made Lo surly. "Got it."

"Wrap the doll in a black cloth and bind it. The spell will hold until you can hand Spencer off to Death."

He didn't want to, but he had to ask. Meeting her solemn chocolate eyes, he swallowed hard. "And how am I to deliver Ebba?"

The question felt more introspective than inquiring. Did he have the strength to let her go?

"I've got the feeling Ebba won't need to be forced to return here again." The gravity of the situation wasn't lost on Clutch. "It'll be easier for you if she comes alone, Lo."

"I don't give a shit about easy. We'll be there unless I can devise another plan in the meantime."

"Death will find her. You, of all people, know that. Don't piss her off. Be here either way, okay?"

"I'll think about it." Disconnecting, Laszlo tossed the phone on the counter and stalked to the bedroom. Ebba's physical self was awake and glaring hatred in his direction.

"Time to give up the ghost, Pig-fucker."

13

It's that time again. Or should I say, "that chapter again"? Chapter thirteen has been omitted as per the Thorne Witch tradition. Although I hope you're as invested in Laszlo and Ebba's story as I was in writing it, you should probably take a break. Hydrate and stretch, my friend. Then, dive back in to find out what happens to our feisty Ebba.

Wanting nothing more than to fade away into the ether to regenerate, Ebba sighed. No rest for the weary, it seemed. She chased after Laszlo, followed closely by Liz and Rafe.

"I swear she was just sleeping," Rafe said, apology heavy in his tone.

"It's okay, babe." Liz rubbed his arm. "You couldn't know when she'd wake."

Oddly enough, Ebba could and did know. Knowledge was coming at her fast and furious the closer she got to Death's deadline.

"He was pretending," she said. "He woke about five minutes after we left."

Spencer's fierce expression superimposed over her physical body's features was disconcerting. Initially, he'd been glaring at Lo, but the instant she spoke, he directed his ire her way.

"What the hell is going on, Lo?" he asked in her normal voice. Anyone who wasn't already aware of his game would believe it was Ebba speaking. Thankfully, those in the room were steps ahead of the lowlife, scum-sucking toad.

She hadn't realized she'd spoken the insult aloud until Laszlo snorted.

"Nailed it in one," he murmured beside her.

"Is the spell to remove him relatively easy?" she asked in a low voice for his ears only.

"It is, but we need a few supplies you might not have available. First things first." Lo held out his hand. The merest hint of blue flashed, followed by a whirlwind of twinkling lights, rising and rotating like a four-inch tornado in the center of his palm. In the blink of an eye, the mini twister flew straight at Ebba's physical form, wrapping around her wrists and securing her to the iron bedposts. Lo repeated the process for her legs.

Snarling and spitting, Spencer did his damndest to break his bonds, but the smirk on Laszlo's face assured him escape wasn't possible. Next, Lo ripped open her shirt with a flick of his finger, tearing it in a way to expose her skin but protect her modesty. The inherent kindness he displayed only added to her love for him. His was the type of thoughtful character easy to fall for.

And she had. Irrevocably.

Sorrow welled within, and the melancholy was too much. In her ghostly state, her will to fight was strong, but the pervading sense of peace became stronger with every passing moment. Welcoming the inevitable would be the final step in her transition. Before that happened, she needed to ensure Laszlo would be all right. Liz had Rafe to ease the loss. Lo was alone. Like Wilder.

His feelings for her were growing with each moment they spent together. Their forming bond resembled threads in varying shades of purple. Emitting from each of them, those threads drifted across the space, attempting to connect. If those strands fused, his grief would be that of a lover or spouse losing their mate, becoming unbearable for him.

This universal knowledge of the metaphysical had grown exponentially since meeting Isis. It seemed being in the Goddess's presence had flipped a switch in Ebba's mind, revealing all the possibilities of the beyond.

Should she tell Lo? Did he already know through his previous work with the supernatural? He was a ghost hunter, after all.

Frowning, she observed the sly way Spencer twisted to expose her breasts in a tempting manner, the easy way Laszlo avoided touching her physical self while placing the clay doll on her chest, and the frustration her unwanted parasite experienced at his inability to get his exorcist to engage.

What would happen if Lo accidentally brushed her skin? Would it open the door for Spencer to escape? These were things she intended to ask when the process was finished. Distracting Lo in the middle of a spell was taboo; even a mortal like her understood the ultimate consequences should she do it.

Liz glanced at her.

"Don't worry," Ebba mouthed with a loving smile. "All will be well."

Tears brightened her friend's warm amber eyes, brimming along her lower lids before she blinked them away. All but one. A single tear, achingly sad in its solitary trek, represented Ebba's personal journey. She'd felt alone her entire life despite the closeness of the Thornes. A lone wolf of sorts. It wasn't surprising she'd die without ever having experienced true love's embrace.

But maybe if the Fates were kind and reincarnation was real, she'd have the whole kit and caboodle in the next life. She hoped so. Her attention drifted to Laszlo, and she prayed it would be with him. That their souls would link up. If she had to wait a thousand years for it to happen, she would.

"PRAESERVO!" LASZLO SECURED THE DOLL AGAINST SPENCER'S chest with a simple command, locking him inside Ebba's body. This way, his soul wouldn't escape to find another host while Lo and the others located what they needed to complete Clutch's spell.

To Liz, he said, "I need a few items from Nash. Think you can find them for me?"

"Are you trying to get rid of me, or are they artifacts only Nash has?"

"Artifacts." He crossed to her and hugged her tightly, resting his cheek against her shiny blonde head. "Our time with Ebba is running out. I wouldn't deny you the chance to spend it with her if possible."

"Thank you," she whispered.

An ache settled in his chest and refused to budge. Never in all the time he'd been dabbling in supernatural affairs like these had the final crossing been subverted. All things ended, and as a magical being, he was well versed in the truth of it, yet for Ebba's life to be cut down this way, this *soon*, it was nothing short of tragic.

Her ghostly presence behind him emitted a transitioning glow and was a beacon for Death to find her anywhere she cared to hide.

Clutch was correct.

Lo wouldn't have a choice.

Pressing a kiss to his sister's temple, he released her to write up a short list of useful tools he was positive could be found in Nash's ever-expanding vault.

"This should do it," he said, handing off the sheet with the four items he sought. "Rafe, you can go too if you want. Nothing more can be done here for the night."

"You're to sit vigil?" his brother-in-law asked, concern drawing his brows together.

"Something like that." After offering a handshake and a grateful smile, Lo drew him into a quick hug. "Thank you for always looking out for my sister. She couldn't have been blessed with a better man as her soulmate."

"This sounds a bit like goodbye. You wouldn't be planning anything foolish, perchance?"

Lo laughed. "No. But this incident has taught me life is short. Things need to be said while we can."

"Fair enough. In that case, you're my favorite of all her brothers," Rafe said with a devilish grin.

"Was there ever any doubt?"

"Not as far as you're concerned," Liz retorted, tapping Laszlo's belly with her balled fist.

"Vicious woman!" He pretended the harmless blow had caused untold pain, and gripped his abdomen, bending double.

Laughing at his ridiculousness, she sandwiched his head between her palms and blew a raspberry on his cheek. "Shut it, you tool!"

Lo caught Ebba watching them, and her longing expression was a literal tug at his soul. Was her yearning to have a familial relationship like Liz's and his, or was it because she loved him and desired his attention?

Charlotte would've stopped their hug by demanding he fetch her something or by saying they were late for one appointment or another. The wedges she used to drive space between him and his family were plentiful. But instead of speaking or complaining, Ebba graced them with a tender smile and nodded, appreciating their bond.

A lump formed in his throat. Why hadn't he approached her

first when they were younger? Believing her too innocent and pure at three years younger, he'd gone for the knockout party girl, who became a constant pain in his ass with her complaining and ultimatums. Love should've been about compromise, not the one-sided wants and endless demands of a spoiled woman.

"You're finally seeing what was there all along," Liz said in a low voice.

"Yeah," he said roughly. "I was a fucking idiot."

"Nah. You were human." She knocked into his shoulder with hers. "Besides, Ebba's like a fine wine aged to perfection. If you'd have partaken too soon, you probably wouldn't have appreciated the flavorful notes."

"We must find a way to reverse all of this, Liz. She's too important to us."

"That goes without saying." With a rub of his arm and a clearing of her throat, she nodded. "We still have time. Not much, but some. Maybe Isis will come around. She's never let us down before."

"Al said he had one other source. I'm hoping he'll pull a rabbit out of his hat."

Liz laughed. "He will. He always does. The man's a world-class magician."

"Truth."

"Okay, we're off to disturb Nash's dinner. It should make him appropriately salty since Ryanne's expecting and insisting on three-star Michelin dishes for every meal."

"He's spoiled," Rafe added with a deep chuckle that turned evil. "I'm going to enjoy eating his dinner while he searches for the artifacts."

"This is why you fit in so well with my twisted family, Rafe." Lo laughed, though he didn't quite feel like it. They were trying for levity, and he'd allow them their illusions.

Thirty seconds later, it was Lo, the two Ebbas, and Spencer, the hitchhiking pig-fucker. Never had he wished a man had a physical form as badly as he did then, to beat the fucker bloody. As it was, Spencer had selected the perfect vessel to hide in because Lo would never lift one finger against Ebba.

"What's next?" Spirit Ebba asked.

"We conjure herbs and wait for Liz to return with my magical security blanket."

She gestured him to the corner of the room away from listening ears and asked, "What do those objects do?"

"The four mirrors are placed in the room's corners, facing the bed. They're intended to confuse his spirit and trap it in place."

"Like a fun-house room?"

He smiled at how fast her mind grasped the concept. "Exactly."

"And the rest?"

"If she can find it, there's an enchanted sword. It helps to sever the soul's link to the Earthly plane."

Dark eyes wide, she met his. "You intend to stab me?"

His laughter escaped.

"Well?" she demanded.

Lo laughed harder.

"You're a jerk."

"So you've said." He wrapped an arm around her waist and hauled her close, happy she'd gathered energy to solidify again. His lips brushed hers once, then twice. On the third go, her mouth opened under his, and he tasted heaven.

"Uhhh!!!!!" Spencer screamed from the bed. "Stop! I feel that shit, too, and it's like tasting shoe leather!"

"That's news to me," Lo told Ebba in a hushed voice. "I've never known the spirit and body to share an experience when separated."

"I've been feeling everything my physical self does up to now. I assumed it was normal."

He looked at her sharply. "Even in the cafe this morning?"

"Yes. I've been unable to leave the apartment, but I've always known what my body was doing when it left."

"Weird, but good to know."

Had Castor's ability altered the norm? What would that mean for her if she crossed? It bore consideration.

"On another note"—he leaned close to whisper into the shell of her ear—"do I *really* taste like shoe leather?"

She giggled. "You taste like cotton-candy cupcakes with rainbow sprinkles. My favorite."

"Whew! I was worried my toothpaste wasn't doing the trick."

"I'd have stopped you at the first kiss if your breath stunk," she assured him.

"Good to know." Biting her earlobe, he chuckled. "How about we drive the pig-fucker over the edge by making out?"

"Mm. I *do* love the way you think!"

15

They were halted by the arrival of Alastair and Castor. Laszlo told himself the interruption was fortunate because crossing into necrophilia territory was frowned upon. Debating the pros and cons of feeling up a ghost or obsessing about how Ebba's body—physical and spirit—was built for hot, monkey sex would find Lo in hot water. Fast! He was quickly becoming addicted to touching her, and it didn't bode well for him.

"Did your friend have a suggestion for stopping Death, Al?"

"You can ask him yourself. He'll be arriving momentarily."

"This is becoming quite the party," Castor said as he flopped on the couch. "Why are there no hors d'oeuvres? Isn't that what you call those little finger sandwiches?"

"I'm a terrible hostess," Spirit Ebba quipped as she jumped up to perch on the counter.

"Why does she do that?" he asked, nodding at the distance she'd placed between her and their group.

Lo was slow on the uptake, but when the truth dawned, he couldn't believe he'd never seen it before. Looking back, he recalled Ebba had always kept to the outskirts of gatherings their entire lives. At every function of four or more, she'd drifted off to sit alone, and Laszlo was ashamed her crowd discomfort had never registered.

"I'm an asshole," he muttered, shaking his head.

Castor grinned his agreement. "No argument here."

Flipping him the bird, Lo joined Ebba.

"I owe you an apology, Sweet."

"For what?" Her brows drew together in adorable confusion, and using his thumb, he smoothed the indention they created with light, caressing strokes.

"For being insensitive to your hatred of large groups."

"Oh!" She laughed and batted his hand away. "You couldn't have known. Besides, I don't hate crowds. I just don't fit in."

"I believe it's called social awkwardness," he replied, toying with a corkscrew lock of her espresso-colored hair. He marveled at the silky feel beneath his fingers. How was it possible she felt so alive?

"I know what it's called, Lo."

"Don't roll those gorgeous eyes at me, woman." He grinned, appreciating the hell out of her sass. In all the years they'd been acquainted, she'd never backed down when teased and always gave it right back. Which was doubly impressive when he thought about it, considering many people became tongue-tied when addressing their crush.

Pitching his tone in the suggestive zone, he said, "When we're alone again, I want to hear about all the ways you fantasized about the two of us."

Her gasp was his reward for shocking her, but she recovered in a flash. "Who said I fantasized about you at all?"

"Didn't you?"

The answer was there, in her smoldering gaze, and the horror he felt from his immediate arousal caused him to step away from her and into the kitchen to hide his body's reaction.

Jesus!

He gave in to his urge to grab a beer, but not to the one to shove it down his pants and cool off his randy dick. Granted, it had been a while since his last sexual encounter, but growing hard from a direct look was downright humiliating.

Taking a few minutes to himself, he popped the lid off and guzzled a third of his drink. Lo blew out a breath and shook his head. What the hell was happening to him? How long had he lusted after Ebba without realizing it? It made him ill to entertain the notion he'd driven Charlotte to her jealousy. Had she seen something in the way he responded to Ebba's adoration?

When he was in control, he circled the counter, placed his bottle next to Ebba's hip, and scooped her into his arms.

"'Nobody puts Baby in a corner,'" he said. "Not on my watch."

Her effervescent giggles triggered his grin.

"I'm thrilled you got the reference," he admitted. "I'd have been embarrassed if you didn't know what the fuck I was referring to."

"Who doesn't know Dirty Dancing?" Her pretend horror tickled him.

"You get me."

"I always did," she assured him, love shining from those devastating eyes.

"I'm sorry if it feels like I overlooked you when we were young, Ebba."

With a shrug, she ducked her head.

Jostling her to get her attention, he said, "I didn't."

"Huh?"

"I didn't overlook you. Remember the day we snuck down and borrowed my uncle Hoyt's boat?"

Frowning, she nodded.

Lo fought the uncomfortable heat traveling up his neck.

"Liz and my brothers saw I was lusting over you in your baby-blue bikini. They pulled me aside and threatened to tear off both my arms and legs if I broke your heart."

"What?"

"Yep. Ask Liz." He pressed his forehead to hers. "They were right to interfere. I was a horndog in those days. It's why Charlotte and I… She…"

His skin felt tight and unbearable under her incredulous stare.

"She put out," Ebba concluded with a scowl. "I'd have put out. For *you.*"

"I think we all knew that." Lo winced when she pinched his nipple. "Ouch! I wasn't being mean, Ebba. I'm saying your crush was evident, and the reality was you were too young for sex."

"I was sixteen, and who were you to make that call?" she asked fiercely.

"The nineteen-year-old boy who wasn't mature enough to keep your heart intact."

Her expression softened. "But you did, didn't you?"

"What do you mean?"

"By maintaining your distance and keeping up the pretense of disinterest, you didn't take advantage of the situation. Therefore, you were mature enough to keep my heart intact."

He laughed at the dumb kid he'd been. "I never considered I was doing the right thing. Mainly I didn't want my brothers to kick my ass."

With an exasperated shake of her head, she peered over his shoulder, then leaned in to kiss him.

"The past can't be erased, Lo. But I'm glad I didn't make you so uncomfortable you couldn't be my friend."

"Never that, Sweet Ebba. Our friendship was the highlight of my life. Nothing could've kept me away from you for long."

As Lo carried Ebba to her favorite armchair, she considered what he'd said.

Sweet Ebba.

He'd called her that since the day they spent at Lake Lure. From the moment those words left his lips, she'd cherished them, secretly believing in her heart of hearts he must care if he'd graced her with a nickname. Over the years, he'd shortened it to "Sweet" and only used it when Charlotte wasn't present. Knowing his endearment was void of artifice and not intended to keep her pining for him, Ebba treasured the sentiment.

The atmosphere in her apartment turned heavy, and the air crackled with what she'd learned was an incoming witch. But she wasn't expecting the jaw-dropping hottie who arrived.

Although dressed casually, he gave off a wealthy man vibe. With a single look at his duds, one could recognize the quality and guess at the cost. The jeans weren't your average off-the-rack brand, or if they were, Ebba couldn't afford to set foot in that store for fear she'd destroy something and spend the rest of her life paying the debt off. Hottie McHotterson's sweater was black and fitted him like an overly friendly glove. With certainty, it wasn't the type to pill or pull, and it was likely to last a lifetime if he cared to keep it that long.

Yet it wasn't his attire that drew the notice. It was the pure perfection of his symmetrical features. His hair was stylish and on the longer side but nothing like Castor's shoulder-length tresses. None of that was the distraction. No, it was his eyes that drew and held one's attention. Almost black, they had the merest hint of a silver starburst, keeping them from blending with his pupils.

With skin a similar shade to Lo's olive-like tones yet not as dark as Rafe's Mediterranean coloring, the man was striking and positively delicious.

Sensual and hypnotic.

Ebba could've stared at him forever and never grown bored.

Those obsidian eyes traveled over her with a thoroughness that would've left her breathless had she needed to breathe. The sweeping glance wasn't sexual, instead leaving the impression he was cataloging everything about her, including her aura, temperament, and place in his magical world.

"Who is he?" she whispered in awe.

As if by some miracle he'd heard her, the left side of his mouth kicked up, and she stilled. He was what she imagined Death *should've* looked like. Souls would willingly go with him if beckoned. Hell, he'd be the Pied Piper of the dead.

"I'm Damian Dethridge, Ms. James."

His tone was smooth, cultured, and seductive to the extreme. She wanted to crawl into his skin and never leave. It wasn't a normal reaction, and she worried his true intent was to capture her soul. Did the others see him?

A look at Laszlo assured her they did.

"What are you?" she asked Damian.

"I'm the Aether and maintain the balance between good and evil."

"*The* Aether, as in only one?"

He dipped his head in acknowledgment. "There were others before me, and there will be others after. However, for now, I'm the reigning one."

"And everyone calls *me* an attention whore," Castor quipped.

Damian laughed, and Ebba was starstruck.

"Holy shit."

"We all say that when he appears," Castor said dryly, crossing the room to shake the other man's hand. They shared one of those brief bro hugs, indicating familiarity, and as they stepped apart, the room lit again.

A mini female replica of the Aether stepped through a rift in space. His muttered curse was immediate, and his chin dropped to his chest, the picture of a harried father.

The girl's chin jerked upward, and she wore an expression of faux superiority. Ebba had to wonder if the child's brave face came from knowing she was about to be scolded.

She had vast experience in the defiance department, too.

"Don't yell at me, Papa. I've never met a real, live ghost before," the girl said, her eyes darting toward Ebba, still held by Lo.

"I'm almost certain that's a lie." With a pained air, Damian pressed his fingers to his temples and sighed. "But please tell me, when have I ever truly yelled at you, Beastie?"

The girl grinned, and Ebba blinked at the sudden transformation. Her elfin face was pure mischief and adorable. Feeling the similar draw to the child as she had to the father, but without the sexual magnetism, Ebba tapped Lo's shoulder to indicate she wanted down.

"I'm Sabrina." Gesturing to Damian with her thumb, she added, "But Papa calls me Beastie."

"Mm, yes. I expect it's fitting," Ebba replied with a warm smile, fighting the desire to hug the child. "I'm Ebba."

"I know. I'm an Oracle."

Frowning, Ebba wrinkled her nose. "Not a witch, so I'm afraid I don't know what that is."

"I see all future outcomes for everyone and every situation."

Awash with hope, she met the girl's knowing gaze. "Even mine?"

"Yes."

"Can you tell me—"

"No," Damian said succinctly, with a meaningful look at his daughter. "She isn't supposed to be here, and she certainly isn't supposed to reveal the future. Her interference could alter the course of the Fates' design."

"Papa's right." Sabrina grimaced and, extending one foot, swung it from side to side, scraping the toe of her shoe along the rug. "The Fates became cross with me and tried to make me disappear."

"What?!" Outraged, Ebba looked at Damian. "They can do that?"

"In the literal sense of the word, yes. They were thwarted, however."

"Thank Christ," she muttered. Although diminutive, the child appeared mature for one as young as her. No kid should be subjected to the whims of fickle deities.

"Actually, it was thanks to a Guardian," Sabrina said, grinning widely.

"A Guardian?"

"They are almost as powerful as my papa and me, but they aren't born with their powers like us. Only the Goddess can choose them."

"I see."

But she didn't. The crazy world of the Thorne witches was beyond Ebba's comprehension, especially when fatigued as she was. She'd expended too much energy in the previous hours and was fading quickly. Soon enough, her strength would wane, and then it would be a literal disappearance.

"I can boost your energy, Ms. James," Damian said, plucking her concerns from the air.

She frowned.

"Can you read my mind?" she asked him silently, testing her theory.

He winked.

"So, like, before, when I, um..."

Don't think about it, Ebba! Don't think about how sexy he is!

"Yes, and thank you. I'll take that as a compliment," he replied aloud.

She almost told Laszlo she was ready to cross over—if only to escape the humiliation.

But Damian's frown made her question what had him perturbed.

"You're a spirit, Ms. James. You shouldn't be experiencing deeper emotions."

"Why did you say that? Is there something I'm missing?" Lo asked. "Is there a private communication between you that we don't know about?"

"With Damian?" Castor snorted. "Always."

Ebba waved them off and shifted closer to the Aether. "Will you explain what you mean, please?"

"Certainly. Your recent emotional responses, the anger on my daughter's behalf, the lustful thoughts—"

Lo swore. "Him, too? Is there anyone you haven't drooled over today?"

She glared. "Really? You're going to rat me out like that?"

"—*And* your justified irritation with Laszlo are all unique for your current state," Damian continued after casting an amused glance his way.

"Unique in what way? Spirits don't feel anything?" Ebba faced Lo. "You're the resident expert. What have you encountered in the past?"

"I can't believe I missed it, but Damian's right. The only thing you should be feeling this close to the transition is peace." Laszlo's eyes widened, and he looked as if he'd taken a blow to the head. "How is this possible?"

Damian's smile was confident. "That's what I'm here to find out."

Ebba chose not to receive an energy boost, preferring to rest and revitalize in her own time, and Laszlo was loath to see her go. If their hours were limited, he wanted to spend as many with her as possible.

And they *were* limited.

Never once in the years since he'd been helping as a liaison between the living and dead had he known a spirit *not* to head into the afterlife. Unless his family and friends came up with something before Death's deadline, Ebba would, too.

Off to the side, feeling he had nothing to contribute, Lo observed the others as they discussed the situation. He felt a tug on his sleeve and glanced down.

"Don't worry, Mr. Laszlo." Like her father, Sabrina Dethridge carried a wealth of knowledge behind her solemn obsidian eyes. How did one as young as she deal with all the ugliness that came with her visions?

"I'm trying not to, Miss Beastie."

A small smile curled her lips. "I like Miss Beastie. My Guardian calls me Wee Beastie."

"I can see where that would be appropriate," Lo agreed dryly. Indeed, she was pint-sized for her age, standing no taller than his waist.

He curbed the urge to run a hand down her silky black tresses, along with the longing for a daughter of his own. Charlotte had never wanted kids, and in one of his many attempts to make her happy, he'd agreed. At forty-two, he wasn't too old, but he'd hate it if his particular gift were passed to a child of his.

With a sage nod, Sabrina turned to watch the three lifelong friends. "They always find a way," she said. "It's why the Goddess brought them together."

"Alastair and your dad are distant cousins. It was bound to happen."

She giggled. "Yes, but Uncle Alex came later. He makes them laugh."

"As I expect do you."

"Can I tell you a secret? You have to promise not to tell my papa."

"I can't promise if I don't know what it is. I'll not agree to something that could place you in harm's way, Miss Beastie."

"No, it won't. It's about Ebba. She—"

"Sabrina Dethridge, not another word!" Damian commanded from across the room.

"Mama says he has eyes in the back of his head, and I believe it," she muttered in disgust.

Lo laughed, unable to hold it in. Her disgruntled expression was priceless. "It's better if you let this play out like it's supposed to," he said, squatting to peer at her too-serious face. "I heard what you and your dad said about the Fates, and I'd rather not know than place you in danger."

"I was just going to give you a little nudge in the right direction." She cast a side glance at her stern father. "Mama said that's allowed sometimes."

"I think she probably meant for immediate family. But if it comes down to the wire and it looks like I'm screwing things up royally, I permit you to issue a course correction. How's that?"

She grinned and sandwiched his face between her tiny hands. "You would make a great papa, Mr. Laszlo."

"I've always thought so. But I'd also ask what you're doing up this late and say things like, 'Shouldn't you be in bed, young lady?'"

Laughing, she patted his cheek. "No, you wouldn't. Like Papa, you'd fix your kid a bowl of ice cream."

"Only if my wife wasn't looking."

"Miss Ebba would want a bowl, too."

The mental picture of Ebba and him sharing dessert with their mischievous daughter caused his heart to contract.

"She'd have made a great mom," he agreed roughly. Clearing his throat, Lo rose and held out a hand to Sabrina. "Let's see what they've come up with to help her."

"I'm sorry you're sad."

"It's the situation."

She slid her hand into his and tugged him toward the others. Other than to cast them a quick, curious look, Damian didn't comment on Lo being led around by a ten-year-old child. He acted as if his daughter taking charge of the room was an everyday occurrence, and maybe it was, but for Lo, the entire episode was strange.

"I think we should tell him, Papa," Sabrina said.

"It's forbidden."

"I have the right to know if it involves Ebba or me, Dethridge." Frustration was building inside him, and he clenched his jaw against the need to spill expletives. Had a child not been present, he'd have given in and swore not only a blue streak but red, green, purple, and black ones, too.

"I agree. You do. However, I won't put my daughter at risk

because of your entitlement. Yes, she is destined to be the Oracle, but not for years to come. How she decides to use her powers when she's taken up the mantle is her choice, but until then, I'll protect her as best I can." Damian stood. "Wouldn't you do the same, Laszlo? Wouldn't you go to any length to protect those you love?"

There was a deeper meaning behind the question. A test of sorts. One Lo couldn't fail, or he'd risk losing Ebba forever.

"I would and will," he said, acknowledging, if only to himself, how much he cared for her.

Satisfaction flared in the other man's eyes, and Damian's lips curled, emphasizing his emotion. With a decisive nod, he gestured to the couch. "Have a seat. We must strategize."

Laszlo frowned. "I thought that's what you were doing already."

"In a sense. But you're an essential part of this equation." Damian cupped Sabrina's cheek. "Please return home to your mother, my love. She'll be worried sick if she wakes to find us both gone."

"But, Papa—" When she understood her wheedling would do no good, she crossed her arms and jutted her chin. "I'm needed here."

"Beastie," he growled.

His irritation gave weight to the room's atmosphere, and taking a deep breath was difficult. Their clash of wills created literal sparks in the air around them. Neither noticed, but Lo, Alastair, and Castor did.

"What the actual fuck?" he whispered to Al. "Is this normal? It's like I'm experiencing altitude sickness."

"I'm afraid it is," Castor replied. He jumped to his feet, scooped up Sabrina, and tossed her across his shoulder like a potato sack. "I'll see she gets home or, at the very least, in the care of her Guardian. Fix my mistake, or devise a foolproof way for me to."

His eerie, light eyes locked with Lo's. "For what it's worth, I'm sorry."

"I get the impression it's not a word you're familiar with," he replied, not unkindly.

"I rarely do things I need to apologize for. But in this"—Castor shrugged his free shoulder—"I believed I was doing the right thing for her. If I need to go back in time to fix it—"

Sabrina grunted behind his back. "That's what I was trying to say, but you wouldn't listen!"

Damian sighed heavily. "When will I learn?" With a finger swirl, he indicated for Castor to set her down. "Tell us the next step, and get to bed, Beastie."

Her superiority was unnerving. "Uncle Alex has to go back, but Laszlo has to go, too."

Castor's brows slammed together, and he shook his head. "I've never traveled with another. Other than to teleport, I'm not sure I can. Taking him back to a place where he didn't exist is impossible."

"I *did* exist five months ago," Lo said, confused.

"Yes, but you weren't at the accident scene. Meaning, I can't take you to that spot."

"Hm." Alastair stroked his lower lip with his thumb while they waited for him to voice his thoughts.

"Jaysus. Spit it out, Al. The kid has to get to bed already," Castor said.

The faint laugh lines beside Alastair's sapphire eyes deepened, though he never cracked a smile. "I was remembering how your future self delivers messages to your past or present self on occasion. What's to stop you from doing it again?"

"If you recall, when I do that, my present self tends to pass out. With no one else around, who receives the message?"

Alastair nodded. "Actually, I *do* remember. Consider going farther back, to when you and I had lunch."

"That might do it." Castor's thoughtful gaze turned distant, and they remained quiet, allowing him to work through his process.

Lo understood the concept of a Traveler and had been subject to a recounting of the man's exploits, but he'd never seen him in action. His curiosity was full-blown. What would it be like to manipulate time? To go back to whenever and wherever you'd been to right a wrong? The idea held appeal.

"What does that mean for me?" Ebba asked.

As one, they turned. Her eyes were dull, and her body was semitransparent, allowing Lo to see into the bedroom behind her. Her expenditure of energy had cost her.

"If I die at the scene, I'll have missed this. All of you." But she only had eyes for Laszlo, and he grasped her meaning. Today's events would never have happened, and they'd miss the precious hours they'd shared bonding.

"No one is letting you die, child," Alastair said, standing and crossing to her. He grasped her hands, infusing her with enough energy to solidify her spirit again.

"Thank you."

The face she turned up to him was tragic, and Lo's heart seized. Undoubtedly, his expression reflected the same emotion. Unable to bear the distance, he joined them.

"If we're meant to be, it will happen, Sweet Ebba," he said, caressing her cheek. The strength of his desperation was greater than any emotion he'd ever experienced. He had to save her. "I'll make sure of it. I promise."

Ebba leaned into his touch, seeking the warmth. "You can't, Lo. You won't remember, and neither will I." Inside, her heart was breaking, an anomaly according to the Aether.

She moved past them and stopped in front of Castor. If this traveling business was dangerous for him, she'd put her foot down. She'd be damned if anyone else would be hurt trying to set this to rights.

"And what do you risk by altering the past, Alex? Is it harmful for you to exist in the same space and time? I'm certain I read or heard a theory that it was."

"Other than passing out and hitting my head, the effects have been minimal." He grinned. "What's a small bump on the ol' noggin' between friends?"

She hadn't known him long, but she'd bet her last dollar the man was seldom serious. "Who doesn't love a man willing to take one for the team?"

His grin was roguish as he lifted her hand and kissed her knuckles. "See? You get me."

She laughed. "You're ridiculous."

"So we keep telling him," Alastair said dryly. "He refuses to listen."

"You're just jealous she finds me intriguing, Al."

"Yes, that's it." His droll expression also held indulgence.

She'd grown fond of the men in the hours since meeting them. Maybe it was how easy they were to be around. Or perhaps they were the uncles she'd never had. Wouldn't Castor be salty if he knew she thought of him as a relation instead of lover material? Either way, she couldn't shake the feeling she would lose something precious if they altered the timeline.

"What is it, Sweet?" Lo lifted his hand, but immediately dropped it.

A glance toward the wall mirror showed her why. Despite the Aether's energy infusion, it had only lasted mere minutes, and she was fading—*fast*. "They won't see or hear me, will they?"

"Papa and I will." Sabrina pointed to Alastair and Castor. "They won't."

"I want to thank you while I can," she told the group. The remainder of the things she wished to say closed her throat. If she could've relayed how much their caring meant, she would've. She'd have also assured them she would understand if their mission to save her failed.

Alastair's warm smile said his empathic abilities were in proper working order. With him, she didn't need to say a word. Although she wanted to hug Castor, she settled for a smile.

"I may miss you most of all, Scarecrow."

"Ah, Dorothy. Don't you worry, love. We'll make it right."

Laszlo cleared his throat. "Also, I object to you missing him more than me."

She laughed, surprised she could under the weight of her sadness. "You'll always be in my life or afterlife, as the case may be."

"No, Sweet." His tone was somber, and she fucking hated it. "If you die for real, you can't linger."

"I don't understand. You talk to spirits, Lo."

"What he's trying to say, Ms. James, is that he's a Reaper's assistant," Damian said. "He helps souls cross over to their proper plane."

"He's a paranormal investigator," she argued, scowling. "Tell him, Lo."

"I'm not, Ebba. You assumed I was. I'm actually a liaison and help the dead see it's best to go."

Awash with panic, she felt sick. "All this"—she waved a hand between them—"has been an act to get me to… to…"

"No!" His alarm seemed legit. "I told you before. I'm not delivering you to Death."

"But you have? With others?"

Closing his eyes, he nodded.

Her mind reeled. Were there people, like her, who'd felt forced to cross before they were ready? She didn't realize she'd voiced the question until Laszlo shot Damian a sickly look.

"There were!" she accused. "You forced them to go with Death."

"It isn't like that—"

"Then tell me what it's like?" The strength of her fury stirred the curtains, but those wisps of air didn't feel substantial enough for her mood. "I trusted you, Lo. I believed you when you said you'd help."

"I *am* helping, Ebba. Why the hell do you think they're all here?" he shouted back.

"Or maybe Spencer was right."

He jerked as if she'd struck him.

"I want you all to leave," she said stonily.

"I'm afraid we can't do that, Ms. James." Damian eased Laszlo away and took his place before her. "If we do nothing, your spirit will stay bound to the earth. Years will pass, and your memories will fade. With the passage of time, you'll become vengeful."

"How do you know?"

"You'll have to trust me on this one."

"He's ancient," Castor supplied helpfully.

Damian rolled his eyes, then nodded. "He's not wrong."

"Death told me she'd come if Lo didn't deliver me," Ebba said, confused by the situational about-face.

"She likely will. She won't, however, be able to reap your soul. Had any other witch bound you, she might, but Castor is descended from a god. I suspect he accidentally supercharged his spell with emotion."

She nodded, running her gaze over Castor's exquisite form. "That explains the perfect looks."

"Right here, Ebba." Lo crossed his arms, and a mulish expression settled on his features. "Not cool."

"I'm done talking to you," she informed him. "You're a liar."

"I didn't lie," he ground out.

"You didn't tell the truth either!"

17

Two hours later, Lo was so damned mad he could drive nails into boards with his bare fists. Ebba's stubbornness was making him insane.

"You have to talk to me sometime," he told her.

Her brows shot up, but she remained mute.

"This is childish." The instant the words left his mouth, he wanted to recall them. Her spiked brows dipped low over narrowed eyes, and she flipped him off. Somewhere behind him, Castor chuckled, and Lo shoved his hands in his pockets to curb the temptation to pass the bird along.

The Aether left for the length of time it took to put his daughter to bed, secure a second Guardian to protect his family in his absence, and return to Ebba's. After his arrival, Damian gave her a much-needed energy boost, helping her to become solid once more.

Him, she spoke to.

"Will I know when things have changed, or will I simply cease to exist?" she asked.

"You aren't dying, Ebba," Lo snapped. "I forbid it!"

Everyone's attention turned to him.

He grew warm under the men's laughing looks, but he concentrated on her. "I'm sorry, Sweet. Whenever people say you are, it triggers me."

"The only thing keeping my body alive is Spencer," she replied coolly. "I'm already dead, Lo. Face the facts."

"You haven't transitioned, and you're not going to, goddammit!"

His magic, fueled by fear and anger, shoved open the window sashes and brought gale-force winds into the room. Vases and books rocked. Curtains billowed. And pillows rolled along the floor like tumbleweeds.

She turned in a slow circle, taking in the destruction. Wide-eyed, she crossed to him. "Stop, or I'll have nothing left."

"What does it matter?" He stood nose to nose with her. "You're so fucking eager to move on. What does it matter what happens to your material goods?"

"My parents or Liz might want keepsakes," she retorted, but tears shimmered in her chocolaty eyes, making them appear larger and more tragic than ever.

With a weary sigh, he shoved his power back into its box and pressed his forehead to hers. Infusing his agony into his voice, he said, "I'm sorry."

"It's okay," she replied in a soft voice.

"It's not. I was an ass."

She smiled up at him, and he ceased to breathe. "Maybe a tiny bit of one, but you're cute, so I'll let it slide."

"Can we talk?"

"I thought we were."

"Funny." He led the way to the kitchen. When they were isolated from the others, he explained what he'd failed to earlier. "The Aether is correct. I'm a Reaper's assistant, and not by choice."

He took her raised brows and curious look as encouragement to continue. "I discovered I could see and speak to the spirits when I turned fourteen. Mom reminded me I had invisible friends as a child, which makes it probable I've always had the gift but didn't understand how to use it, or I subconsciously suppressed it until I got older."

"How did you learn what it was?"

"Hiking along the train tracks behind our home, I encountered one too many people dressed in period clothing. I thought my brothers were punking me at first."

She grinned. "I can see that. Wilder, Health, and Coleman were gremlins."

"Were? Still are!" he scoffed. "Death visited on occasion, explaining what came with my gifts, but I ignored her. Clutch was another matter altogether."

"He taught you to be a Reaper's assistant?"

"Yes. He showed me how it eased the fear of the unknown and provided a smoother transition for the living and the dead. When people believe they are speaking to their loved ones through a medium, they experience peace. And on the flip side of that, when the deceased feels the person left behind has grasped some measure of comfort, they go without regret."

"But they always go," she said softly.

"They do."

"And I will, too."

"No." He shook his head. "No, Ebba. I won't allow it."

"Laszlo."

"Don't give me that it's-all-for-the-best tone. Your place is here. With me." His throat was raw and aching with unvoiced emotion. "Say you understand."

"Our moment has passed, if it ever existed at all." She caressed his jaw. "You need to know I'll be okay on the other side, whatever comes. You've eased this transition for me."

"We haven't put our plan into action. There's still a chance."

Closing her eyes, she shook her head. "When Castor

returns and unbinds my soul, Death will be waiting. We both know it."

"I'll negotiate. I'll—"

She kissed him silent. Drawing back, she smiled, and the love shining in her eyes branded his soul.

"No."

In his distraction, he didn't at first register what she'd said. Once it sunk in, he slammed his palms on the counter. "Don't do this. Don't fight me, Ebba. I need you to fight *for* me. For *us*. It's the only way this works."

"What works? What part of the plan haven't you told me?"

"There is nothing we haven't told you," he snapped. Reining in his pique, he said, "Castor is to go back to his previous self to explain the situation. I intend for my spirit to hitch a ride."

"What?" she screeched.

"I—"

"I fucking heard you the first time. I just can't believe you're that stupid."

"I'm trying to show you I love you, and you're saying I'm stupid?" he asked, incredulous and with building irritation. "Seriously?"

"You're leaving your body open to have the same thing happen to you that Spencer did to me. No fucking way am I letting someone hijack your body."

"I'll have Clutch and Alastair stand watch."

"What good will that do? Alastair can't see spirits," she retorted.

"Clutch can. If he sees one, Alastair whisks it away. Easy-peasy."

"In the whole history of the term 'easy-peasy,' never has anything been truly easy," Ebba said sourly.

He grinned. "It will be this time."

"Bullsh—"

Cutting her off with a hard peck, he followed it with a lovebite. "You didn't react to my declaration of love."

"Meh. I think it's because you secretly looked at my naked chest earlier. My girls are always love at first sight for boob men."

Laughing, he drew out the top of her V-neck and glanced down. "I did my best not to peek, but your girls *are* beautiful."

"Thank you. Both for properly appreciating my C cups and for loving me."

"You're an easy woman to love, Sweet Ebba James."

"How do you always know the perfect thing to say?"

"Let's go." He flung an arm over her shoulders. "I have to save the girl."

***

EBBA REFUSED TO ENTERTAIN THE NOTION OF SURVIVING. "NOT to be a Patty Pessimist, but what about Spencer? Is he willingly going to move along?"

"First, we have to remove him from your body," Damian said. "That's trickier than expected."

Lo's head whipped up from the spell he'd been memorizing. "How and why?"

"We'll need to remove all trace of him from Ebba's body, memories included, or she could experience an echo of this timeline if she returns."

"When," Lo ground out. "When she returns."

Damian nodded dutifully. "When."

"Memories? You can do that?" she asked him, not caring for how it sounded. Did that mean she'd recall none of this at all? What about Laszlo's confession of love? The sweetness of the moment shouldn't be lost.

"I can, and it *is* necessary, Ms. James. I'm sorry."

"Call me Ebba," she replied with an absent wave. "What is

tricky about the memory removal? I'm assuming that's the worrisome part since Lo hasn't seemed all that concerned about ejecting Spencer."

"I was and still am concerned," Laszlo protested. "My concerned face obviously needs work."

She cracked a smile but remained focused on Damian, who obliged her by answering her question.

"Memories aren't stored in one particular area of the brain. There are multiple, all working together. The hippocampus, neocortex, and amygdala store explicit information, while implicit memories depend on the basal ganglia and cerebellum. The prefrontal cortex is used for short-term storage," he explained. "I'll need to go into the temporal lobe and access the hippocampus to remove episodic memories. These are what you'd consider specific and long-term. It's tricky in how these all exchange information."

"Did we need the science lesson?" Castor asked, rising from the couch to cross to the liquor cabinet.

"It wouldn't hurt you to learn how that block you call a brain works," Lo said.

"Hardy har har. You're hilarious." Castor's tone was anything but amused.

Damian carried on as if the others weren't behaving like bratty children, and Ebba admired his calm.

"For example, the amygdala stores emotional memories. How something made us feel. The stronger the emotion, the harder it is to forget." He cast a significant glance between her and Laszlo. "Whatever you're experiencing together could result in a lasting impression."

"You'd have to remove my feelings for Lo?"

It seemed inconceivable that he could. She'd loved Laszlo Thorne for what felt like forever.

"Those are woven into my entire life," she confessed.

Expression soft, Damian shook his head. "I wouldn't do

that to you, Ebba, and I imagine the damage would be significant should I try. No, I'm suggesting eliminating all your memories since the accident. From the moment Spencer wormed his way in onward. One insidious thought left behind can cause eventual madness."

"This sounds more dangerous by the minute." Lo sat straighter and gripped Ebba's hand. "If it isn't safe for her, it's not happening. I'll find another way to save her."

"There isn't one." The Aether's intent look tried to relay the truth. "Earlier, my daughter gave us the solution. For as young as she is, she's still able to view and weigh every possible outcome. If she said Ebba's survival depends on you and Castor going back in time to five months ago, then that's what it will take."

"You really think I'll survive this?" Ebba asked, afraid to hope.

"There's a twenty percent chance of failure, according to my calculations. Less if you ask Beastie. But yes, I do."

Ebba shared a concerned glance with Laszlo. "I'm worried about you more than anything. Should this go wrong—"

"We've got this, Sweet. Trust the magical process."

His smile was both a comfort and a bittersweet blow to her heart. Losing what they'd shared would be devastating.

Maintaining eye contact with Lo, she turned her head enough to ask, "Will you need to remove Lo's memories of this time, too? Won't the echo affect him?"

"That's going to be trickier. He'll need them when he returns," the Aether said.

"Why?"

Lo answered for him. "To deal with Death if she comes for you."

Ebba's mouth rounded in an O as she processed the trials ahead.

"Shall we get to it?" Damian asked. His tone was kind but prodding, indicating their time had run out.

18

The living room furniture was pushed against the walls, creating a large blank space for the coming ceremony. Laszlo thanked his lucky stars Ebba wasn't a pack rat, because there'd be no room to move despite the spaciousness of the apartment.

Castor and Alastair teleported the bed and its occupant to the center of the living room floor, but not without a wisecrack or ten from the Traveler.

"Dude, are you ever serious?" Lo snapped.

When Castor's icy blue eyes met his, they were void of amusement. "My life has been a series of one trauma after another. I had a murderous family, and enemies who forced me to fake my death to protect my son and the woman I loved. Strangers had to raise Quentin so no one knew he was related to me. His entire life, he believed his father didn't give a shit when, in fact, it was the opposite." Sucking in a stabling breath, he dropped his shoulders. "If I seem blasé to you, Laszlo, it's because I've had to put on an act since the day I learned to walk. But I wouldn't be here if I didn't care or take my responsibilities seriously."

Feeling like an ass for his waspishness, Lo pressed a hand to the other man's shoulder. "I'm sorry."

"Aw, does this make us besties?" Castor quipped, batting his eyelashes.

"Nope. Still don't like you." But the constant annoyance he'd felt for the man was gone, and Lo smiled to soften his reply. It helped that the guy had saved Ebba and was willing to do whatever it took to keep her alive.

"I know you," Spencer stated. "You were there that night. You caused the accident."

The accusation was dismissed by those who knew the truth, and his attempt to stir trouble among their group failed.

"Shut up, pig-fucker. No one believes a word out of your lying mouth," Lo said.

"Pig-fucker?" Caster crowed his delight. "Careful, Laszlo Thorne. I'm beginning to see potential in a friendship."

"Spare me." To Ebba, Lo said, "Please wait in the farthest spot of your apartment. We can't take the risk you'll be pulled in with this spell, Sweet."

After she was gone, they cast their circle and positioned themselves with one man at each corner of the bed.

"Damn! I forgot the globe." Leaving the protective circle once created was never ideal, but he didn't have a choice.

"What globe?" Damian asked with a frown. "You shouldn't need any tool for this but the doll."

Earlier, under the Aether's advice, he'd texted his sister and suggested she and Rafe head home. With Damian here, they didn't need the added artifacts. The man's power was formidable, and although objects could enhance his abilities, in this instance, they weren't needed except for a vessel for Spencer's soul.

"It's one Clutch gave to me. You remember, Al. I had it in the clearing."

"Yes." Alastair gave Damian a considering look. "Why would McClutchin give it to him if he didn't need it?"

"I don't know, but I'd like to find out." Waving his hand, he extinguished the candles and swept the salt into a pile. "Please fetch your globe, Laszlo. My curiosity is aroused." With a stern glance at Castor, he said, "Don't say it."

"You spoil all my fun." Castor plopped on the bed, extended an arm along the headboard, and crossed his ankles. With his free hand, he tapped the clay doll. "How does this work?"

"Don't touch that!" Lo gripped his wrist. "It's the only thing keeping the pig-fucker's soul locked in place."

"Jeez. It's like working for the Authority all over again. 'Don't do this. Don't touch that. No killing the bad man,'" he mocked in a falsetto with a flip of his blond hair.

Stifling his amusement, Lo went in search of the globe. Finding it on the dresser, he picked it up and turned to go, but a picture stuck in the mirror's corner caught his notice. Sixteen-year-old Ebba, dressed in that fucking hauntingly hot bikini he remembered so well, was tucked beneath his arm and laughing up at him. His younger self was looking down at her with a wolfish grin. Plucking the picture from its home, he studied it, seeing what he'd missed all his life.

He'd always been in love with Ebba, like she had with him.

Nineteen-year-old Laszlo wore such an expression of adoration, it was embarrassing to see. He didn't recall who had snapped the picture, but the moment was imprinted within every section of his brain Damian had droned on about. She'd smelled like sunshine and goodness that day. So good, in fact, he'd wanted to eat her up. Touching her had become a secret obsession, but he'd kept his hands to himself because she was underage. Although, now that he thought about it, it hadn't been so secret if his family had to threaten dismemberment.

Lo felt Ebba's approach. The hair on his body stood at attention, and a restless energy zinged through him as it did whenever she was near.

"Why didn't you make me see, Ebba?" he asked hoarsely.

"I thought it was all in my head. Something I desperately wanted and that my view was skewed."

"We missed *years*." His voice sounded accusing to his own ears.

"What was I supposed to do or say, Lo? By the time I turned eighteen, you were with Charlotte. Did you want me to break up a happy couple because of a two-year-old picture I happened to have?" She cupped his cheek. "You were engaged by then, and I believed you loved her."

"No. Not the way I should've." Closing his eyes, he leaned into her palm. "Something always held me back, and I gave her whatever she wanted because I felt guilty I couldn't love fully."

"Maybe that's why she was a raging bitch to any innocent female who smiled in your direction. She probably sensed it."

"Fuck! I'm such an idiot."

"No. You're a kind man with a big heart who takes his obligations seriously." She dropped her arm. "Liz told me you cast a spell to make Charlotte leave and your cousin set her up for life. Your family cares about people's welfare."

Laszlo jerked. *"What?"*

Ebba's stomach tightened. "Am I wrong?"

"Not about the spell. Alastair helped me with that," Lo said with a distracted air. "But I didn't know about the money."

He chuckled, then fell into hysteria, leaning against the dresser and holding his ribs, laughing like a damned loon.

"She's a fucking millionaire!" he gasped out. "Between everything she made off me and the lifetime annuity I suspect Alastair gave her, she won the damned lottery."

"And that's *funny?*" Ebba was inclined to be pissed the woman took the Thornes for a ride.

He sobered, but a small smile lingered. "Are you mad on my behalf, Sweet Ebba?"

"Yes! She's a damned gold digger."

"You wouldn't take what was offered without coercion?"

Ebba shook her head. "No! I'd tell you to shove it up your ass."

His grin flashed, and he wrapped his arms around her. "That, right there, is why I adore you."

She grew lightheaded, and her pulse hammered, threatening to burst her heart had she been corporeal. The sensation wasn't the pleasant one caused by attraction, but a feeling that made her sick.

"Lo?" Her voice was faint, and she struggled to stay alert. "Why—"

Firm hands hauled her away and across the room. She was as stunned as Laszlo, based on his slack-jawed expression.

"Sorry to interrupt, but that globe you're holding just came to life," Castor said. "It's glowing."

"Fuck!"

Ebba's knees buckled, and she was grateful for the strength of Castor's embrace. "I feel like I'm going to vomit."

Retching noises filled the room, and she peered out the door at Spencer.

"Turn him on his side," Damian ordered.

"No! The doll!" Lo rushed forward.

"It's secure," Alastair assured him, pressing it in place.

A second wave of dizziness assailed her, and Ebba swayed.

"I've got you, love." In a smooth, novel-hero move, Castor swept her into his arms and carried her to the living room. He laid her on the couch and, from thin air, produced a cool washcloth for her brow. If her heart didn't already belong to

Laszlo, she'd have fallen for the blond, godlike man leaning over her.

"You're dangerous," she said in a low voice.

His brows shot up, but then he grinned. "Not to you."

"Especially to me. To any woman in your general vicinity."

"I'll remind you of this when I save you from Death's door *again*."

Ebba tsked. "Sorry, but my memory will be wiped. I won't remember your roguish smile or your gentlemanly way of rescuing damsels in distress."

With a laugh, he rose. "I'll have to arrange a proper meeting. Preferably at a time before you lose your heart to that one." He jabbed a thumb in Laszlo's direction.

"Christ, I can't leave you two alone for a second," Lo complained as he crossed to them. "Flirt, flirt, flirt."

"It keeps you on your toes, babe." She smiled at him and was pleased to see his grin. "*You*, I will remember," she promised.

"I'm counting on it. But if not, we'll make new memories."

The globe lit again, and Ebba curled into a ball as a wave of nausea struck. Pain pierced her abdomen, causing her to cry out.

Spencer resumed retching.

"Back up, man!" Castor snapped. "Whatever punch that thing is packing, it's lethal to her."

Lo dashed to the kitchen, and the loud slamming of cabinets jolted her from her misery curl.

"What the hell is he doing?" she croaked.

"Filling a pot with water." Castor appeared confused, but then he grinned. "Clever."

"What is? What's clever?"

"He immersed it in water and shoved it in the oven with a lid on the pan. It's his way of getting it as far away from you as possible without throwing it out the window."

And it appeared to be working. Spencer had stopped dry heaving, and Ebba's pain receded, leaving behind a clammy sensation.

She sat up and pressed her thumbs to her eye sockets, then inhaled deeply, attempting to regain her composure. Her reaction to the pain was cringy, but at least she hadn't tossed up her cookies like Spencer. Although, if the fucking body snatcher was physically feeling *her* pain, it would make sense that he had. Still, she hated to give him any grace.

Lo returned and knelt at her feet, rubbing his hands along the outside of her thighs. "I'm sorry I was slow on the uptake. Are you okay, Ebba?"

His worry was endearing but unnecessary.

"I'm fine." She brushed back a dark lock of hair shielding his intense eyes. "I swear."

"Did I see markings illuminated on that globe?" Damian asked.

Laszlo nodded, and the Aether shot a thoughtful look toward the stove.

"I'd like to take a few minutes to study it." When they protested, he held up a hand. "I'll create a force field around Ebba, and it won't affect her in any way."

With their main objection neutralized, they agreed.

Damian approached her with a warm smile, and Ebba had difficulty remembering to breathe. *Not* that it mattered, because she wasn't living. But the stern-eyed stare from Lo was flattering. Call her twisted, but she liked his jealous act.

"It's best if all of you stay inside the dome I create. No matter what happens, don't break the barrier until I say," the Aether warned.

Pressing his palms together, he shut his eyes. The language was undecipherable to Ebba, but there was a musicality to the way he spoke it. Around them, the atmosphere grew heavy and crackled, as it had when he first arrived. Growing between his hands was a ruby-colored ball, and like the gemstone, it appeared faceted. How it differed was in its density. Instead of a solid rock, it resembled a soap bubble, expanding as he separated his hands. Inside, sparks ignited, popping off like miniature lightning bolts.

She was supposed to stand inside that thing? Was he mental?

His lids flew open, and his gaze locked with hers. Ebba gasped at how his eyes had transformed from their obsidian color to molten-silver.

The ruby bubble expanded until it consumed the entire space between them, and with a flick of his wrist, he chucked it in their direction.

She screamed.

Laughter from the men caused her to open her scrunched-tight lids. Looking around in wonder, she shook her head. Where there was nothing before, a filmy, see-through wall stood, its depth similar to a wood-studded one. The lightning bolts existed within the confines of its structure, unable to reach them.

"Are you all right, Ebba?" Damian asked with a humor-filled smile.

"Peachy."

Laszlo appreciated the kindness the others showed Ebba. Curiosity endless, she plagued them with questions about magic and the barrier the Aether had created. Through it all, they displayed nothing but patience and understanding.

For himself, he wanted to be in the kitchen with Damian, examining the artifact. Periodically, the man would nod to himself as he scribbled notes, silently confirming a theory only he suspected. With an abrupt slash of his pen, he drew two lines, dropped the globe back into the water, and shoved it into the oven.

As he approached them, his expression was grim. The removal of the barrier consisted of a single-hand swirl and pull of the crumbling wall toward himself. It folded in on itself, shrinking until it was golf-ball-sized. Instead of dispelling the magic completely, he tucked it into his jeans pocket.

"Saving it for later use?" Alastair asked before taking a sip of the drink he'd conjured.

"You never know when a force field comes in handy," Damian deadpanned.

"For those who don't know"—Castor gestured between Ebba and Lo—"this is the lull before shit gets real. Damian becomes all business when he's in planning mode."

The Aether's lips twitched, and he gave his friend a look that was shy of an eye roll.

"Tell me I'm wrong. Tell me you're not plotting something," the Traveler taunted.

"No."

"I thought so." His chuckle was packed with satisfaction, and he rubbed his hands together. "Hold on to your hats, kids. Things are about to get fun!"

Alastair barked a laugh.

"Don't encourage him, Al," Damian scolded good-naturedly. "If he believes he has a rapt audience, he'll double down."

"I'd double down anyway," Castor retorted.

"Are they always like this?" Ebba laughingly asked Alastair.

"Yes. It's a trial."

Her giggle brought a smile to everyone's lips.

The skin along Laszlo's neck prickled, and he cast a searching glance around the room.

Spencer watched them with hatred tempered only by envy. Was it their effortless magic he coveted or the easy friendship?

The man's ire was redirected, and Lo got a sinking feeling when his gaze locked on Ebba. The jealousy was associated with *her*! Had he fallen for her only to be rebuffed? She'd said she was ending things the night of the accident. Perhaps there was more to the incident than they'd believed. Spencer's reasons for hanging on could have more to do with unrequited love than any attempt to prolong his life.

"What the fuck are you staring at?" he growled, finally noticing Lo's attention on him.

"You."

There was no heat in his answer, and confusion shone on Spencer's face.

Laszlo approached the bed.

"You can't have her," he said quietly. "Even if she did love you—which she doesn't—your life has ended. Your body cannot be revived."

"I'll keep this one, and she'll remain repulsed by you with me at the helm."

"Spencer. Come on, man. You know that's not cool."

Sullen, the guy shrugged. "Cool or not, she's mine."

"No. She was mine from the start," Laszlo said as Ebba joined him and clasped his hand. "And I was hers."

Alastair came to stand on the opposite side of her. "You can't fight the pull of soulmates, Mr. Barlowe. Their bond is too strong, and that's to say nothing of the Fates' design. As a witch, you should know this."

"Who said I was a witch?" Spencer snarled.

"Aren't you?" Ebba asked, inching forward.

Laszlo tugged her back. "Careful, Sweet."

A knock sounded.

"It's the cops," Castor said in an aside. "Quick, everyone form a line and hide our prisoner so it doesn't look like we're doing shady shit."

"How does he—"

Alastair pressed a hand to Ebba's shoulder, silencing her. "He's teasing. The presence on the other side of your door is magical in nature."

She shot the Traveler a glare. "Tool."

"Your face was priceless, Dorothy," he tossed over his back as he strode to admit the newcomer.

Clutch stepped over the threshold, followed by Wilder, and Laszlo couldn't have been more surprised by seeing his brother than if someone had taken a tire iron to his kneecaps.

"Wilder?"

His brother's frowning glance around the room deepened when it landed on the bed. "I didn't know y'all were into weird sex games. I'll show myself out."

"Stay!" Ebba surged forward, causing Wilder to do a double take.

"What the fuck?" His eyes widened in horror and met Lo's. "Why is she blinking in and out that way? And why are there two of her?"

To an outsider, it had to seem bizarre that she was tied to the bed but also standing by the door. Wilder couldn't know one was her possessed body and the other her spirit.

"Blinking in and out? What do you mean?" Ebba asked.

The rest of them shared a confused look. To them, she appeared solid.

"It's like you're here, but not. Ghostly," Wilder explained, stepping closer to her and touching her shoulder. "You're solid now. What the hell's happening?"

"Fascinating," Damian murmured, studying her with new eyes.

"Thanks, Doctor Spock, but that's a real problem," Castor said.

Lo's stomach dropped. "How?"

"It indicates a time disturbance. Like a computer glitch before the hard drive crashes. It's bizarre only he can see—"

Flinging her arms out wide, Ebba gasped. Her eyes grew opaque an instant before her head dropped back.

Lo swore and dove for her, but Wilder reached her first, catching her before she fell.

Behind them, Spencer thrashed and released a cry as Ebba called out, "Save me, Wilder! I love you, my wild boy."

The blow was crushing, and Lo sucked in a breath. His heart rate increased, and the thudding against his chest wall became painful.

"How...?" Wilder swallowed, and the haunted eyes he turned on Lo added to the betrayal he felt.

"When did you and Ebba...?" He didn't really want to know, did he? Surely, that path led to heartbreak. The little voice in his head sneered in derision. It wasn't as if his heart hadn't just been trampled to death.

"What? *No!* Christ, have you lost your last fucking brain cell?" his brother shook his head. "Ebba and I have never been an item. There's never been anyone for her but *you*, you idiot."

"Then why did she say she loved you?" Lo demanded, growing angrier by the second. But not at Ebba or his brother. At himself for his instantaneous lack of faith in the two of them. And had she and Wilder hooked up, there wasn't a damned thing he could've said about it. Until recently, he'd been married and didn't realize he'd buried his feelings for Ebba when he was nineteen.

"I have no idea. Abbie was the only person who called me 'wild boy.'" Wilder's voice cracked, and he looked away to hide his anguish.

"Do you think Ebba's channeling her?" Castor asked.

"It's possible," Clutch said. "She's got one foot in the spirit world. But why would Abigail need saving if she's crossed?"

"Perhaps you should ask Death the next time you see her," Lo suggested. "Also, you and I are having a conversation as soon as Ebba wakes. I want to know what the fuck is up with that glowing globe you gave me."

Guilt flashed in his friend's eyes.

Waiting be damned!

He grabbed Clutch by the shirtfront.

"What did you do?" Laszlo shook him, praying he had the self-control not to pummel him after he heard the answer. "What is that thing, and why give me something so dangerous?"

"It absorbs renegade souls," Damian said with a meaningful

look at Clutch. "Those spheres are rare. Four exist in the entire world." He shrugged a shoulder at Lo's accusing glare. "I recalled where I'd seen it before. What I'd like to know is how one came to be in your possession, Mr. Adams? Those soul transporters aren't meant for Reaper's assistants."

"I'm not an assistant. I'm a Reaper," Clutch confessed. Expression apologetic, he met Lo's disbelieving stare. "Five months ago, I replaced the one who failed to collect Ebba. I didn't know what she meant to you, Lo, but either way, I'm here to finish the job."

Laszlo growled low in his throat. "You can fuck all the way off. You're not taking her."

"I tried to make this easy, but you're being stubborn. She's mortal and has been on this plane too long. It creates ripple effects, man."

"I don't give a shit if the earth blows apart." Lo released him with a hard shove. "She's staying with me."

"You always were stubborn," Clutch muttered. "Aether, please talk sense into him. He'll bring Death's wrath if he keeps this up."

Damian smiled. "I'm inclined to side with Laszlo. Had you been upfront and presented your case in a reasonable manner, this conversation may have gone your way. Likely not, as I'm a sucker for love, but there was a slim chance."

Clutch glanced down at Ebba held in Wilder's arms, and Laszlo stepped between them and his ex-friend.

"Don't even think about it," he snarled.

"Lo."

"I will kill you where you stand."

With a shake of his head, Clutch teleported away.

"Now we know why the globe lit up," Castor said.

Alastair placed a calming hand on Lo's shoulder. "Don't worry, son. We're still within Death's window."

Wilder stood with Ebba draped over his arms. "When this is over, I'm going to need a rundown of what the fuck is going on."

20

as she dreaming?

Ebba wasn't sure anymore. Her conscious self floated along a mist halfway between the Wild West and the present. She cast a look the way she'd come, but no one remained in her living room.

Where had everyone gone?

A chill gripped her, and she rubbed her arms for warmth. Squinting at the town's wooden buildings, she tried to make out the name of what appeared to be a saloon.

Abbie drifted closer, wearing filthy clothes, ripped in various places. Her long ash-blonde hair was a tangled mess, and she shook her head with disbelief on her face.

"I know you," she said in a dazed wonder. "I don't know how, but I do."

"Yes." Ebba attempted to touch her, to offer comfort, but neither was corporeal. "How did you get here?"

Gaze wide with anxiety, Abbie shook her head, tears shimmering in her pale blue eyes, and Ebba's stomach clenched in response.

"Do you know who you are?"

"No," she replied with a choked sob.

Ebba felt genuine fear. Were they in purgatory? Did memories fade here? The thought was crushing. What must it be like to wander aimlessly for months or years with no sense of self?

"Your name is—"

The woman latched onto her wrist, and a shock wave rippled through Ebba's system, causing her to black out. When she awoke, she was back in her apartment, cradled in Wilder's arms as he stalked across the living room to the couch.

"What the fuck?" she whispered.

"You went all exorcist, mumbled some shit, and passed out," he told her.

"What did I say?"

Stark anguish transformed his face from grim to tragic. "It doesn't matter," he said gruffly.

"Wilder, please tell me."

He set her down on the sofa and squatted in front of her. With a heavy sigh, he ran a hand through his hair. "Ebba, hon, it doesn't matter. Really."

"I disagree." Without considering the consequences of her confession, she said, "I just saw Abbie."

He plopped on his ass, appearing shellshocked.

"What?" Laszlo knelt beside his brother and placed a hand on his back as a gesture of solidarity. "You saw her? How?"

"I don't know. We were both in some misty, in-between place. It was strange."

"Were there other people there?"

She shook her head. "No. The town was empty, but so was my apartment. It was like no one else existed where we were."

"Town?" Alastair shifted closer. "You saw a town? Can you describe it?"

"It was old, reminding me of those Wild West movies. Buildings with wooden storefronts and a saloon."

"But you're sure it was Abbie?" Wilder asked, despair mingling with hope and contorting his features. "*My* Abbie?"

"I'm sure. But she doesn't know who she is. It's like she's lost in time." Ebba felt foolish for suggesting it. "Do you think I dreamed it?"

"No, child." Alastair shot Wilder a concerned glance. "I don't believe you did. None of us do."

Lo sat beside her and clasped her hand. "You fell into a trance and called out to Wilder, telling him you loved him and asking him to save you. But we think it was Abbie."

"She touched me, and it short-circuited my brain. Everything went black until I woke just now." Ebba shook her head. "It was real?"

"I think so."

"I can't help thinking that place was purgatory. It's so cold there."

Wilder's face turned sickly. "Can it be good if it made her soul cold? Lo?"

"I don't know." Laszlo addressed Damian. "Earlier, you said a soul could become lost and vengeful if not reaped. Is that what happened to Abbie?"

"Without all the facts, I can't begin to speculate." The Aether's expression was grim. "But if we can reach her again, we'll help her transition."

Folding his arms over his legs, Wilder dropped his head against them. His breathing was erratic and bordered hyperventilation. Ebba dove off the couch and wrapped her arms around him.

"I'm so sorry," she whispered.

Shifting, he returned her embrace with a tighter one as if holding onto her like a lifeline. Together, they rocked back and forth as his hot tears trailed down the skin of her neck. She shared a worried look with Laszlo.

Was that her fate if she wasn't unbound and available to go when Death beckoned?

RISING, LO USHERED THE OTHERS TO THE KITCHEN, LEAVING Ebba to comfort his brother.

"What the hell does any of that mean?" he asked the others. "Have you seen anything like this before?"

The three men shook their heads.

Alastair removed his suit jacket and draped it over a kitchen stool. After loosening his tie, he added it to the pile and rolled up his cuffs.

"What are you doing, Al?"

"An experiment," he replied. "Alex, I need you to stab me with a butcher knife."

Lo's face went numb. "Fuck no!"

But both of Alastair's friends looked intrigued.

"What do you have in mind?" Damian asked as Castor rummaged for a weapon.

"Is anyone listening to me?" Laszlo demanded. "I said, *fuck no!*"

Alastair's expression was droll. "I'm doing this, son."

"How about you tell me your theory first?"

"I don't believe Abigail is dead." His cousin sent Ebba a considering glance. "In fact, I think she's very much alive, and I hope to prove it."

"How?"

"If my soul can follow Ebba's path to her perceived purgatory, I might encounter Abigail for myself. Then I can get answers." He shot the Aether a warning look. "But revive me before I cross completely or Rorie will never forgive either of us."

"There's an alternative way to do that," Damian replied. "Isis."

"I think she's provided all the help she plans to in this case," Alastair said grimly. "She's holding back, but the precise reason remains a mystery."

"She always has one," Castor agreed. "Personally, I think she likes being an enigma wrapped in a sexy exterior."

Damian cracked a smile.

"No," Wilder said from behind them, with Ebba lingering at his elbow. His red-rimmed eyes spoke of his heartbreak, but there was determination in them, too. "Abbie's been gone for two years, and whatever is happening with Ebba should be addressed today. Right now."

He met Lo's gaze. "You know I'm right. You both deserve to be happy if you can."

"Wilder." Ebba's concern caught his attention.

Glancing down at her, he smiled. "It's okay, kid. You've given me a reason to hope, or at the very least, to move on if she's lost to me." He impulsively hugged her again and released her to embrace Lo.

"Does this mean I don't get to stab Al?" Castor complained.

Wilder laughed. The sound rusty and odd after so much time had passed. "No stabbing Alastair. Now, someone catch me up."

For the next few minutes, they did, answering his plethora of questions. He looked at the group with considering eyes, pausing overly long on Castor. Twice, he opened his mouth to speak but decided against it.

Finally, Wilder hugged Lo. "This has to be difficult for you since you've loved her forever."

"I'm not even going to ask you how you know that." Lo shook his head in disgust. "Hell, I didn't until today."

"I was the one who encouraged Cole, Heath, and Liz to dissuade you from pursuing a relationship. I'm sorry, but in those days, I didn't think you were serious about her."

Ebba punched his shoulder. "Next time, mind your own damned business, Wilder Thorne!"

"Oww! Who knew a spook could hit so hard?"

"Aether energy," Lo supplied with a wide grin.

"What about the sleeping Ebba on the bed? What happens to her body snatcher?" Wilder asked.

Fuck!

They'd forgotten about Spencer in all the commotion, and Laszlo ran to check on him.

"Does anyone else think it's odd that he didn't wake when Ebba did?" Castor asked.

"Abso-fucking-lutely," Lo said.

"We can't worry about him. We've delayed long enough." Damian approached Ebba. "Before I remove your memories, I'd like to see what you encountered on the other plane. Would you permit me to tap into your mind?"

Casting a wary look at the rest of them, she nodded. "If it will help Abbie, yes."

"Excellent. Have a seat, my dear."

21

The sensation of something rooting around in Ebba's brain was disconcerting. She didn't want to liken the process to worms crawling through underground passages, but she had no other fitting comparison. When he'd retrieved what he was after, Damian sat back and looked at Wilder.

"It's not purgatory," he said before adding, "We'll find Abigail."

He didn't wait for Wilder's grateful nod before turning back to Ebba. "Ready?"

"I don't think so," she croaked.

"What do you need?"

"To say goodbye to Laszlo. Just a few minutes."

"Of course." He rose and gestured to the others to give Lo and her privacy.

"Lo, if I don't make it—"

"Ebba, stop. You will."

"But if I don't, I want you to know I was never mad at you for choosing Charlotte. Disappointed, yes, because I wanted you to pick me, but I wasn't angry at you for it."

"I know, Sweet." He wove his fingers into her curls and tipped her head back. "But I love you in a way I could never love her, and I can't imagine a world without you in it. Having said that, you need to do whatever it takes to survive."

Their metaphysical bond had fused completely, revealing the truth of his words. Those strands were a starburst of happy colors with gray threads of sadness woven in. Still, she wanted him to be okay.

The smile she sent him was wry. "Don't be overly dramatic, babe. Six months ago, you didn't know I was alive."

"Shut it, woman! You know I did. I was at peace believing you were living a good life without me to muck it up."

"I'd have given anything for you to have done that." She grinned when he leaned in to kiss her. "This love we have, I'm taking it with me. When I finally meet Death again, I'm going to throw myself on the altar of her mercy and beg for leniency." When he would've protested, she covered his mouth. "I won't let you blow me off so easily in the next life, Laszlo Thorne. If she allows me to return, I'm going to be that burr in your shoe."

His eyes gleamed with love and intent. "You'll be my burr in this one. Count on it."

"If stubbornness can make it happen, you'll do it."

"Damn straight."

Flinging her arms around him, she buried her face against his neck. "I love you so damned much."

"Don't give up, Ebba. Whatever you do, you hold on, okay?"

She nodded, and her nose brushed the strong column of his neck. Although she breathed deeply, hoping to memorize his delectable scent, she understood it would be forever lost the instant Damian plucked it from her brain. Still, she savored the smell of crisp, clean linen and the peppermint from the candies he consumed at an alarming rate.

"Do witches get cavities?" she asked against his throat.

Laughter rumbled inside his chest, causing friction with hers. "That's random."

She drew back and grinned. "I was thinking about all the candy you eat. Not only would I be twice my size, I'd need every tooth in my head filled."

"You're going to despise the fact we don't age, gain weight, or get cavities, aren't you?"

"I fucking knew it!"

He laughed. "Goddess, I love you."

"Thank you."

Taken aback, he asked, "Why?"

"It's the one thing that makes my life complete."

"Stop sounding like you're transitioning, Ebba James. I swear by all that's holy; I'll hunt you down and bring you back."

His determined look cemented his promise.

"I believe you would, Lo," she murmured against his lips before deepening the kiss. When she drew away, she caressed his stubbled jaw. "I'll see you on the other side of this."

"That's my girl."

He cradled her face, staring into her eyes. What he saw, he didn't say, but his love seared itself on her soul. She might not remember their time together, but she'd feel it somewhere deep inside whenever she saw him again.

"It's getting late," Damian said from behind him.

"Yeah," Lo said roughly. Still, he made no move to release her, and Ebba grabbed his wrists.

"You have to let me go," she said softly.

"It's like asking me to cut out my heart," he replied, equally as soft.

But he released her and rose, leaving room for Damian to do his job.

The memory removal wasn't necessarily painful, but it was damned uncomfortable. Five minutes into the process, he sighed. "Ebba, you must stop fighting this, or it won't work."

She blinked back tears. "Can you put me to sleep or something? I can't look at him and not resist."

"I can, if you're all right with it."

"Yes."

"Close your eyes."

Within seconds, she'd drifted off.

"It's done." The Aether sounded weary or perhaps a little sad.

Pulse pounding, Laszlo took his spot next to Ebba's comatose spirit and smoothed the hair from her forehead. He wasn't certain what he'd expected to see, maybe a lobotomy scar, but it wasn't the smooth, untouched skin beneath his fingers. "Is she okay?"

"Yes. But it's time for the next step. I'll stand guard in place of McClutchin, with Alastair. I'll create a spell for us to see any spirits as they enter the room."

"I don't know how I'll repay you for this, but if you ever need me, I'm there," Lo promised.

"No need. I wasn't lying when I said I was a sucker for love, Laszlo."

Damian directed him to lie next to Ebba's physical self on the bed. "I'm going to move her body over, but don't touch her if you can help it."

"What about Spencer's soul?"

"I'll extract it at the same time I cast the spell to separate yours." Leaning in, Damian touched Lo's temple.

The zing felt like the minor shock one got from static electricity, and with it came the Aether's thoughts.

This is the only way I can convey what my daughter said

without the Fates learning of it, so pay attention," he said through their telepathic connection. *"You cannot prevent the accident from happening, but it's imperative you're there to meet Death and Isis. Plead your case, and it won't fall on deaf ears. Nod if you understand."*

Lo nodded.

"Find your familiar. The key lies with the wolf."

"I don't have a familiar. I don't know where to begin looking," Lo told him.

"You will."

Damian severed their link and gave him a meaningful stare.

How the hell was he supposed to find a familiar while in his bodiless state? Laszlo was so caught up in his tumultuous thoughts he barely registered the removal of Spencer or the separation of his soul from his body.

One minute, the Aether was standing at the foot of the bed, and the next, he held a voodoo doll in hand with Laszlo staring at his and Ebba's sleeping bodies.

"Can you see me?" he asked them.

"They can't. I can." Damian handed the doll off to Alastair, who handed it to Castor. "Tell Alex not to play with it. It's not a bloody toy."

"Telling him anything is a wasted effort, but I'll watch to make sure he doesn't set our friend loose."

"That's all I can ask." Turning back to Laszlo, Damian beckoned him closer until they were touching. *"Fac nobis visibiles."*

Make visible to us.

Simple. Effective.

Oh, to have his abilities!

"To have my abilities, you'd have to do the terrible things others won't," the Aether said somberly.

"'With great power comes great responsibility,'" Castor mocked.

"You ready, wiseass?" Laszlo asked him. "We've got a girl to save."

"Ready, hero."

Alastair's brows shot up, and he shook his head. "Is it smart to send these two without a referee, Dethridge? I doubt they can stop arguing long enough to accomplish anything."

"We're the best of buds." Castor flung an arm around Laszlo's shoulders. "Aren't we?"

"Sure. When this is over, we'll sit around a campfire, drinking PBRs and singing Kumbaya."

Castor snorted. "You had to take it a step too far, didn't ya?"

Lo walked to the sofa.

Ebba was eerily still in her coma-like state, yet the glow of her aura was brighter than it had been whenever Lo had observed her while inside his body. He'd never seen anyone's as brilliant and pure as hers.

"What about Ebba? Will you find a way to restore her soul while we're gone?" he asked Damian.

"Of course. Consider it done."

His next question was harder to voice. "When we go back, and if we fail, will she cease to exist in this timeline?"

"I don't know, but it seems likely," Damian replied.

Leaning down, Lo brushed a kiss on her mouth. "I love you, Ebba James. I'll be back soon."

With one last lingering glance, he turned on his heel and stalked to Castor.

"Let's go."

22

The trip to the past took no longer than an average teleport. According to Castor, they'd arrived three hours earlier than Ebba's accident. Laszlo desperately wished he could call and tell her to stay home, but fate didn't work that way. Something else would cause her death if it was meant to happen.

But was it destined? If so, shouldn't Death's Reapers have been there to collect the souls? Clutch said one of them failed to do their job, and he was assigned the position. Why had an experienced Reaper failed? Castor's interference?

Together, they walked the path from the clearing where they'd landed to Alastair's home. The woods were dense, and mystical energy flowed throughout the forest, cresting over everything from the ground to the tops of the trees.

"Can you see the magic?" he asked Castor, and surprisingly, he didn't need to elaborate.

"Only as I'm traveling through time. Not once I arrive. Everything returns to normal, and the colors fade." Castor paused and cocked his head. "I'm assuming you can in this form."

"Yes. It's wondrous and humbling to know we are but a spec in this vast world." He struggled to explain. "My abilities allow me to see the supernatural, and I know magic exists in every living thing. But I've never actually viewed it outside a spell or conjuring." Pointing, he said, "Take that mushroom for example. The fuchsia color is pulsing and absolutely exquisite."

"Sounds like you're tripping balls," Castor replied dryly.

"It does, but I'm not."

"I know. I've witnessed it all in Traveler form."

"So then you get it."

Castor nodded. "I do. We don't have time to stop and smell the roses, though. The longer we're in this timeline, the greater the chance of fucking things up."

"Got it."

"For what it's worth, Thorne, I'm sorry about your girl and for my part in binding her."

"If you hadn't, she'd have died. I'd have gone my entire life without realizing she was my soulmate." He smiled his thanks. "I'm not sorry you helped her, Castor. I'm grateful."

As they exited the woods, Lo saw two figures on the terrace. "That's you and Al."

"Yep. In about ten seconds, present me will drop like a stone. Alastair's defenses will go up, and he'll become untrusting of our motives. Remain calm and radiate honest energy."

"I'm well aware of how his empathic abilities work."

"Right. I forgot for a second." With a heavy sigh, he said, "Showtime."

On cue, his present-day counterpart's head listed to one side, and the hand holding a coffee mug dropped to his side, spilling black liquid on the stone.

Alastair reacted as predicted. Throwing up one hand, he

created a barrier between them, guarding against the enemy he couldn't see. Next, he checked Castor's still form, first pulse, then his pupils, before sniffing what remained of the cup's contents. He nodded as if assuring himself his friend wasn't poisoned before scanning the horizon.

His gaze fixed on them, and he gestured them forward.

Alastair frowned. "Laszlo?"

"Hello, Al." Lo grinned weakly. "We're from the future."

Dismissing him, Alastair focused on Castor. "Start explaining, Alex. Why is my cousin a fucking ghost?"

Both Castor and Lo clenched their fists, hoping to stem the plague of locust the vehement curse would bring.

A half smile curled Alastair's mouth. The wariness fell away, and acceptance shone in his sapphire eyes. "You're the real deal if you know that about me."

"I've traveled enough times to make this seem normal," Castor replied with an answering grin. He gestured to Lo with a nod of his blond head. "He's not dead if that's what you're worried about. Dethridge separated his soul from his body, allowing him to hitch a ride with me."

"Why would you both need to be here? One warning from you wouldn't suffice?"

"I—"

"You need to call my present self, Al," Lo cut in. They had to act quickly or all was for naught. "Get him here ASAP."

The standard ease with which Alastair carried himself disappeared as he tensed, and his expression tightened. "Tell me what's going on."

He peppered them with the occasional question as they relayed the coming events. When they were finished, he drew his phone from his pocket and shot off a text.

"To me?" Lo asked, nodding to the device.

"Yes, but I doubt you'll get it in time."

"What do you mean?"

"You're off with Heath in the Grand Caymans, celebrating your freedom, son."

"Jesus!" He recalled the cell coverage was spotty in that location. "I need to teleport there right away."

"Not sure that's possible in your current state."

A clawing sense of panic ripped through his chest. "How long can we remain, Castor?"

"Another minute at most," he replied grimly.

"We came too soon." Disbelief that he wouldn't be here to save Ebba rocked him. "Can you leave me and come back for me?"

"I could try, but there's no guarantee it would work." Castor looked as devastated as Lo felt. "Christ, this is a mess."

"Why not simply call her and tell her to stay home?" Alastair asked.

"According to Sabrina Dethridge, this has to play out this way. Ebba has to hit that tree, and I have to be there to persuade Isis and Death to let her live." Lo shook his head. "But how?"

"Then you'll remain and hope we can catapult you back to your timeline afterward." Alastair tugged each of his cuffs down. "If Isis is feeling generous, she might do it."

"She hasn't been generous regarding this mess so far," Lo said, fighting the feeling of hopelessness trying to smother him.

"Don't lose faith, Laszlo. We'll save your friend."

"I love her, Al. She's the one." His nerve endings were raw, and he belatedly recalled Damian saying spirits shouldn't feel as deeply as Ebba was. But Lo did. Maybe their love was the kind to strengthen those emotions even after death.

"We have to go back, Thorne," Castor said, urgency in his tone. "Delaying is dangerous."

"Go without me."

The two friends shared a speaking glance, and their silent

conversation was one Lo wasn't privy to. Nor did he care to be. He wasn't leaving without saving Ebba, and if he couldn't, he didn't care if his soul found his body again or not. Life would be meaningless without her. Recalling his brother's ongoing pain, Laszlo vowed not to continue on that way. It was all or nothing.

"I recognize the stubborn look," Alastair said. "You should return, Alex. I'll take care of him."

With a frustrated glare, Castor nodded and turned on his heel to jog back the way they'd come.

"Thank you, Al."

"Don't thank me yet, son. We haven't saved your Ebba."

THE FOLLOWING TWO HOURS DRAGGED, WITH NO WORD FROM Lo's present self.

"Did you try Heath?" he asked Alastair.

"I did."

"What about sending someone to the island to find me? Ryker?" Lo suggested Alastair's brother-in-law and best friend. Ryker Gillespie had been trained as a master spy by the Witches' Council. If anyone could locate a target, it was him.

"Already on it. I contacted him after Alex returned."

"Why hasn't Castor's present self woken? Is that normal?"

"It's odd, that's for sure," Alastair agreed with a check of his watch. "I'll give him another ten minutes of beauty rest, but he'll—"

"What the actual fuck!" Castor shouted, surging up from the lawn chair they'd laid him on.

"Ah, right on time and surly as ever upon waking." Alastair shot Lo an amused smile. To Castor, he said. "Your future self paid us a visit."

"Fucking hell! What now? What was so damned important that I had to break cosmic rules to fuck with a timeline?"

"The accident scheduled to happen in fifty minutes."

"What accident?" Castor growled, dropping his legs on either side of the recliner and leaning forward to cradle his head in his hands. "The hangover from that shit is off the charts," he muttered, tapping the heel of his palm to his forehead. "Stop doing that."

"Weird. Does his future self ever listen?" Lo asked in a quiet voice.

Alastair chuckled. "Alex never listens to anyone but Damian, and that's selective."

"Who the fuck are you?" Castor asked, still testy but curious.

"Laszlo Thorne. Cousin to Al and brother to Liz."

He grunted as he rubbed his temples. "Why are you translucent?"

"It was the only way I could hitch a ride with you to the past, or what's considered your present."

"Got it." He sighed heavily and met Lo's watchful gaze. "Out with it. What am I preventing?"

"It's what you're not preventing." Alastair held out a hand to help him up. "You need to get to the bend in the road—"

Lightning zigzagged across the evening sky, and thunder shook the earth.

"No rain in the forecast, Al. What do you make of it?" Castor asked with a sharp glance around.

"Magical. Goddess, if I'm not mistaken."

The next streak of light was vertical, splitting the veil between worlds. Isis stepped through the gap and looked none too happy. But her pique might've been because of the woman trailing in her wake. Death sauntered forward, and although her black hood hid most of her face, Lo had the sense her expression was smug.

"Laszlo Thorne," Death purred his name. "You've been a bad boy."

"Not yet," he quipped, stealing a snarky comeback from Castor's bag.

She hissed her displeasure.

Lo met Isis's amused gaze and almost lost control of his jaw when she winked.

"You've come to circumvent the demise of Ebba James and Spencer Barlowe," Death accused. "Deny it if you will."

"I *am* denying it." He met the deities in the middle of the lawn. "I'm here to stop the Traveler from binding Ebba's soul to earth after the accident."

"I do that?" Castor sounded impressed. "Who knew I had such a cool superpower?"

"I did," Isis replied with a warm smile. "Your execution needs work, though."

He laughed.

Death waved them off and stepped closer to Lo. "I don't believe you. You've repeatedly claimed you won't turn over the renegade soul to me, failing in your job as a Reaper's assistant."

"So fire me." He shrugged. Up close, he saw beneath the hood, and she didn't look thrilled. "Or write me up for insubordination if you must. But I'm telling the truth."

Suspicion clouded her visage as she studied him. After a long moment, she shrugged. "You'll be unable to do anything about it anyway. The incident is too far away for you to get there in time."

His stomach relocated to his big toe, but he stood his ground. "But you can do something about it. You can let her live. *Please.* In all these years, I've never asked you for anything."

"I don't make the rules, Laszlo." She disappeared.

"Who does?" he demanded, spinning to face Isis. "Who makes them? You?"

"Did your familiar find you, beloved?"

"No, but I was so concerned about Ebba, I forgot that part."

"Hmm. Come with me." She held up a hand to prevent Alastair and Castor from following. "You two are—what's the sports term you men like so much?—*benched* for this game."

Touching Laszlo's arm, she transported him to the scene.

Death, along with Clutch, were moving toward the crumpled vehicle when the air stilled around them.

"I despise being benched," Castor said as he stepped from behind the tree trunk and summed up the scene. Circling the vehicle, he ripped open the driver's door. His curse was savage when he viewed the inhabitants. With a troubled look at Laszlo, he said, "I heard what you said to them, boyo, but I can't leave her to suffer."

When Lo would've run to him, the Goddess halted his motion. "Wait," she said in a low voice. "Let him go."

Castor positioned his arms like he was drawing a bow back for release. The steering column eased out of Ebba's chest with each inch of space he created in the air.

If he were in physical form, Laszlo would've puked up his guts. To see her laid open, ribs piercing her lungs, and heart halfway shredded was brutal. He was so focused on the carnage that he almost missed her appearance beside him. How many times had he urged her to get rid of that stupid '94 Wrangler, arguing with her that it was dangerous without today's standard safety measures or even a single fucking airbag? But she loved that old relic from her dad. She'd once said it was the first vehicle she'd learned to drive.

"Wow." She whistled softly. "That's a mess."

"Ebba!"

"I guess I don't need to ask what's happening here." Her expression was sad as she observed Castor lift her body from the driver's seat and lay her on the ground.

Time rebounded.

"No!" The anguished cry had originated from the slope above them. *"No!"*

Laszlo's present self had arrived.

His physical body stumbled as he ran down the hill at breakneck speed.

"Why isn't my physical self teleporting?" Lo asked Isis.

"Death filed for a temporary restraining order of sorts," she murmured beside him. "She was determined to gather her souls when she brought the Reaper through time with her."

"She's a Traveler, too?"

"Of sorts due to her status, but not born to it like Alexander," Isis replied. "Wait here."

As she sauntered toward Castor, her filmy dress caught around her legs from the tropical-storm-force winds building around them.

"Pull it back, Laszlo Thorne," she called over her shoulder.

He hadn't realized *his* was the magic stirring within Death's dome—or rather his physical self's. But they weren't linked, and he couldn't convey her wishes.

"He can't hear—"

"He can," she replied, and the winds died down with her answer, although his counterpart never took his eyes off Ebba.

"Alexander," Isis said.

The Traveler held his hands over Ebba's body, pushing a green healing light into her chest cavity.

"Alexander."

He looked up but didn't pause his actions.

Isis touched his shoulder. "If you continue, you'll bind her to this plane, and we'll be back where we started."

"I can't let her die."

"Place this around her neck and step away." An amulet dangled from the fingers she extended toward him. "It will prevent her condition from worsening."

$\mathcal{D}$enied her reaping, Death looked fit to be tied and turned accusing eyes Laszlo's way.

His spirit self was on borrowed time!

In a move to make conquering heroes everywhere proud, he swept Ebba's spirit into his arms and gave her a kiss that promised forever.

Her eyes were dazed as she stared up at him, and Lo grinned when she touched her fingertips to her lips.

"What is happening right now? Am I dreaming?" she asked.

"Nope. This is all too real, Sweet." He cupped her face. "Five months from now, we fall madly in love."

She snorted. "I'm *definitely* dreaming."

"Ebba, I'm out of time and need you to listen. Magic exists, and things are about to get extremely weird and hard for you to comprehend. But trust me, and trust the process."

Turning her head, she watched his physical self stumble toward their group. "This isn't real."

"It *is*," he insisted. "You were driving and impulsively

thought to teach Spencer a lesson. You wanted to break up with him, and he wouldn't take no for an answer."

"That's not right." She shook her head. "I mean, it is, partially. But there was a dog in the road—*Ohmygod!* The dog! I think I hit it!"

Tears gathered in her large chocolaty eyes as her head pivoted back and forth, seeking the injured animal.

"Laszlo, help me save it," she cried.

"Ebba, please! *Listen* to me. Don't follow Death. She'll want to take you with her." He gave her a gentle shake. "Stay with me until I find a way to save you. Can you do that?"

She spoke, but the words were indistinguishable and sounded far away as if they were at opposite ends of a tunnel. Dizziness caused him to sway on his feet, but from the corner of his eye, he caught movement.

Clutch stalked toward him, regret in every line of his face.

Predictably, Death went for Ebba.

Lo's building anxiety turned to outright panic, and he shoved Ebba behind him, continuously shifting to block them both.

"I'll fuck you up, Clutch. I swear I will," he warned his friend, while keeping one eye on Death.

"Lo, it's her time."

"I don't give a shit. Make an exception. *Please!*"

"It doesn't work like that. You've done this long enough to know that." Clutch's scold was filled with compassion. "Hand her over before Death decides to take you, too," he said in a low voice.

The wind kicked up again, shoving Clutch back.

"Fuck off," Lo snarled.

A whimper came from the ditch beside them, and it was all Ebba needed to remind her of the injured dog. She ran before he could stop her.

"Enough!" Isis's voice rang out, halting everyone except

Ebba, who was determined to save the animal. "That goes for you, too, Ebba James."

Standing at the lip of the ditch, she cast an anxious glance down and wrapped her arms around her stomach.

"Please help it," she called to the Goddess. "I'll do whatever you ask. Just help it."

"*No!*" Laszlo and his physical self hollered simultaneously.

A smile curled Isis's lips, and Death bore a smugness Lo wanted to slap clean off her face.

"She doesn't know what she's promising, Exalted One," Castor argued, standing guard over the body. "It's not fair to hold her to it."

"When did you become the defender of mortals, Traveler?" Death sneered. "As I recall, you couldn't be bothered to protect your own *son*."

The fury in her voice brought Castor's head around, and he peered through the darkness at her. She eased back the hood of her black cloak, and his harsh expletive echoed off the trees when he recognized her.

"Divina. How the hell did you get this gig?"

"I had no choice!"

Isis cleared her throat. "You always have a choice."

"It didn't feel like it after my passing," Divina said with a sour look. "It was the only way to protect my son from the constant evil the Thornes send his way."

"Whoa! Wait a fucking minute!" Laszlo snarled. "My family isn't evil, lady. If anything, they've tried their damnedest to prevent evil fuckers from hurting others."

"Quentin has repeatedly stood in the line of fire to save that silly girl!" Divina argued. "As has anyone who loves a Thorne. You have no respect for human life."

"*Holly?*" Castor scoffed. "He loves her. And she loves him equally as well. They have a daughter. Francesca," he added, his voice softening on their granddaughter's name. "She's beautiful, love. You should see her."

"I have." Her tone was haughty, but the wary glance toward the Goddess indicated she'd done something wrong. When she received no rebuke, she allowed a soft smile. "She's beautiful and looks just like Quentin at that age."

"She does."

"I have a job to do, Alex," she said tiredly. "This game of jumping through time or binding souls to Earth has to stop. They are to be collected when their bodies die."

"But her body isn't dead," Castor countered.

"The Tyet amulet has suspended her transition." Isis shrugged a delicate shoulder. "It was necessary while we resolve this dispute."

Hope tried to gain a foothold inside Lo, but resolving disputes meant compromise, and he didn't know what sacrifice would be required. Another wave of dizziness assailed him, and rather than expend the energy to argue, he knelt at the Goddess's feet.

"If you know anything about my family, you know we only *truly* love once. But this isn't about my happiness. It's about *hers*." He gestured to Ebba's body, still unable to look at her broken form. "She doesn't deserve an end like this. She deserves the freedom to choose."

"You're correct. And I'll give her the choice."

"Wait—" Death's objection was cut off by Isis.

"All those present answer to me, with the exception of the girl and you, Divina. You receive your orders from the Fates."

"Yes, Exalted One. So you must see why I need to do my job properly. Balance must be maintained in all things."

"I agree." Isis produced a scroll. "These are your new orders."

Death's perfectly arched brows shot up as she read the

parchment. After handing it off to Clutch, she strode to the vehicle and gestured to Spencer. "He's all yours."

"You'll need to wait until his powers are confiscated, my dear," Isis said, adding a smile to soften the command.

As Laszlo had said, things were getting extremely weird, but Ebba paid no attention to the Goddess or Death, not caring about their silly games. Instead, she focused on the poor animal suffering in the ditch, hoping to find a way to ease its pain. With a fleeting glance toward the others, she scrambled to comfort the beast.

It wasn't a dog, as she'd initially suspected, but a wolf with a beautiful shiny, black coat. The wary golden eyes watching her approach reminded Ebba of Laszlo. Throughout their lives, he'd worn that same look as if he were weighing the trustworthiness of others.

The beast growled low in its throat as she inched closer.

"It's all right, sweet baby. I intend to help you." But she wasn't sure how she could with no physical form. And *that* particular thought was difficult to wrap her mind around.

"And how would you help this poor creature, child?"

Ebba gasped at the Goddess, who hovered on the ledge, and she quickly dipped her head as she'd witnessed the others do.

Think fast, Ebba! Think fast!

But her brain cells abandoned her right when she needed them most.

"I'll ask you again, Ebba James. How would you help this creature?"

"I'd heal her if I could."

"You cannot. She's dying."

Ebba met the wolf's pain-glazed eyes.

"Then *you* do it," she cried. "Please, don't let her suffer because I'm a shitty driver."

"She darted in front of you, and there was nothing you were able to do." Isis gestured behind her. "The accident should tell you as much."

"Please," Ebba begged.

Kohl-lined eyes narrowed, and the Goddess stepped off the edge, heedless of the drop. The breeze kicked up, and it was as if a set of invisible stairs existed beneath her feet as she descended into the ditch.

"This creature cannot be healed, child. Her soul is transitioning."

"But *you* can save her. I know you can. You're a goddess, for fuck's sake! What good are you—"

"Ebba!" Laszlo's warning came too late.

The freezing wind bit into her flesh, and Ebba was surprised she felt anything at all. But it was nothing in comparison to the icy tones of the pissed-off Goddess.

"You *dare* speak to me in such a manner?"

Well, no. She wouldn't have been brave enough if she hadn't been worked up over tonight's events. She'd quite literally screwed the pooch on this one—right along with herself.

The spirit of the wolf sidled up to her and rubbed its head along Ebba's hip before bounding up the dirt wall to stand beside Laszlo. They looked perfect together—the beast and the man. Dark-haired and dangerous-looking, yet worried for her.

"I'm sorry," she whispered, unsure if it was meant for him, the wolf, or the Goddess.

"I'll allow your outburst this once because you fear for this poor creature. But mind your tone. Disrespect will *not* be tolerated."

Ebba nodded, but inside, she was miserable. Her foolishness had cost at least one life. How many more needed to die?

"Step aside," Isis said.

After she complied, the Goddess bent and placed a necklace around the wolf's throat.

"It will suspend her death," she said in an aside to Ebba. "All will be well, child."

"Will it go to heaven or wherever souls go?" she asked, struggling against tears.

"I've another plan. For *both* of you." With a pat on Ebba's cheek, she drifted back up the hill. Once at the top, she tilted her head back and spread her arms wide.

"Aether!"

The air around them crackled, and the invisible dome lit up, highlighting its honeycomb design an instant before dissolving into millions of sparkling lights. A golden fissure appeared beside the Goddess, and a black-haired man stepped through the veil. Behind him, Ebba caught a glimpse of a country estate with a house older than America.

The man was divine, perfect in every way, and it was a wonder any one person could be so beautiful. His eyes, nearly as black as his hair, summed up the scene in a single glance.

Bowing his head, he said, "Exalted One."

His voice was deep, smooth, and seductive, a symphony to the ears. He had the barest hint of a British accent, and Ebba could've listened to him speak all day.

"The man in the vehicle is Spencer Barlowe, and he's been ungovernable," Isis said.

Laszlo's physical self approached Ebba, ignoring the byplay between the Goddess and the beautiful man she'd called Aether.

"I got the call too late," he said achingly. "But I'll fix this."

Ebba frowned, turning to seek out his spirit self, only to find him fading.

"What's happening?" she cried.

"He cannot exist in two places without causing a ripple effect," the Aether said, and with a wave of his hand, he sent Spirit Laszlo away.

24

*E*bba cried out, but it was too late.

The single understanding glance from the Aether and Isis did nothing to ease her fear for Laszlo.

"What happened to him?" she demanded, immediately forgetting their "disrespect" conversation. "Is he okay?"

"He was sent back to his time," the Goddess replied with remarkable calm. "Trust the process, child."

Laszlo's warm hand brushed hers and traveled through, creating a chill where he attempted to touch her. Frustration contorted his features before he pasted on a brave expression. "I'm here, Ebba. I won't let anything happen to you."

"You can't promise that, and you shouldn't," the dark-haired man said, not unkindly.

"She's a family friend, Dethridge," Laszlo argued.

An amused smile curled the other man's lips, and Ebba became transfixed by his beautiful mouth.

"I'm well aware of who she is, Thorne, and what she will become to you."

"What? What will I become?" Ebba's mind was spinning faster than ingredients in a mixing bowl. "And what's with this supposed time-travel shit?"

His amused smile turned to an engaging grin, and the Aether thoroughly hypnotized her with that single action. All she wanted to do was stare at him until her dying day.

"If I'm not mistaken, it *is* your dying day." A devilish twinkle entered his obsidian eyes. "But I'm here to correct that."

His words had the impact of a bucketful of water over her head, and she jerked back from the reality dousing.

"You read my mind?" she croaked.

"Normally I wouldn't intrude on another's thoughts unless I had an inkling they intended harm to me or mine, but you transmit louder than most."

Fucking fantastic!

He fought a smile, and she wanted Death to simply take her at this point and end her suffering.

"Power is to be collected," Isis said. "When you are done, Aether, transfer it equally to the amulets."

"Mr. Barlowe's, I'm assuming?" Dethridge asked though it sounded more like a statement of fact.

Her nod confirmed his question, and with one last considering glance at Ebba and Laszlo, the Aether did as she bid.

"I don't understand," Ebba said to Laszlo. Her mind was officially blown. Goddesses, Death, two Laszlos, gorgeous men who appeared from thin air. It was all like a fantasy novel or chaotic movie script. These things didn't happen in the real world. "What power? What's she talking about?"

"I come from a long line of witches—"

"My line," Isis said, interrupting him. "And magic does exist, my dear. Mr. Barlowe is descended from my brother and, like him, feels he can do whatever he wants. Including persuading women that they are attracted to him. Yet you, for any number of interesting reasons, were not."

Ebba didn't want to admit aloud she'd been in love with Laszlo since childhood. Somehow, she suspected the Goddess knew, and she didn't want to voice it in front of her lifelong crush.

"There's no getting between fated mates," Castor said. "Believe me, I'd have stolen Damian's love years ago if that was the case."

The Aether snorted. "My wife would chew you up and spit you out before breakfast, Alex."

Castor grinned. "Yeah, but what a ride!"

Instead of displaying jealousy or anger, Damian laughed. "I'll be sure to let Viv know you're lusting over her."

"She knows," Death said with an eye roll. "Alex can't keep it in his pants."

"Ouch." Castor placed his hands over his heart. "I'm wounded."

Her laughter was surprising. "Doubtful, darling."

"I agree. It's unlikely," the Aether replied, reaching into the car.

Ebba didn't want to consider the idea of fated mates, the relevancy to her situation, or why Castor had brought it up. She was too fascinated with Damian Dethridge and his power-removal process.

It took less than a minute, and her letdown was great. "I thought there would be more to it than him placing his hands on Spencer's head and chest," she said to Laszlo.

"He's the balance between good and evil in the witch community, and he's been around as long as I can remember. I imagine he doesn't break a sweat over these things."

"He doesn't age?"

Laszlo shrugged. "He does, but not at the speed mortals do."

"What about you?" she asked, her curiosity about his claim subduing her fear of the present situation.

"I'm somewhere in between."

Castor, who had been standing guard over Ebba's body, stepped aside to allow Damian to infuse the necklace with the reclaimed power.

With a questioning glance at the Goddess, the Aether knelt and pressed a hand to Ebba's forehead. The other, he placed about five inches above her chest. A green ball formed in his palm and shot strands of light into her wounds. Her body finished knitting back together. The ribs eased from her lungs, and the tissue reattached, pinkening to a healthy color. Her heart took the longest, but eventually, it appeared whole. New skin grew from damaged old, covering her organs.

"Can he do that for the wolf, too?" she asked, hopeful he could and would.

"Bring the animal and place it beside the girl's body," Isis directed Laszlo.

With a respectful nod, he jumped into action, skidding down the side of the ditch to retrieve the wolf. Its spirit followed him like a faithful companion with her tongue lolling on the side of her mouth as she stared at him with adoration.

Ebba understood the urge.

"Your souls are ready, Divina," Isis said.

Laszlo topped the ditch and stopped short, denial on his face.

"Not your mate, Beloved. Spencer Barlowe and the unfortunate creature you hold," Isis informed him.

Anger at the unfairness bubbled inside Ebba. "I thought you said it would be okay? That you'd heal it?"

"Then you mistook me, child. But if you don't wish to be the third soul Death reaps, I suggest you learn to control your temper."

Once again, she'd pissed off the Goddess with her spontaneous outbursts. Heart aching for the wolf, Ebba nodded and dropped her gaze to the canine spirit beside Laszlo.

"I'm sorry," she whispered, but her apology was more for the magnificent beast than her behavior. "But you made me believe you would save her life. That means her soul."

"What would you give to save the creature?" Isis asked with a thoughtful tilt of her head.

"My life."

Laszlo tightened his grip on the wolf and ran to her. "Ebba, no!"

"This beautiful girl doesn't deserve to have her life cut short," she said with a catch in her voice. "What if she's pregnant or has pups to care for out there?"

"And what about you, Sweet?" he asked achingly. "What about your family and those who love you?"

"No one counts on me, Laszlo. No one needs me."

"Liz does. You're her best friend. And me. Based on what I've done to save you, I suspect I'm about to need you a great deal."

She wanted to weep, but bottled it inside. "I've waited over half my life to hear you say that. But I won't allow her to be sacrificed on my behalf. If the Goddess can save her, I'll gladly do what is required of me."

The animal's spirit approached Ebba, and she squatted to touch the beauty's massive head. "You're a gorgeous girl, aren't you? I'm sorry your life was cut short. If I could do it over, I'd never get in that vehicle tonight."

"It was fated, Ebba. You had no choice," Divina said, holding her hand out for the wolf.

"Fated? It was fate that I should kill her because I got in an argument with Spencer? How fucking stupid is that?"

Her anger caused the wolf to whimper, and she swiped her tongue over Ebba's upturned face. Rubbing against her, the wolf whimpered again. Tears gathered as she watched the proud beast's soul shimmer.

"Please save her, Goddess. I'll go with Death."

"No!" Laszlo gently laid the body at her feet. "No, Ebba. That's not happening."

"I ask you again. What would you give to save the creature?" Isis asked her.

"My life. My soul. Whatever it is you demand of me," Ebba promised.

The Goddess nodded her satisfaction. "Then I shall hold you to that, child."

Laszlo dragged Ebba behind him. "I don't want to defy you, Exalted One, but there has to be another way. Something other than taking Ebba. Please."

"And if I say there is no other way? What would your response be, Laszlo Thorne?"

His expression turned mulish. "There's always another way."

"Perhaps." Isis gestured to the Reaper. "Take Spencer Barlowe's soul."

A male spirit materialized beside Ebba. "I'm sorry."

She straightened to meet Spencer's apologetic gaze. In this form, he wasn't as handsome, and she had to wonder if he'd used his powers to amplify his looks. She'd have to ask Laszlo if it was possible. Perhaps he'd lost his luster in the face of her disappointment with him.

"Go in peace, Spencer," she said, hoping to sound gracious instead of bitter. His inability to understand she had free will and didn't want him had led to tonight's tragedy.

With a regretful nod, he approached Death's companion. And within moments, he disappeared in a cloud of shimmering light, consumed by the Reaper.

A shiver skated along Ebba's spine. Was she next?

"Ebba James, I shall now pass sentence upon your soul," Isis said.

"Excuse me?" Surely she hadn't heard correctly, had she?

Laszlo placed his hand on Ebba's arm, locking her in place. "Sentence? Why?"

Castor was more emphatic with his, *"What the fuck?"*

Terrified she'd find herself in the fiery pits of hell, she brushed Laszlo off and moved at a snail's pace toward the Goddess. Only when she was standing before her, awaiting judgment, did she meet Isis's exotic eyes.

"I'm sorry," she said, suitably contrite for the pain she'd caused. If she were being honest with herself, it was great. Her accident had caused Laszlo and another to come from the future, the Goddess, Death, and a Reaper to appear on this plane of existence, the Aether to steal a man's power, and a wolf to lose her life. Ebba's sins were many. "I'm prepared for whatever punishment you see fit to dole out, ma'am."

"Good."

"Wait!" Lazlo lunged forward. "Take *me*! If payment has to be extracted, I'll pay it on her behalf."

The Goddess looked between them, then at Castor. "Nothing to say, Alex? No supreme sacrifice on your part?"

"I've been around longer than these two. I'll await your decision, then argue in her favor after."

She smiled and faced Damian. "I've one more request of you, Beloved, and then you may go home to your family."

"Of course."

"Assist me in merging the bodies."

Ebba's mind blanked, and she looked to Laszlo for answers. He appeared as gobsmacked as her, though. Castor's confusion was great, too, and it seemed only the Aether understood what the Goddess intended.

Damian knelt beside the wolf and offered a hand to Isis, who knelt on the far side of Ebba's body. After clasping his proffered hand, she placed her other over Ebba's heart. He did the same to the wolf.

Their combined power shot upward and collided with the molecules in the air, producing a light show to rival the aurora borealis. The result was so bright, Ebba was forced to shield her eyes. When she sensed it had died down, she dropped her arm.

The wolf was gone, and only her physical self remained.

25

"What happened? Where did the wolf go?" Ebba asked, transfixed by the pulsing amulet.

"You've become one, child."

Unable to comprehend, she shook her head and looked down at the patiently waiting spirit between her and Laszlo. Once again, the wolf's pink tongue lolled out the side of her grinning mouth, and this close, Ebba registered the scale of the beast's intimidating teeth. Lying beside her, the length of the wolf's body was the same as hers.

"What about her mate? Don't they only have one? I'm sure I read that somewhere." What made her ask that, other than the worry in Laszlo's burnt-amber eyes? When had they darkened? Was it the effect of the dark light or the deep emotion he was experiencing?

"He was shot by hunters last month. She has no offspring awaiting her care." Isis rose to her feet and crossed to their small group. "You and the wolf are now one, child."

"You mentioned a choice," Laszlo said. "What is it?"

"She made it when she claimed she would do anything to

save the creature." Isis smiled. "This is what is required for them both to survive."

"I still don't get what's happening." Ebba rubbed her forehead and glanced down. "Do you?" she asked the black beauty.

"Yes."

"What?" Surely it hadn't answered her?

"Yes. I understand."

"Who are you talking to, Sweet?" Laszlo's concern for her sanity had skyrocketed based on the horrific look on his face.

"Herself," Isis replied on her behalf.

Ebba opened her mouth, but the words wouldn't come. This bizarre dream had gone on way too long.

"It's not a dream, my dear," Damian said. "You've been offered the opportunity to extend both your life and that of Laszlo's familiar."

"Wait! What?" He did a double take and then stared at the Aether. "The wolf Ebba struck was to be my familiar?"

The dark-haired man simply smiled as Laszlo shook his head in wonder.

"The power will transfer to your mate," Isis said. "She'll be your familiar moving forward."

"A witch like him?" Ebba asked in disbelief.

"Not quite," the black wolf said.

"Ohmygod, I'm going mental," she whispered. "I dove off the deep end, and there's no fucking water in the pool."

"Your magic will enhance Laszlo's. In return, you'll live as long as he does," Isis explained. "The wolf, too."

"How is it any life for her?" Ebba tangled her fingers in the black fur, wanting to bury her face there and cry. "It's not fair. She'll miss out on running and—"

"No, she won't." Damian's smooth, seductive tones cut through her building hysteria.

Isis squatted down and rubbed the wolf's shaggy head.

"She'll have three days during the full moon to be herself. The rest of the time, you're in charge."

"You're turning her into a werewolf?" Castor asked from the sidelines. His tone conveyed intrigue, but there was an underlying concern. "A woman who has never experienced the smallest scope of magic before? I hesitate to ask if it's wise, but is it?"

"I'm with him," Laszlo said. "I don't like it."

"The alternative is death for them both," Isis snapped. "Is that your wish?"

A calmness settled over Ebba. "Why? There's a reason you're doing this, but I can't figure out what it is. You claim the Fates have decided. What do they care about me? A nobody in their grand scheme of things?"

"She's clever," Damian murmured. In a louder voice, he addressed them all. "I believe my job here is finished. I bid you all a good night."

"Wait! How do we separate the wolf? Did anyone ask her opinion?" Ebba demanded. "You both assumed a dumb animal—"

Watch it, the wolf warned with a low growl.

"Sorry." Ebba patted her head. "I don't even know your name."

"Focus, Ebba," Laszlo scolded. "Please."

"I'm trying! You deal with a second voice in your head, why don't you!"

Isis sighed her exasperation. "Clearly, I didn't explain it well enough. I'll rectify my mistake now."

She held out a hand to Damian. "The amulet, please."

"I almost forgot." He dropped the pendant into her outstretched palm, and Ebba got her first good look at it.

Shaped from a ruby stone with a loop at the top and flat on front and back, it had handless arms dangling halfway down each side. Weirdly, it resembled the body of a person wearing a dress. Carved into the flat surface of its center was an ankh symbol, which Ebba was more familiar with and understood to be the Egyptian symbol for life.

"This is the Tyet," Isis said, holding the necklace up and shifting to face Laszlo. "I've engraved the surface with the ankh. Together, they will provide protection and life to the wearer." She looped it over his neck. "Your mate will keep its match on her person at all times."

His gaze locked with Ebba's. "Mate. You've said that before, Exalted One. What does that mean?"

"I believe you know, Beloved." Her tone shifted, deepening as she said, "You need only *remember*."

Frowning, he pressed his fingers to his temples and swayed seconds before his eyes rolled back in his head. As his knees crumpled beneath him, Isis was prepared with a golden staff and waved it in his direction, suspending his body in midair.

"He was always going to be a problem," Isis said without concern. "Now, let me truly explain. Death needs two souls to reap today. Spencer's and yours."

The sick feeling lingering in the pit of Ebba's stomach grew exponentially.

"However, there's a third in the mix. Kyrella."

"Who—"

"*Me,*" the wolf said.

"Oh." Ebba nodded. "Gotcha."

"By merging the souls and removing the impurest parts to combine and create another, Divina will have the two needed to maintain the balance," Castor concluded with an admiring grin. "Brilliant, really."

"Thank you," Isis said without a hint of pride or vanity. "The trade-off is the shift every month."

"Why does it sound so ominous?" Ebba shared a wary glance with Kyrella.

"It's painful," Damian said. "Your bones will break and

reform into that of a wolf. Your consciousness will disappear, and the animal will take over for three full days until the moon wanes."

"Is she vulnerable to danger?" Ebba asked, unconcerned for herself but fearful another car might strike Kyrella while on a nightly run.

"That's up to you and Laszlo," Isis said.

"You may use my estate during that time," Damian offered.

"And I'm certain Alastair will offer his or the woods behind Thorne Manor, in Tennessee," Castor added with a supportive smile.

"But she'll be okay?" Ebba asked.

"Yes," Isis assured her. "While human, the amulet is simply a necklace designed to protect you. When you transition into Kyrella, the stone will burn through her fur and become one with her skin. It serves as a shield of sorts."

"*Burn?*" Ebba's fingers tightened in Kyrella's fur. "No! She's suffered enough!"

"She won't feel it, child. *You* will. The broken bones and seared flesh are your penance for taking her life and prolonging your own."

Nausea churned in her gut until she thought she might vomit. But ghosts didn't puke, did they? Still, she felt weak and plopped on the ground to lean into the wolf's strong shoulder.

"Are you okay with this, Kyrella?" she asked in a low voice. "Tell me if you aren't, and I'll go with Death. You can live the rest of your life."

The wolf's golden eyes glistened with something akin to compassion and love as they met hers.

"*Yes. We will be joined. True soulmates.*"

"You're too generous."

"*No, friend. You are, and it makes you the perfect human to bind souls with.*"

"If, at any time, you change your mind—"

"I won't. My mate is dead. You deserve to experience the type of love we did." Kyrella nuzzled Ebba's face. *"Maroke would say the same if he were here."*

"Will you miss the chance to see him if you stay? Like, can't you meet up with him in the afterlife or something?"

Her wolf counterpart looked to Isis to explain.

"The part of Kyrella transitioning to the next stage will be with her mate again. There, she will be a wolf for all but three days," the Goddess said.

"So, the reverse of her time here?"

"Yes."

Ebba smiled at Kyrella. "Not so bad then since I get to consume your pain."

"Not so bad then." Her canine grin was a sight to behold, and Ebba laughed for the first time in what felt like forever.

Sobering, she asked the question they'd avoided all night. "Why would the Fates allow this?"

"Because I asked them," Isis replied. Her sudden smile was startling and a thing of wonder.

"I still don't understand why. Was it for Laszlo?" Ebba couldn't say why her need to know was so strong, but she couldn't seem to let it go without the full truth.

"It was for you both, child." The Goddess's expression was one of deep affection, the kind reserved for a friend or relation. "You were my handmaiden, and when it was your time to be reborn, I couldn't bear to part with you. That delay cost you years of happiness with Laszlo."

"My mother's miscarriage four years before I was born?"

Isis nodded.

"It's why you bothered yourself to get involved in mortal affairs," Ebba concluded.

"Yes."

"It would also explain the familiarity I feel around you."

"If by that you mean your inability to curb your tongue, yes.

You've always been outspoken," Isis replied with a laugh. "It's what makes you unique, my darling girl."

"I wish I remembered."

"It's part of the process. When your time comes to leave the earthly plane for the Otherworld, those memories will resurface," the Goddess assured her. "If you choose to join my court again, you will be welcomed."

"Thank you for this chance, Exalted One." Ebba bowed her head.

"It was the least I could do for my favorite pet and handmaiden. Treat Kyrella well."

"I will."

But there was one possible objection left.

Laszlo.

"Will you wake him?" Ebba asked, climbing to her feet. "He should get a say in whether he's tied to me forever or not."

Castor snorted. "Somehow, I don't think that will be a hardship."

26

PRESENT DAY

*L*aszlo jolted as his spirit rejoined his body. He woke slowly, vaguely aware of the conversation around him. Words like *wolf* and *Ebba* were spoken in hushed tones, and the sense of dread he experienced was staggering.

Panicked, he bolted upright and looked around the living room. Seeing only Castor, Alastair, and Damian caused his heart to slam painfully against his chest wall.

"Where is she?" he demanded.

"How much do you remember from the accident scene?" Alastair asked him.

"Other than Ebba fawning over Damian, not much," he admitted grimly.

"Yeah, that was annoying for me, too." Castor crossed his arms and sent a sour glance toward the Aether. "He's honing in on our territory."

"*My,*" Lo snapped. "My territory."

Alastair tsked as Damian's black brows shot skyward.

"Who raised him to be such a barbarian, Al?" Castor wanted

187

to know. "Women aren't chattel. They're meant to be honored for the queens they are."

"I know my wife just stepped into the room, Alex," Alastair replied, extending his hand for Aurora to take. "You can drop the act."

"Nice try, Alexander," she said in her cultured British tones as she cuddled up to her husband's side. Tilting her head to study Laszlo, she smiled. "How are you, darling boy?"

How was he? It was a damned good question! He took stock of his person.

"I've got a raging headache and a desperate need to know what happened to Ebba, but these yahoos refuse to tell me anything."

"Ah. Clearly they've forgotten how the uncertainty can be stressful." She shoved off Alastair with a reprimanding glare. "Unkind, darling. Very unkind."

"Rorie—"

"We were just about to tell him," Damian said. "But now that he's awake, I'll leave that to the rest of you."

Laszlo blinked, and the Aether was gone.

"He's a man of few words," Lo said with a rub of his neck.

"Unless he's droning on about areas of the brain," Castor said.

"What's this?" Alastair appeared confused. "When did Damian drone on about the brain?"

"When he told Ebba he had to remove her memories." Lo shot Castor a worried glance, but the other man shook his head. "What am I missing?"

"He won't remember. The timeline shifted," Castor said simply. "You only remember because your spirit made the journey with me."

"But he was there. So was the Aether," Lo argued.

"Yes, but they recall what happened *then*, not what led to it or your spirit taking a side trip tonight. Or rather, Al won't.

Damian might remember both because he holds pieces of every magical ability."

"I'm not sure I understand."

"Think of it as two roads at an intersection." Castor created a V with his hands. With a small shake of his left, he said, "This was the road we were on, but when we rewound to this juncture"—he tapped the heel of his palms—"also known as Ebba's accident, we all took this road instead," he concluded with a shake of his right.

"So they never traveled the other road," Lo said softly.

"Correct. I did, along with your spirit, so we'll retain the memories."

"But I don't remember much—" Sharp, stabbing pain in his head caused Lo to gasp and press the heels of his hands to his eye sockets. "Agh!"

"What is it, son?"

Before he could answer Alastair, he was cut off by Castor. "The new memories are shuffling around in his brain. Reorganizing to match the new timeline. The effect is a wicked migraine."

As if Lo's headache wasn't bad enough when he woke!

Gritting his teeth, he scrunched his eyes.

"Just tell me where Ebba is," he ground out.

"She gave Kyrella control two days ago, and she's running around Alastair's woods." Castor shoved him back down and dropped a sopping rag on his forehead, chuckling when Lo swore. "Sorry."

There wasn't an ounce of remorse in his tone.

"Fucker," Lo muttered.

With a laugh, the Traveler moved away and, from the sound of it, sank into the closest chair. "I'll give you the cliff notes while your memories unscramble," he said. "Ebba and Kyrella became one—"

Lo lifted the edge of the washcloth. "Who's Kyrella?"

"The wolf."

"What—*oh!* Oh, god!" His stomach revolted, and he swallowed back the threatening bile. When he could speak again without vomiting, he asked, "Is this physical reaction normal?"

"Somewhat." Ice clinked in Castor's glass tumbler. "Al, you want to field this one?"

"Actually, I will," Rorie said, crossing to Lo and stroking the damp hair back from his temples. "I experienced something similar not that long ago. It's a normal reaction when your soul reunites with the body. You came back mere minutes ago, am I right?"

He nodded with great care, incapable of any other physical movement. Hell, he'd do well to hold on for dear life while the world spun off its axis.

"Not the world, just your equilibrium," she told him, alerting him to the fact he'd spoken aloud. "The headaches, the lack of coordination, and the discombobulated thoughts will disappear after your body self-corrects. You weren't gone that long, so it should only last a week or two at the most."

"Why are you all here?" he asked.

"Alastair insisted on it, suspecting when your soul rebounded, you would need someone who had experienced it to discuss the symptoms and ease your transition."

Lo peeled back a corner of the rag and managed a half smile. "Thank you, Rorie. And thank you, Al. I appreciate the support."

"Always," Alastair said, and it sounded like a promise.

"Does—what is her name? Kyrella?—does she know me?" The new memory surfaced. "Scratch that. My brain downloaded the information. I see that she does."

It also registered he and Ebba weren't together as a couple, and his stomach tightened at the unexpected knowledge.

"Relax. The calmer and more open your mind is, the quicker the new info will flow," Castor advised. "And because you're about to ask, Ebba hasn't dated anyone else, as hard as I tried to convince her she should. She's faithful to you."

With an amused snort, Lo eased into a sitting position and set aside the damp cloth. When Alastair handed him a tumbler of scotch, he happily drank.

"I think I'm okay now, gang. I appreciate the support."

Alastair nodded and set his glass aside. "My security team has watched over Ebba and Kyrella in the months since they merged, and will continue to do so. She's as safe as can be, Laszlo. I promise."

"My main concern is Charlotte. It seems my divorce isn't finalized in this timeline."

"No, but it will be in two days."

Two days. The timing seemed perfect. Ebba would be human again, and they could plan their future, if indeed they had one. As best he could recall, they hadn't discussed their feelings since the night of the accident, despite his separation. He had a harder time remembering why.

"Are you okay?"

He glanced up to find Castor studying him, and the concern was warming, all things considered. "Yeah. Thanks." He held out his hand to shake. "For everything, both the first time and this time. You saved her and gave us a chance at a future."

"Don't think I wouldn't seduce her if I could." The Traveler laughed when Laszlo tightened his grip. "Calm down, killer. I'm teasing."

"I don't believe you are, but I'm assuming nothing's changed as far as your potential mate."

Castor's dark frown lightened Lo's mood. "Not cool, man."

"Why are you running from it?" he asked softly.

"Every female I've cared about has died and/or moved on. I'm not looking forward to the fallout from another relationship gone bad."

"Why does it have to?" Alastair asked.

"Come on, Al. You know why. Guys like me, the ones always walking into danger, are a risk to anyone we care about."

"You're wrong, Alexander." Rorie kissed his cheek. "You've got a lot of love to give, and any woman worthy of that love will not care about the risks."

"Leave Al and run away with me," he urged, wrapping an arm around her waist. "You, me, Mai Tais on the beach. What do you say?"

"I'd say Alastair would tear down the world to find and murder us both."

"Just Alex, my love. You, I could never harm," Al responded gallantly. "But I do love the idea of Mai Tais on the beach."

She laughed as Castor released her. With a hug for her husband, she said, "You hate frou-frou drinks, darling. Admit it."

"For you, I'd pretend to enjoy them." He kept his arms locked around her as he gazed deeply into her eyes.

"And because I love you, I'd never make you," she replied with an adoring smile. "Let's go home, darling. It's late, and I have something that requires your attention."

Alastair's answering grin was worthy of the devil and pure wickedness as they teleported away.

The wistful expression on Castor's face said how much he craved a relationship like theirs, and Laslzo felt a kinship with the man.

"Maybe you should take their advice to heart," Lo suggested. "It might ease the loneliness."

"I've had my great love, boyo. It's not fair to promise the next woman forever when I'm still crazy about the last one."

"What happened?"

Castor took a long chug of his drink, making it appear his past trials still weighed on his heart. Finally, he said, "I faked my death and disappeared for almost a half century. My lover was shot in the heart by her half-brother and met her soulmate in the Otherworld."

"My cousin Preston's wife, Selene? *She's* the one you love?"

"She's the one."

Lo cast him a compassionate look. "Sorry, man."

"I didn't just tell you all that for my benefit, Thorne. You owe both Charlotte and Ebba one hell of an apology for marrying one when you were in love with the other."

"Because Thornes only love once," Lo said with a nod.

"Personally, I think that's a load of shit. A secondary love may not be as consuming as the soulmate love, but it's just as beautiful if it works out."

"But all my family eventually found their soulmates."

"True, yet Preston loved Rorie for a time, and Al loved his son's mother. Both were content." Castor shrugged. "Hell, Holly married another man before returning to Quentin."

"Wait—"

"Separate timeline. Quentin and Francesca reset the one you remember."

Lo's brows met. "How often does that happen?"

"Not often at all. Seems to be specific to my line." Castor removed the empty glass from Laszlo's hand. "Refill, or are you good?"

"I'm good."

"Okay. Then clean up this place so your girl doesn't come home to a mess," he ordered. "Add vases of her favorite flowers to each of the rooms and leave her a note. Tell her you'd like to take her to dinner to celebrate your divorce if she's willing."

"You think it's as simple as that?" Lo asked dryly.

"I do. Ebba loves you, boyo. Try to recall the night of the accident and how she wanted to make sure you were okay with having her as a familiar for life." Castor nodded his satisfaction as Lo's face registered the shocking memory. "That's right. She was willing to give up her life if you weren't good with it. A woman who would sacrifice everything for you is the one woman you should sacrifice everything for in return."

"Understood."

"Good, because if you treat her poorly, I'll gladly steal her away." He winked. "It only takes a time hop."

"That's disgusting. You're old enough to be her father."

Castor grinned. "Yeah, but I look the same age as *you*, and I'm a helluva lot better looking."

27

*E*very bone in Ebba's body ached.

"Such is the price I agreed to," she muttered as she exited the shed after pulling on her sweatclothes.

Inside the building, Alastair and Laszlo had created an exact replica of her apartment for her monthly shift. With careful consideration, they'd provided all the comforts of home, with the addition of a super-sized doggy door for Kyrella to come and go when the mood struck or she wanted to curl up and sleep.

After sliding the panel into place to prevent unwanted critters from using Kyrella's entrance, she turned the key in the lock.

A twig snapped.

She whirled with a snarl, hackles up, and fighting stance at the ready.

Her instincts were on point. Or rather Kyrella's were. They shared acute hearing and smell, along with a heightened distrust of strangers.

"It's just me, Sweet Ebba."

Laszlo.

His dark hair fell over one brow, giving him a roguish look. Or perhaps it was the appreciation in his amber eyes that held the appeal.

"What are you doing here?"

"I returned last night and couldn't wait another second to see you," he said, walking toward her with purposeful steps.

Her heart picked up its pace. "Returned? From where?"

"The past."

"Oh!" She grinned as her tension eased. "I was wondering when your past and present selves would collide."

"Yeah, I'm told it's going to take anywhere from a few days to weeks to acclimate." He twirled his finger in her hair, tangling it with one of her corkscrew curls. "It's a bizarre rush to have all my memories shift and mesh."

"Alex said it would happen once the timelines intersected."

"How so?" he asked.

His gaze ate up her features, landing on her mouth, and Ebba's blood began pumping like Kyrella's on an invigorating run. The desire to lean into his hand and be petted was strong. She suspected it had nothing to do with her wolf.

"The new timeline finally reached the five-month mark when you traveled to the past and your soul returned three hours later," Ebba said. "Alex warned you about the rebound effect of the flood of old and new memories merging."

"Did it happen to you, too?"

"No. I can't recall anything but the events surrounding the accident."

He frowned and stopped playing with her hair. Putting some distance between them, he asked, "You don't remember me telling you I love you?"

"Not exactly. I believe you said we were going to fall in love in five months. I assume that's now."

"Fuck! It just occurred to me that day we spent together

didn't happen." He shook his head as if dazed. "You didn't show up at the café, asking for help, and we didn't spend time together trying to reunite your soul and body. Worse, I didn't wake to the fact I've loved you since we were teenagers."

She gasped and pressed her hands to her mouth.

"It's true, Sweet." His gaze searched her face. "Please tell me I'm not too late."

Ebba shook her head, and Laszlo closed his eyes in apparent relief.

"Thank Christ!"

"Maybe thank the Goddess instead?" she teased, coming down from the lofty heights of wonder. Since the accident, she'd met with Isis a few times to learn about their friendship. The Goddess had been forthcoming, and Ebba understood why they'd been close. Those meetings had left her with a deep appreciation for deities, magic, and nature.

"Yeah, her, too." The softness left his eyes, and they shimmered with wickedness. His mouth kicked up at the corners to match, and that devilish smile weakened Ebba's knees.

"We kissed in the previous timeline," he said with a twinkle. "I got to feel you up a little while we were at it."

"Hmm." She closed the distance between them with purpose and a boldness she'd never have dared before he spoke of love. Reaching up, she wove her fingers in his dark mane and dragged his head down to hers to nip his lip. "What about me? Did I get to feel *you* up?"

"There wasn't time." His tone was regretful.

She trailed her fingers down his chest, hesitating oh-so slightly when she reached his waistband. "We have time now."

"Mm." He glanced behind her at the shed. "What are you suggesting?"

"I—"

He hauled her up and over his shoulder. "Yep. I agree."

Laughing, she slapped his butt. "I didn't say anything!"

"You didn't?" he asked, suspiciously innocent. "I was sure I heard you say, 'Rock my world, Lo.'"

"Nope. I didn't say it." He hesitated at the door, and she giggled. "I *did* think it, though."

"Must be the familiar-witch connection."

He blasted the door off its hinges, tossed her like a sack of potatoes on the bed, and secured the door with a wave of his hand. With a jubilant bounce, he joined her on the bed.

"Your seduction needs work," she scolded, dragging his T-shirt over his head and tossing it away.

"You want the princess treatment or the real-woman treatment?"

Ebba locked her legs around his hips and rocked upward. "You've known me my entire life. What about me screams princess?"

"Not one fucking thing," he growled as he captured her mouth.

His playful kiss deepened, becoming more consuming, and Ebba met the demand, giving him all she had to offer. Laszlo's weight pressed into her, grounding her in the here and now. His lips trailed down her neck, and he lingered at her collar-bone, planting kisses that sent shivers through her and caused her to gasp. Every movement was purposeful as his hands traced her curves, and he seemed to be memorizing the contours of her body, his touch reverent and unhurried.

Her breath hitched, and her fingers threaded through his hair as she surrendered to the sensation of being wholly, undeniably alive. His movements slowed further, turning deliberate and setting her ablaze. Yet each caress reflected the emotions they could no longer contain. It wasn't only about the physical —it was about everything they'd endured to get here, the walls they'd torn down, the fears they'd conquered. It was about trust, love, and finding something real from all the chaos that came before.

Ebba's heart raced in her chest. Her emotions were born of exhilaration and a vivid realization that this moment was forever theirs. From this instant until forever, she'd think of him as hers. Tugging him closer, she threaded her fingers through his hair and smiled as his lips traveled upward to meet hers again.

This kiss was different from the others—deeper, almost desperate. It carried the weight of everything unsaid, a culmination of his longing and a silent plea for forgiveness that he'd chosen Charlotte all those years ago.

Laszlo stripped her bare, worshipping every square inch of her with his mouth and leaving her skin tingling under his touch. She arched into him, and her breath caught as he murmured, "I love you, Sweet Ebba," against her neck. His voice was low and reverent, as if she were something sacred. "Tell me this is real. Tell me you're mine."

Her chest tightened at hearing his raw vulnerability, and she cupped his face, her thumbs brushing over the faint stubble along his jaw.

"I've always been yours, Laszlo Thorne," she replied, her voice trembling but sure. "Even when you didn't know it."

He closed his eyes as the weight of her words sank in. The moisture in his, when he opened them, threatened to undo her. His amber gaze burned with an intensity that quickened her pulse.

Their lips met again, and there was no holding back this time. The air between them shifted, and the laughing way they'd started developed into something more profound. His hands moved with purpose, and his touch ignited an all-consuming fire within her. Letting herself fall into him, Ebba trailed her hands down the defined muscles of his back, feeling the strength that had carried them through their trials.

She cried out when he entered her, and with each stroke, they lost themselves in each other. Their passionate love-making was a testament to her life that he'd fought so hard to save.

Time blurred, and the outside world was forgotten as they created a space that was entirely theirs—a place where magic didn't complicate, where ghosts didn't linger, and where love could flourish unbound.

Eventually, their sexual energy dwindled into a quieter intimacy, and as they rested, he held her as if he feared she might disappear. She understood the emotion. Hell, she half feared this was all a bizarre fantasy she'd concocted in her mind to cope with the trauma of the accident. As she rested her cheek against his chest, she counted his steady heartbeats and smiled. The rhythm was soothing, creating a sound that felt remarkably like home.

"I'm annoyed you didn't court me properly," she said, circling his nipple with the tip of her finger before flicking the tip. "Really, your assumption wasn't cool."

"I thought you said you weren't a princess?"

"I'm not, but a little work on your part would be nice."

His chuckle rumbled through his chest beneath her ear. "How do you suggest I make it up to you?"

"Who says I want you to?"

Wrapping his hand in her hair, he tugged lightly until her head came up and their eyes locked. "You wouldn't bring it up unless you wanted me to show proper remorse."

"True. Pure penitence is totally appropriate." She rolled on her back and sprawled her limbs wide. "You can start at my neck and work your way down. About a thousand kisses should do."

"A thousand." He whistled and rose over her to admire her naked form. "That's a steep demand, considering the hours I just put in."

"I've suffered many, *many* years of neglect."

"Mm. It's true and entirely my fault."

She giggled. "Not entirely. Your siblings were horrible to you and determined to intervene."

"They were. We shall never forgive them," he vowed.

Laszlo commenced with his punishment, and Ebba lost count after forty-seven.

The distraction was great.

"I'm hungry," she complained twenty minutes later. "And the worst part is I'm craving raw meat. This wolf has disgusting dietary habits."

His laugh was entirely too amused.

"If I were a witch, I'd turn you into a frog," she grumbled.

"Come here." Laszlo tucked her between his legs and wrapped his arms around her. Whatever he said next was lost because her mind was focused on the feel of him pressed against her back.

"Focus, Sweet."

His low voice next to her ear caused her belly to somersault.

"I'm having a difficult time," she admitted.

"Food or sex?"

"Don't make me choose," she whined.

With another laugh, he cradled her hands in his, palms extended about eight inches apart. "I'm making the call. Food first, sex after."

"See? Your practicality is why I adore you, Lo."

She could practically feel his eye roll.

"Mm-hmm." He dropped a kiss on her exposed neck. "Focus."

"Okay. What are we focusing on?"

"First, a wooden platter."

She twisted to look at him. "Like a charcuterie board?"

"That works." He gestured with his chin. "Concentrate on our hands, Ebba. Feel the wood against your palms—"

She snorted. "'That's what *he* said.'"

"It's supposed to be *she,* and your bawdy humor is not going to help you learn magic."

"Wait! You're trying to teach me magic?" Excitement thrummed through her.

"What do you think I've been doing?"

"I didn't. The feel of your dick—"

He clapped a hand over her mouth. "None of that, or it's going to grow hard."

After prying his fingers away, she sniggered. "Too late."

"Jesus, we're never conjuring food," he muttered.

"Conjuring food? That's a thing? I can do it, too?"

"Yes, and sort of." He nuzzled her throat. "You can through me, so you'll feel what it's like. It's doubtful you can manage it on your own, though. I'm sorry."

She considered it and shrugged. "It's cool you're willing to share this experience."

"That's my Sweet Ebba." Tucking his chin on her shoulder, he talked her through the process. "Visualize the wood in your hand—and don't you dare make a snarky comment about wood. Consider the texture, the color, the grain."

A low-amp current ran through her body, making the hair on her arms stand up and her skin tingle. "Ohmygod! Is this normal?"

"Yep. Now, see the spark of light? Grow the board in your mind until it resembles the platter you initially envisioned."

The result astounded her. One second there was nothing but a hum of electricity, and the next, she was holding a charcuterie board.

"We can do that with food, too?" she asked, awed by the power and coolness of what he could do.

"We can. Start visualizing what you want to eat in the same way."

Together, they created a feast for a queen.

"I'm going to love being your familiar," she blurted as she reached for an apple.

His arrested expression stopped her.

"What did I say wrong?" Nerves ate at her belly. Did he not want her in that capacity?

"I'd forgotten for a minute," he said.

"Is it a problem? The lifetime thing?"

Please say no. Please say no.

His smile was slow to form, but when it did, it consumed his entire face. His eyes sparked with joy, and his grin was engaging, making her want to crawl into his skin and live there forever.

"Like I said at the accident scene, it's no problem at all, Sweet Ebba." He leaned in and stole the apple with a chuckle. "I'm going to enjoy having you around for life. I can't say the same for you." The laughter died from his eyes. "You're going to get sick of me pretty quickly, though."

"You mentioned that. But why would you believe it?"

He shrugged. Listening to his words back in her head, she realized how hollow they'd sounded.

"Lo. Look at me."

When he did, his underlying worry was present. Shoving aside the tray, she straddled him and hugged his face between her palms.

"I love you, Laszlo Thorne. I have forever and a day. Those who hang around the outskirts see things. *I* saw things. Yes, you can be moody and absent-minded, but I don't care." She rubbed her nose against his. "Because now I understand why. The ghost thing distracts you, I'm sure. But you care about your family, more than anyone I've ever known. They only have to ask, and you're doing for them. Maybe *too* much."

His brows met, and he looked troubled. "I'll always go when they need me, Ebba. I—"

"And I want you to. I'm not Charlotte, Lo. Whenever you want me to, I'll be right beside you."

His uncertainty fell away. "I absolutely do, in *every* situation."

"Good." She gave him a hard peck. "Now stop stealing my food. I'm starving. Shifting burns a shit ton of calories."

"Does it?"

"Could be all the running and the muscle-building thing. I'm not used to exercise. Give me a good book and a cupcake any day."

He laughed and drew her down on top of him. "I'll conjure you different flavored cupcakes every day."

"See?" She poked his chest. "That right there is why I love you. Who couldn't love a man who conjures cupcakes?"

"Clearly the way to your heart is your stomach," he teased.

"It has been recently."

"Are you okay with me coming back to your place?" Lo asked.

"Of course. Why wouldn't I be?" Ebba appeared disconcerted.

"I thought you might need rest. After."

She snorted a laugh. "After the sex or the three days of wolfing out?"

"Both."

Stretching up on tiptoe, she kissed him. "Thank you for your consideration, but I'm fine. I do need sleep, but I'm happy to have you lying with me."

"Good."

As she inserted the key into the lock, a form stepped from the shadows. Ebba's reaction was immediate. The snarl from her throat was pure Kyrella, enough that it raised the hair on

Laszlo's neck, and she whirled so quickly, he barely registered the movement.

The newcomer was facing a massive black wolf with snapping jaws.

"Holyfuckingshit!"

"Clutch?" Heart pounding, Laszlo stroked Kyrella's neck until her hackles lowered. "It's all right, girl. Promise."

Kyrella or Ebba, whichever was in charge, believed the opposite and growled low in her throat.

Trusting their instinct, he eyed his friend. "What are you doing here?"

"I came to talk. Death wants you back."

"Death can go fuck herself."

"Careful, Lo. She's more powerful than you imagine."

"I'm a fucking warlock who helps reap the dead and has a werewolf for a familiar, Clutch. I'm able to imagine a helluva lot."

Kyrella leaned into his side, and Laszlo experienced a power punch along with a sharpening of his vision. Darkness formed around Clutch, and underneath his skin, something shifted, similar to Spencer's possession of Ebba.

"Can you do something about your wolf, man? And did anyone check it for rabies before they merged the bodies?" His friend's eyes watched Kyrella with something akin to malice.

"Yeah, sure thing. Wait here."

Flattening his hand over the deadbolt, Lo envisioned the tumbler shifting to unlock. Once he opened the door, he gestured Kyrella to follow.

"Give me one sec to secure her, Clutch."

Once inside, he pointed toward the bedroom. Needing no verbal communication, she bounded away. He quickly conjured rock salt and, drawing his elemental magic to him, used the air to lift the salt, creating a protective circle on the ceiling. Satisfied it remained unbroken, he waved his hand

and placed the candles in the shape of a pentagram in strategic places within the circle. One on top of the counter, one on the foyer table, and three more where they looked inconspicuous. At first glance, they would appear like ambiance.

"Contineo."

Satisfied the containment spell would work, he opened the door.

"Come on in." Walking only far enough to keep Clutch beneath the circle, he stopped and turned around. "Can I make you a cup of coffee or offer you a beer?"

He had no idea if Ebba kept any in the fridge, but he assumed she did since they drank the same brand.

"I'm good."

"What did you wish to discuss?" Lo asked, tucking his hands in his back pockets in a casual pose. The move exposed his chest to attack, but nothing would pass the circle he'd created. Whatever magic Clutch threw at him would be held within the walls of the invisible cage.

"Ebba. More importantly, your relationship with her."

Lo's brows shot up. "Can't see where that's any of your business."

"You've made it my business by jumping back in time to mess up the timeline."

"Your job is to assist Death. Or that's my understanding, at least. Where she directs you to go, you go. It has nothing to do with what went down."

Frustration flared on Clutch's face, and his eyes narrowed. "Like I said, Death wants you back. She's not happy with the way things turned out and needs you to return to your Reaper status."

Laszlo was never a full Reaper, and whoever was possessing his friend had just made a fatal mistake. "Who are you, really, and where's Clutch?"

"I don't know what you're talking about," fake-Clutch said. "You've known me forever, man."

"Right. So tell me. How did we meet?"

Face savage, fake-Clutch charged. When he slammed into the invisible wall holding him, he turned into the rabid beast he suggested Kyrella might be.

Ebba stepped from the room and approached. Tilting her head and narrowing her eyes, she said, "It's Spencer."

"Yeah, I got that impression, too." Feeling decidedly grim, Lo asked, "But what happened to Clutch?"

29

FIVE MONTHS EARLIER

Clutch couldn't show it, but internally, he was smiling for Laszlo and Ebba. He'd hoped by stalling Death when she'd initially met Ebba, it would give Lo enough time to come up with a plan. Fortunately, it had worked, but not without annoying his lover. They were currently at odds, with him trying to make it up to her. Hence taking the job as a full-time Reaper, which he'd never wanted.

Now, as he waited to consume Spencer Barlowe's soul for the journey to the waiting room, Clutch basked in satisfaction. Soon, Laszlo would be as happy as he deserved, and with any luck, Divina would view Clutch as an equal instead of a boy toy. The stubborn woman refused to be tied down, stating she'd been burned in the past and wouldn't be vulnerable again.

It was a surprise to learn that the "past" was the Traveler.

He understood Alexander Castor's appeal. The man had charm to spare, and the jealousy Clutch was experiencing because of it had no place in his well-ordered life. Yes, he loved Divina, and like him, she'd fallen into feelings. Yet he was the only one willing to do something about it. Until she was ready to move forward with him, Clutch would bide his time, do his job, and respect her boundaries. And he'd deny her what she sought whenever she turned up at his apartment.

Movement from the corner of his eye indicated the approach of Spencer, and Clutch turned to greet him. But what he saw threw him.

Malice.

At this game stage, spirits were at peace and ready to cross, not belligerent or prepared for battle. It appeared his latest charge wasn't going without a fight. Clutch opened his mouth to speak but was gripped with a disconcerting dizziness. Around them, lights shimmered and sparkled, cloaking them from the others.

A taunting smile curled Spencer's mouth.

"Ebba stays. I stay." He lifted an enchanted metal talisman. "It's time for you to enter the circlet, Reaper. If you're a good little boy, I'll release you in twenty years or so."

Clutch shifted to block the spell, but the object was designed to draw his soul out, similar to the globe he'd given Laszlo to exorcise Spencer. The warlock shouldn't have had the magic to pull a stunt like this one.

"Bastard!" He grunted as he twisted back and forth, fighting the pull. "How?"

"I was awake and privy to the conversation. There was no way in hell I was letting the Aether take all the magic and knowledge I've accumulated. I hid just enough to exchange places with you inside this little trinket." With a tsk, he pressed the wreath-shaped talisman to Clutch's throat, cutting off his scream of pain. "None of that. We can't alert the others to my plans to woo Ebba—as *you.*"

Lip curled in rage, Clutch wanted to blast the man, but his strength was bound by whatever black magic resided in the object.

"This group was dismissive, assuming I'd fall in line. The Aether didn't question the fact I didn't possess the level of magic of a Thorne or Reaper." Spencer's triumphant smile grated on Clutch's last nerve. "It was a simple matter to store my power inside this until no one was looking. And I know what you're thinking, but I *will* get away with it. Just like I got away with possessing Ebba. The difference is that you don't have anyone who knows you well to notice a personality change when you return to your proper timeline, do you, McClutchin Adams?"

PRESENT DAY

SPENCER GLARED AT LASZLO THORNE. ALL HIS PROBLEMS could be laid at that man's door. If Ebba hadn't been ridiculously enamored with the asshole, Spencer might've had a chance. He still could if he removed the dickhead from the playing field. It required being smart about it. Perhaps a body hop from the Reaper to Laszlo. Ebba was sure to want him then.

When she entered the room, she appeared as luminescent as she always did to him.

Her flat, "It's Spencer," hurt his heart, but it was only because Laszlo's handsomeness dazzled her. That would be rectified soon enough. To remove his soul from Clutch's body, Laszlo would need to get close. That's all Spencer needed with the excision circlet in his pocket. Like the Reaper's, Laszlo's spirit would be drawn in and contained, giving him the freedom to take over.

The downside? Ebba would know. But if she was only hung up on Laszlo's physique—and honestly, how the hell did she tolerate the jerk's overbearing personality?—then Spencer could put on his meat suit and be all that she could dream of and more.

Satisfied with his plan and confident Clutch was physically stronger than his rival, Spencer beckoned Laszlo closer. "Come into the circle, and we'll settle this like men."

Ebba stepped forward and placed a hand on Laszlo's chest before he could answer the call to action. "No, Lo. Kyrella is about to bust out again. She doesn't trust him."

Yeah, the wolf was a problem. Spencer had to find a way to separate the woman from the beast, and soon, before it ripped his throat out.

Laszlo studied him with considering eyes. It was disconcerting to feel like an object under a microscope, and Spencer fought the urge to fidget. What did he see? Was he gifted with the ability to delve deeper and recognize the threat, like the wolf?

Lifting her hand from his chest, Laszlo kissed the inside of her wrist. "Thanks for the save. Are you okay here on your own with him if I leave for a bit?"

"Of course."

"Don't be tempted to engage. It might be a good idea to wait in the other room, if only to keep Kyrella from shifting."

"Yes. This close to the moon, she's stronger."

"I get it. Safety first, Sweet."

With adoration in his gaze, Laszlo smiled down at her, and Spencer experienced a moment of doubt. The urge to pull them apart was stronger than any he'd experienced, and yet, it might work to his disadvantage.

"I'm not intending to hurt anyone," he lied. "When I was ready to transition, something strange happened to the Reaper, and I found myself inside his body. I came here looking for help."

Ebba's eyes turned golden brown and flared wide with

rage. The low growl she released raised the fine hair all over his body.

"Liar," she snarled in a voice deeper than her norm.

He froze.

What would happen if the wolf took over and charged through the protective wall? Could he remove it with his talisman?

"Don't try it," Laszlo warned him with a hard edge to his voice. "It will kill them both."

A chill chased along his spine, and Spencer fought off a tremor. How had Laszlo guessed his thoughts?

***

EBBA KEPT AN EYE ON SPENCER FROM ACROSS THE ROOM. LO HAD been gone for over thirty minutes, and Kyrella was getting antsy.

"Kill him and be done with it," she said.

"You know we can't, Ky. If we cross that barrier, he could hit us with whatever spell he used on Clutch."

"He deserves to die."

"Not going to disagree, but we'll wait for Lo. We're stronger together."

"I'm strong enough now," Kyrella retorted.

"We are not having this argument. Period."

"Humans are fearful creatures. The strongest reigns supreme in every species, and we kill the weak."

"Not fearful. Civilized. We don't go around maiming or killing without a damned good reason," Ebba told her.

"Wrong. Maroke was shot by those wishing to kill my kind."

A pang struck Ebba's heart, a mere echo of what Kyrella must feel to have her mate taken in such a brutal way.

"I'm sorry, Ky. I can't begin to imagine what it must feel like to be hunted because you're different and have people fear you."

"It is why your mate and others like him don't reveal what they are. It would mean persecution and death for their kind."

"Yes. He told me about the Witches War."

The wolf stilled. *"When?"*

"What?"

"When did he tell you? Not while I've been merged with you."

"I'm sure of it. When else..."

The entire conversation returned and, with it, a migraine of epic proportions. She bent over and clutched her head with a cry, alerting Spencer to her pain.

"Ebba! Ebba, what is it? Are you okay?" He banged his fists on the wall of his cage. *"Fuuuuccckkkkk!* Hold on, baby. Hold on!"

"Blech. Please let me rip his vocal cords from his throat. I can't take the noise coming from his mouth." Kyrella shuddered inside her.

"I'm not your baby," Ebba croaked. "When will you get it through that thick skull? I'm not your *anything*, Spencer! I love Laszlo!"

His look turned to one of horror, and Ebba experienced a similar sensation. She'd let her anger get the better of her, leaving Kyrella room to take over.

All of Ebba's bones began the excruciating breaking process as the skin of her arms tingled, then thickened. The amulet around her neck heated, and as the temperature of the stone rose, a scarlet light pulsated and lit the room. A scream was torn from her throat as it seared her flesh, and from a distance, the slamming of a door registered.

Her last conscious thought was that Niall, her ever-vigilant protector, would be charging into the apartment at any second. There was no telling what he would do if he saw Spencer in the foyer with a wolf at his throat.

· · ·

"Yesssss."

Kyrella padded toward Spencer, taking great pleasure in seeing his fear. Since her merge with Ebba, she'd grown to double her size. Her prey always froze when they saw her, allowing her the advantage.

"Kyrella, *no!*"

She hadn't heard Laszlo return but had felt him the instant he materialized beside her. Head positioned at his chest height, she tilted her chin to meet his worried gaze.

"Please, Ky. If he hurts you, it's the end of Ebba, too."

"He's not strong enough to beat me."

"Perhaps not physically, but his magic is," Laszlo replied, scratching behind her ear. "Please stand down."

"You know nothing about me or my magic," Spencer said, but his fear hadn't resided.

"There's a man at the door," Kyrella warned.

"Fuck." Laszlo closed his eyes and teleported. Leaving her alone with the evil entity.

She grinned a second before she lunged.

30

*L*aszlo teleported behind the Mountain, aka Niall, sparing only a moment to knock him out. Although he should probably feel bad because the lug was only trying to protect Ebba, he experienced no remorse when Niall's head thudded off the tiled floor.

After a quick check to make sure the guy was still breathing, Lo teleported back into the apartment. Not in time to prevent Kyrella's lunge, but at least he was able to create a rebound effect for the wall, causing her to bounce off without penetrating the barrier.

Spencer looked both relieved and disappointed. With a certainty, the guy had something up his sleeve.

"If you want to get out of your cage, my dude, I'd suggest you show whatever you're packing." When Kyrella and Spencer did a double take with a shocked stare, Lo replayed what he'd said and cringed. Yeah, it sounded dirty to the most innocent of minds. "Not that! For Christ's sake! The artifact."

Spencer's expression turned crafty. "I don't know what you're talking about."

The wolf growled and scratched at the barrier.

"Yeah, sure you don't," Lo replied dryly. The guy was fooling no one, especially not Kyrella, whose innate instincts were like a built-in lie detector.

Whipping out his phone, he dialed Alastair. "Can you contact the Aether? We've got a serious problem on our hands."

Within minutes, the magical dream team had gathered.

A knock sounded during their discussion.

"I invited your cousins, Spring and Nash," Alastair said. "If an artifact exists that allows a body swap, they'll know about it."

Though she refused to budge from her spot in front of the circle, Kyrella lifted her head and yipped, assuring Laszlo their company was friend, not foe.

He opened the door and offered a moment of silence for the beautiful couple before him. One had to do that when they met Spring and her husband, Knox. If or when AI robotics gained traction, inventors should design robots to look like this couple. The word *flawless* came to mind. With her chestnut hair, sparkling green eyes, and dainty build, she was the perfect foil to his blond-blue-eyed gorgeousness.

"Lo!" She kissed his cheek in passing, pausing only when she sensed the circle's rim. As she edged around to reach the others, she called back over her shoulder, "Did you know a guy was lying on your doorstep? I healed his headache and sent him on his way."

"Appreciated," Lo said, then offered Knox his hand to shake.

"Sorry for barging in. Where she goes, I follow."

"Understood." And it was. Laszlo had secondhand knowledge of Spring's story, revolving around her abduction a few years back. Knox had been destroyed when he reached her too late. To keep him from tearing the world apart with his godlike powers, Isis had cut a deal with him, returning Spring to the bosom of the Thornes.

And it was necessary for their family. Spring was their jewel, spreading light and love. With her photographic memory, she was also the primary source of their knowledge. Isis's compassionate act healed the fracture her death had caused.

As Laszlo was closing the door, another person approached.

Nash. Alastair's son, similarly to Spring, held a wealth of information in that big brain of his. Lo wished he could retain half of what they managed to do.

"Welcome."

"Thanks for hosting this shindig." Nash grinned, and his smile was so like his father, it was easy to see the charming rogue Alastair had been forty years earlier.

"Beer's in the fridge, and if you want something stronger, the liquor cabinet is on the far wall."

He, too, sensed the circle wall and glanced upward. "Nice. I don't know if I'd have considered attaching one to the ceiling."

"You would've in a pinch," Lo assured him.

Kyrella rose, crossed to Laszlo, and rubbed her massive head against his chest, showing affection and allegiance.

His cousin whistled low and long. "She's beautiful."

"Yes. As is her counterpart," Lo said, stroking the inky fur between her golden eyes. "You can let Ebba return, Ky. She'll be okay."

She padded toward the bedroom but stopped to nudge the Aether's hand.

"Hello, Kyrella," he said with fondness. "Are you adjusting well?"

"Yes."

They all froze.

"She can speak?"

Her black head swiveled in Lo's direction, and he swore she winked.

Narrowing his eyes with promised retribution, he said, "This better not be your way of flirting with that man, Ebba James."

The wolf's husky laugh was eerily similar to hers. "As king to all creatures and our magical community, he deserves deference."

"A talking wolf. Now I've seen almost everything," Castor quipped.

"The actual shift is brutal to watch," Spencer said with a surly tone. "Forcing her to—"

"Let me stop you right there." Damian approached him. "Ebba and Kyrella were given a choice, with the former knowing the painful toll it would extract. She did it willingly so Kyrella would have some semblance of a life."

"She's just a dumb animal!" Spencer shouted.

"Watch your tone, Barlowe. You won't like how I react." The chill in the Aether's words raised the hairs on Laszlo's neck. Even his voice wielded power.

Their staring contest ended with Spencer dropping his gaze and nodding his understanding.

Lo released a breath he hadn't been aware of holding, and based on the other exhalations, he wasn't the only one. Only Alastair appeared unfazed.

With an irritated huff, the wolf stalked away.

"I think she was hoping you'd smite him," Castor told Damian. To Lo, he said, "Your wolf is bloodthirsty."

"Don't I know it!"

EBBA SHOVED ASIDE HER NEED FOR SLEEP AFTER TRANSITIONING to human. Her standard practice was to fall into bed for about twelve hours after Kyrella's three-day takeover.

This time, she'd had hours of on-again-off-again sex with Laszlo to add to her exhaustion in addition to a spontaneous shift on Kyrella's part. Jaw-popping yawns from fatigue aside, she needed to be party to what was happening in her living room. She splashed water on her face and fought the urge to pass out. Once she touched Lo, she'd receive an energy boost.

After checking all her shirt buttons were fastened properly and no skin was showing, she joined the group. Five feet into the room, she stopped short and gaped at the blond male beside Laszlo. Next to the Aether, he was the most gorgeous thing she'd ever seen. Yes, Castor was hot, but whoever this new guy was, he was unbelievable and utterly delicious.

"Oh, for fuck's sake," Lo muttered. "Am I going to be constantly picking your jaw up off the floor?"

Ebba jabbed his ribs. "Yes, if you keep hosting house parties for hotties. Is he single?"

"Ebba James, I swear to—"

"I'm fucking with you. I can see the wedding band."

Lo's scowl was priceless, and she lost the fight not to laugh. "Okay, and yes, I'm with you."

"Better."

"Who knew you were so territorial?" She didn't give him time to answer before standing on tiptoe to kiss him. "I like it," she confessed. "It turns me on."

His wicked grin woke the millions of butterflies living in her belly.

"Okay, stop that right now, mister. We have the hottie house party happening, and I can't be all flustered and shit."

"Too late," he murmured with a kiss of her temple. "You passed that point the second you cleared the doorway and registered Knox's presence."

"Knox." She tried the name on for size. "It fits him."

With a snort and exaggerated eye roll, Laszlo guided her forward for introductions.

After, he asked, "Do you need some coffee to get through this? You look exhausted."

"I want to see Spencer dispatched for good. Of course, I don't remember his possession the first time, but his behavior is over the line."

"Dispatched?" Spring's light laughter caused Ebba to smile.

"It sounds antiquated, but I don't know how else to say it. Would 'ejected from Clutch's body and sent to hell' be better?" she asked.

"Works for me." The other woman's wide smile was like a beacon of light, and Ebba appreciated the friendliness offered. With looks like hers, Spring could easily head up a Mean Girls Club. Yet she exuded nothing but sweetness.

Ebba had long since realized the Thornes were beautiful people, both inside and out. Their innate kindness set them apart from the rest of the world and had her gravitating toward them, creating lifelong connections.

Spring approached the circle and cocked her head to study Spencer. "Will you show me your artifact, Mr. Barlowe? Please?"

She'd said it so prettily, and Ebba was surprised he didn't fall right down at her feet, holding the object up like a sacrifice to a goddess. His expression was dazed, though, and she smiled, feeling her first kinship with him.

Knox walked up beside her. "She's something, isn't she?"

"Yes," Ebba gushed. "I think I'm experiencing my first female crush."

He chuckled. "I was a goner the instant I laid eyes on her."

"I can see why." She glanced up and tried like hell to keep from batting her lashes. "Also, why she was a goner when she saw you."

"It's a glamour on my part. A scar runs here to here." He drew a line from temple to jaw. "Courtesy of my father."

"Ohmygod! I'm so sorry."

"Thank you, but there's no need for you to be. My uncle and aunt acted as foster parents and were the best influence a kid could have. And the Thornes have welcomed me with open arms."

"They do that, don't they?" she mused aloud, glancing back at the gathered family as they discussed options. "I don't think I'll ever get used to the fact magic actually exists in the world."

"And yet, you're magical yourself now," Knox reminded her.

"Yes. I'd feel like I'm dreaming if it wasn't for the pain when Kyrella takes over."

"Talk to Spring when this thing with Spencer is resolved. She may be able to concoct something to ease your discomfort while still allowing your wolf to be alert."

"I never thought of that," Laszlo said as he joined them, indicating he'd been listening to their conversation.

Likely, it was one part jealousy, and the other two-thirds was his need to stay informed.

"It hurts like a mofo, but either way, I'm happy to do it if it means Ky can live on," Ebba said.

"Thank you," Kyrella said.

She clutched the amulet to feel the connection to her wolf and show support. A warming peace filled her, assuring her their bond was real.

"What's the next step?" she asked them.

Knox winked. "I believe it's my turn to shine."

31

"He's the stuff of heroes, isn't he?" Lo said with a smidgeon of envy in his heart as Knox stepped away to join Spring.

"So are you," Ebba assured him. "You time-traveled back to save me. Who does that if not a hero?"

"Don't say that too loudly, or Casto—"

"It's nice to be recognized for my better qualities," Castor quipped.

Laszlo hung his head. "Damn. I thought we'd be able to avoid all his preening."

Their grins were his reward.

"I'm discovering everyone has a different skill. What's Knox's?" Ebba asked, her focus on the couple by the circle.

"His element is metal. He's able to bend and transform it," Castor explained. "And unlike standard witches, his magic was infused in his soul. No matter how often he's reborn, he'll possess the same power."

"And he's able to call metal objects to him," Alastair added, joining their trio. The keen satisfaction in his voice said it all. "He's a master."

Although Laszlo wanted to see the man in action, he focused all his attention on Ebba's expressive face. It tickled him to see her so fascinated by each new bit of information revealed to her. Currently, her eyes were rounded with wonder as she watched Knox hold out his hand and draw the molecules from the room to create a blue ball. It crackled and sparked, causing the metal objects in the room to rock.

Fear lit Spencer's eyes, but he hid it well. Still, Lo could see the color of his emotions beneath Clutch's faux-calm exterior, thanks to *his* particular gifts. Alastair's empathic ability would make his cousin aware of Spencer's innermost feelings, too. There was no fooling one as clever and experienced as Al.

"My wife asked you nicely, Barlowe. I won't be as nice," Knox said, tone solid steel.

"I would hand it over, but I'm the only one capable of controlling it." Spencer smirked to hide his worry. "We wouldn't want her to be sucked inside it, would we?"

The Aether approached him, and sweat broke out on the man's head. One solitary bead of moisture dripped down his temple and ran to the hard edge of his jawline. "Your time is limited, Barlowe. There are a few ways this can play out." Damian crossed his arms to show he meant business. "One, I can simply kill your host, leaving you nowhere to go but hell. Two, I can drag your soul from that body and decimate it, which is excruciating, by the by. Three, you can place the object on the floor by the edge of this circle and back away from it. Then, you'll tell us exactly how it works."

"He doesn't need to," Nash said as he lifted an ancient-looking book up. "I know. It's all right here."

"Oh?"

"I suspect he's holding an excision circlet. Its primary use is to draw a soul out of a body so another can enter. As long as one retains possession of the object, they control the physical form they inhabit." He skimmed the page. "But it can also draw multiple souls into its center, leaving a body open for a spirit to possess, so be careful."

He didn't need to elaborate. If Damian's soul were drawn in and Spencer jumped into his body, he would possess unimaginable power at his fingertips.

"Informative. Thank you, Nash." The Aether's expression darkened, and the temperature dipped a good ten degrees. "Decimating the soul it is."

"Wait!" Spencer quickly withdrew the circlet and tossed it away. "Just wait, please!"

"Who did you intend to use this on next, Barlowe?"

"Him." He pointed to Lo. "Ebba doesn't love him. She's physically tied to him because of the wolf. But if I could possess his body, she might love me instead."

Oddly, Laszlo understood the man's pain and obsession. When he would've stepped forward, Ebba placed her hand on his arm.

"Let me." She walked to the edge of the barrier. "Spencer, I've loved Laszlo since I was sixteen years old. I only dated you because he was married, and I refused to do anything to destroy his happiness." Compassion softened her face. "That's what true love is. The willingness to bury your wants and desires so the other person can find their joy."

"But I love you, and if given a chance—"

"You're not hearing me. The answer will always be no. Remember our conversation in the car the night of the accident?" She hugged herself and shook her head, looking pained. "I tried to tell you then. I don't feel any chemistry with you. There's no love. Friendship would've been nice, but you wouldn't settle for that, and I had nothing more to offer you."

"It's the bond with the wolf. The excision circlet can remove her, too. Give me a chance," he begged.

"If she dies, Ebba dies, and with them, so does Laszlo," the Aether informed him. "You'd be killing three separate souls. You weren't paying attention that night."

"It's hard to hear the truth, isn't it?" Ebba asked Spencer softly.

His face crumbled before them, and tears filled his eyes. "Why can't you see we'd be perfect together?"

"Because we wouldn't be."

"What if I could take that feeling away?" Damian suggested, not unkindly. "It would allow you to move on without the earthly ties, and I can speak to the Goddess on your behalf. Perhaps they will allow you to reincarnate with your fated mate in the next life."

The light died from Spencer's eyes as he watched Ebba. "I *do* love you, Ebba."

"If that's true, let Damian help you move on so I can be happy." She dropped her arms, and her voice was raw when she said, "Please, Spencer. Let me be happy."

"Okay." He nodded his agreement.

The Aether glanced over his shoulder. "How do we neutralize the object and release McClutchin Adams, assuming he's still alive in there?"

"There's the catch. He has to reverse the spell."

Damian didn't appear pleased, but he faced Spencer. "Barlowe, are you willing to release your host while inside the protective circle?"

"Yes."

"Pick up the artifact and make the switch. If I detect any artifice or duplicity, I will destroy you immediately. Understood?" The Aether's no-nonsense tone left little doubt that he'd follow through on his promise.

"Understood."

"Good." With a nod toward the circlet, Damian said, "Proceed."

Spencer inched closer to the object as if afraid the Aether would go back on his word. Placing it against his throat, he said, "I release you from this hold, McClutchin Adams. Come forth from the prison to which I sent thee."

Sparkling lights filled the circle, obscuring their view, and Lo hated that he couldn't see what was going down. He prayed Damian and Alastair would sense deceit. When the shower of sparkles landed on the ground, Spencer's ghostly self stood beside Clutch.

"Thorne, you know him best. Please ask your friend a question only he'd know," Damian instructed.

Spencer appeared resigned, while Clutch was enraged. But there wasn't the standard malice in his gaze that Spencer always failed to hide. Satisfied the switch was made, he turned to Ebba. "Present a question only Spencer would know the answer to, and I'll do the same."

"Where did we first go to dinner?" she asked Spencer.

"We met for coffee or lunch. Once a movie, but no dinner."

She nodded. "That's right."

Turning to Clutch, Lo asked, "Where was our first training session?"

"The church graveyard, where I held services prior to my reaping career," his friend replied in a gravelly voice. "Now, can I throat punch this motherfucker or what?"

Lo laughed. "Yeah, that's Clutch."

"You still hold the excision circlet, Mr. Adams. Toss it to your left and step to your right with Mr. Barlowe." Damian put himself between Lo and the barrier. "Please usher the others to the far side of the room."

After he did as instructed, Lo rejoined him.

"You were meant to stay there, too," Damian said dryly. "You shouldn't be in temptation's path."

"I'm the last line of defense between him and Ebba."

"No. You're the reason she'll die if he finds a way to attack and kill you."

Lo swore, turned to go, and came face-to-face with Ebba. "What the hell are you doing?"

"He won't hurt me," she replied in a low voice with a glance beyond his shoulder. "But I want to put myself between him and Damian, just in case he tries something with the circlet."

"No."

"I wasn't asking, Lo."

"Ebba—"

"If he manages to trap the Aether's soul, he gains an undefeatable weapon." She placed her hands on her hips. "Tell me I'm wrong."

"You're not."

"Right. So if someone has to go, it should be me. Everyone is here because of my mess anyway."

He shoved his fists deep into his jeans pockets. "And what about me, Sweet? You go, I go, remember?"

"We'll beg the Goddess to pair us up again in the next life, if it comes to that."

He considered her words.

"Okay. You go, I go." Wrapping a hand around her neck, he hauled her close and kissed her hard. "I fucking love you and your warrior's spirit."

"I'm getting that impression." After delivering a saucy wink, she marched toward Damian.

32

"I can't let you risk yourself, my dear," Damian said as Ebba approached.

"I'm not asking," she said, repeating what she'd said to Lo. "Consider me your protective shield."

"I don't allow women to fight my battles." His tone was firm and his look unrelenting.

"Sexist much? I know you're old and all but…"

He rolled his eyes, and she grinned.

"Anyway, who said anything about fighting them? I'm here to make sure he stays in line." With a nod to Spencer, she asked, "I'm assuming we're not going to have a problem here, right?"

A wry smile curled his lips. "No, Ebba. No problem."

"My wolf will sense a lie and kick your ass, Spencer. You have to know that up front."

He nodded.

Inside, Kyrella grunted, and Ebba got the distinct impression the wolf wanted him to pull a fast one. Her disappointment traveled through their link.

"Sorry, Ky."

"Stay alert," Kyrella cautioned. *"I'll do the same."*

In the end, the warning wasn't needed.

Damian removed the protective barrier and booted the circlet across the room to Knox. "Melt that down, please."

"Gladly."

After picking up the object, Knox clasped Spring's hand and teleported away.

"I wanted to see him do that." Ebba was disappointed he didn't do it on the spot. She'd have loved to see his magic in action.

"He'll gladly show you, using another not-so-harmful item, I'm sure." The laughter in Damian's voice made her smile.

"Sorry. I'm a nerd."

"You're adorable, Ebba," he assured her. Facing Spencer and Clutch, he said, "Reap his soul, Adams, and keep him in a holding area until I can speak to Isis and the Fates. I intend to honor my promise to intervene on his behalf."

"Thank you, sir," Spencer said.

"I'm only doing this because I don't believe you're a bad man, Barlowe. Don't prove me wrong in the next life." With a tight smile, Damian said, "You can't help who you care about, but as Ms. James said, love is seeing to the other person's happiness. It isn't obsession or about harming them in your need to own."

Spencer swallowed, and his expression was pure misery. "I understand. I'll do my best."

"Do better than your best. Aethers live for centuries. I will find you and obliterate your soul should you ever harm another."

The reaping took seconds, and then Spencer was gone.

"What is something only Laszlo would know?" she asked Clutch.

"Clever," the Aether murmured.

With a grin, Clutch gestured Lo over. "You got a bright one here, man."

"Don't I know it," Lo said, smiling ear to ear.

"You didn't answer me, Clutch," she reminded him.

"Something only he would know… hmm." Narrowing his eyes, he studied her. A face-splitting grin appeared. "I got it. He once told me you were so sweet, his teeth ached to look at you."

When she looked up at Laszlo, it was to see him flush. "Really?" she asked, delighted he'd said something so romantic about her.

"That was supposed to be kept between us, you ass." Lo shoved him, but not hard enough to hurt. "You couldn't come up with another moment?"

"Meh, she should know you've always carried a torch for her."

"She's going to think I'm a scumbag because I was married to Charlotte," Lo countered with a scowl.

"Thornes only *truly* love once, Laszlo," Damian said with a laugh. "The fact you were pining for her while trying to stay faithful to another doesn't make you a bad person. Quite the opposite when the pull is strong between fated mates. Your control was admirable."

"Is it wrong to admit I like being the subject of your locker-room talk?" Ebba teased.

"Not locker room," Clutch said, clapping Lo on the back. "We were attempting to reap a serial killer. Your man wanted me to tell you in case he didn't make it through the mission."

Her heart thunked in her chest. "Oh!"

"It's true." Lo drew her away and tangled a finger in one of her curls.

"That wouldn't have been fair to Charlotte."

He shrugged. "Our marriage had already crumbled to dust. It wasn't going to hurt for you to know I cared."

"I'm glad we're here now. It feels like a dream, though."

"Why's that?" he asked gently.

"I'd always hoped we'd wind up together. In love."

"I'm glad, too, ya know."

Ebba wrapped her arms around his waist and leaned her forehead into his chest. "Will you be mad if I leave you to entertain everyone and go to bed? The shifting has taken a toll."

"Not at all. Go, Sweet. Get rest. I'll clean all this up."

She called a thank you to the others and went for a shower. Her need to cleanse the day from her skin and hair was more pressing than the promise of sleep. If she could scrub her soul clean of the worry and sadness she'd experienced, she'd do that, too.

"Thanks for the assist today, Ky."

Her wolf didn't answer, but the mutual understanding was there.

Sunlight peeked around the edges of her blackout curtains, and Ebba blinked, waiting for her eyes to adjust. She reached out, but she was alone, and no indentation appeared on the pillow. Clearly, he'd not shared her bed last night. As she lay there, she listened for an indication he might be somewhere else in the apartment.

Nothing.

No one.

"Gone," Kyrella confirmed.

Reaching through her familiar's bond with Laszlo, she realized she couldn't sense him. How close did he have to be for their link to work?

"He's not on this plane," her wolf said.

That tidbit of info had her shooting up and dragging jeans

over her ass. She didn't know what the hell it meant for him to be absent from the earthly plane, but it struck her as off.

Whipping open the bedroom door, she stopped short and squinted at the hulking figure sprawled facedown on her sofa. The white-blond hair gave him away.

"Alex?"

He grunted and pulled the lightweight throw blanket higher on his shoulder.

She pressed her fingers to her mouth to stem a giggle. The man looked absolutely ridiculous with his saggy-socked feet sticking past the end of the sofa.

"What are you doing on my couch?" Ebba asked.

"Babysitting," he muttered as he gave up on comfort and sat up.

"Why didn't you wake me and take the bed?"

"You looked too peaceful. I almost climbed in, but then I remembered your boyfriend's threat of castration if I went within an inch of you." He scrubbed his hands over his face and gave her a lopsided grin. "I'm going to conjure coffee. Want some?"

"I'd love a cup."

He rose, stretching and displaying the perfectly sculpted muscles of his expansive chest.

Her eyes developed a will of their own and refused to look away. If he called her out, she'd blame Kyrella and her base urge to mate.

"Not cool, Ebba."

"Sorry, Ky. A girl's got to do what a girl's got to do."

"And that means eye-fucking the Traveler?"

"I'm not—"

"Sure, keep lying to yourself," the wolf scoffed.

"Shut up."

Kyrella's silent amusement came through as loud as her voice.

"Where's Lo?" Ebba blurted, ripping her eyes away as he wrapped the blanket around his hips. With his muscled thighs exposed, it was apparent he wasn't wearing pants. Her brain was playing the guessing game of boxers or briefs.

Blue eyes dancing, he strutted toward her, laughing when she gulped. "I won't tell him you find me attractive, but you might want to work on your poker face when he's around."

"Shut up and conjure that coffee already," she ordered, climbing onto the island and bracing her back against the wall.

"You like being up high?"

"I must've been a cat in a previous life," she said, smiling as Kyrella growled.

"How do you want it, love?"

For one heart-stopping moment, she thought he meant sex.

"Mind out of the gutter!" she scolded herself.

"At this point, I'm enjoying the show," her wolf replied.

"Ebba?"

She shook her head, attempting to focus on Castor. "Sorry."

"No problem. Sugar? Cream?"

"Just a dash of the vanilla creamer in the fridge, please."

As if her ghostly self still existed, the refrigerator door opened, and the container floated through the air before settling on the counter beside the mugs.

"Did you do that?" she asked in awe.

He chuckled. "Yeah, I'm lazy in the mornings. I prefer to conjure breakfast in bed and feed tempting morsels to my partner rather than expend the energy on other, less-interesting tasks."

As she sipped her coffee, she considered the scenarios for why Castor might sleep over. He'd mentioned babysitting, and she suspected he meant her.

"Where did Laszlo go, and why?"

"To testify at Spencer Barlowe's tribunal." Castor held his hand over an empty platter and produced a heaping mound of bacon, cooked to perfection. Not one limp or burnt slice in the batch! Next, he formed a U with his hands, and from the flat of his palms sprung a wicker basket full of steaming muffins. "I hope you like blueberry. If you prefer another kind..."

"Nope. Blueberry is my favorite."

"He knows because I told him that," Lo said, appearing from nowhere. "Don't let him con you."

Ebba gasped, and her amulet fired up as Kyrella bristled.

"Easy, Ky," Lo said in a soothing voice. "Sorry to startle you."

"What the fuck? How did you do that?" Ebba glanced between the guys, noting Castor's smirk. "That wasn't a teleport!"

"Actually, I *did* teleport, but you'd already left the bedroom. I saw you eyeballing the playboy's chest, so I thought I'd let you have your fun." Lo laughed and caught the muffin she chucked at his head. "Granny Thorne's cloaking spell seemed harmless enough."

"Did you know he was there, Alex?" she demanded.

Castor grinned as he bit into his bacon. "I suspected."

"*Assholes.*"

"Why do you think I put on the show?" After giving her a mischievous wink, he addressed Lo. "How did the tribunal go?"

"They gave him a pardon for reincarnation. The issue of a future mate was still up in the air when I left."

"That was fast," Ebba said.

Lo frowned, and she got an uneasy feeling.

"Uh, how long do you think you slept, Sweet?"

"Six, eight hours, maybe."

"You were asleep for over twenty hours, love," Castor said gently. "Laszlo got worried and called Damian, but he said you needed the rest."

Dropping a kiss on her temple, Lo snatched a handful of bacon from the platter. "He said eventually it would even out, but extended activity this close to Kyrella's takeover may require longer recovery periods."

"Since Laszlo was required at the trial for Barlowe, he asked me to watch over you."

"It felt like leaving a fox in charge of the henhouse, but Liz and Rafe were off on an anniversary trip," Lo added, shooting a wry glance Castor's way. "When I asked Al, he assured me the fox could be trusted."

"And I was a fucking Boy Scout. Your girl was undressing me with her eyes, though."

"I saw that." Lo laughed when she glared. "She's sex-starved. I'll have to do something about that."

Ebba's face flamed. "I hate you both."

"Nah. Not even a little." He scooped her up in his arms. "Grab that basket of muffins." As he headed for the bedroom, he called over his shoulder, "Thanks for watching over her, Castor. Now don't let the door hit you in the ass!"

Before they reached their destination, pounding alerted them to a visitor.

"Dammit!" Lo glanced at her. "Do we ignore it?"

"It sounds urgent—"

Castor's voice boomed a greeting from the hallway.

"I have a like-hate relationship with that man," Lo muttered as he spun and returned to the main room.

Ebba bit her lip to hold in her laughter. "He probably answered to thwart your plans."

"Hence the hate."

33

"Wilder?"

The arrival of his brother confused Laszlo. He'd been reclusive since Abbie's fall, never intentionally seeking out anyone. Yet here he was, hat in hand—literally—and shifting his weight from foot to foot.

"What is it?" Ebba asked, expressive face filled with concern.

Lo was positive she avoided asking his brother if he was all right, knowing the answer she'd get would be a resounding no.

"I have a favor to ask you, Ebba," Wilder said, continuing his embarrassed shuffle. "You can say no, but I hope you'll consider it."

"Of course." She patted Lo's chest as an indication she wanted down. Once free, she hugged Wilder. "What can I do?"

A fond smile flitted across his too-solemn face, but it never reached his eyes. "You may want to wait until I explain before saying yes," he warned.

With an impatient wave of her hand, she led him to the kitchen table and shoved the basket of muffins in front of him.

"You can tell me over breakfast. Do you still take your coffee black?"

"How does she know how he takes his coffee?" Castor asked in an aside. "Should we be worried your brother's honing in on our girl?"

"I hate you," Lo growled, equally as soft.

With a sputtered laugh, Castor returned to the kitchen to fetch a coffee cup and the platter of bacon. After setting it down in front of Wilder, he said, "If you want anything else, you'll have to conjure it yourself."

"I'm good. Thanks."

"If this is family business, I can leave you to it."

"Actually, I'd like you to stay, Mr. Castor," Wilder said. "I'm beginning to suspect something else was off about the day our magic went on the blink and could use another perspective."

They gathered around the table and waited for Wilder to make his request. He relayed the tale of his and Abbie's climb, pausing now and again to swallow his grief. When he got to the part where the equipment failed, he buried his face in his hands.

Lo, Ebba, and Castor waited him out, letting him finish in his own time.

"With no magic, I couldn't save her," Wilder said roughly. "And as Lo knows, we never found her body." He turned beseeching eyes to Ebba. "It's been a long time, and it could be a fool's errand, but will you search in your wolf form?"

"She's not a fucking rescue dog," Lo snapped.

Ebba placed a soothing hand on his wrist. "I'll do it."

He shook his head. "No way. You have zero climbing experience. How will your wolf manage those mountain passes alone? It's stupid to try."

"I'll be with her," Wilder assured him. "I'll rig up slings and extra safety measures. We'll go when the weather conditions are perfect."

"You're risking her life! Wasn't Abbie's death enough to tell you that fucking mountain is too dangerous?" Laszlo retorted.

His brother recoiled, and the hopeful light his eyes held was snuffed out. The standard bright amber color was tarnished brown.

Ebba shot up from her chair, an avenging angel with flashing eyes and a fierce growl. It shocked Lo to realize her fury was directed at *him*.

"Get out!" she snapped.

"What?"

"How fucking insensitive can you be?" She shoved his chest. "I said go! You can come back when you apologize to Wilder for being a dick."

"Jaysus, I think I love you, Ebba James," Castor said with a broad, appreciative grin. "Fierce and beautiful, what an intoxicating combinat—I'm shutting up now," he assured her when she turned her anger on him, adding a mimed lip zip.

Lo shoved back the chair as he rose. "You're being ridic—"

"Don't say it," Wilder warned under his breath with a kick to the shin. "Trust me, man. You don't want to go there."

Ebba crossed her arms and narrowed her eyes. "No. By all means, Laszlo, say what's on your mind."

Both Castor and Wilder frantically shook their heads, panic on their faces. He ignored them to focus on her.

"You want me to tell you I think you're being ridiculous? Fine. I do."

"Because I refuse to allow disrespect in my home? Or because I intend to help your brother?"

He closed his eyes and sighed. "The second one." He splayed his arms wide. "I love you, Ebba. I don't want to see you risk your life on an unstable mountain. We've searched."

Looking at his brother, he silently urged him to take back the request.

Wilder remained silent, dogged about finding Abigail to the last.

"Come on, man. Don't make me out to be the bad guy here. Tell her, Wilder. We searched and searched. We scryed. When our magic was restored, Liz and I went up there with you and did everything we could to clear the peaks and weather just to get a better view." Lo squeezed his brother's shoulder. "Tell her there was no trace. We found a few deceased climbers, but none were Abbie."

Wilder shut his eyes and nodded his confirmation.

"Ebba, Sweet, I'd never forbid you to do what you think is best." Lo was solemn and sincere. "Hell, you'd castrate me if I tried. But the risk is great for no chance at a reward."

"I dreamed she spoke to me through Ebba," Wilder croaked.

Castor leaned his elbows on the table and gave them all a considering look. Only he and Laszlo knew it wasn't a dream. Abbie had reached across the void and communicated through Ebba's spirit. Surely that meant something, right?

"What are you thinking?" Lo asked Castor.

"I'm intrigued by the mystery, and I'm bored enough to help." He grinned. "Count me in, Thornes!"

Hope once again filled Wilder's face, and the emotion was contagious. Laszlo felt the flutter in his chest as he considered the Traveler's usefulness. He locked eyes with Ebba, but addressed his brother.

"I'm sorry for being a dick, Wilder."

She uncrossed her arms and raised a brow.

"And I'm sorry for saying you're being ridiculous, Sweet Ebba," he added for her. "I'm scared for you."

Her stance softened, and her lips curled in half smile. "Was that so bad?" she teased.

Holding his index finger and thumb an inch apart, he shrugged.

"I have questions," Castor said. "The first one is for you,

Wilder. Was your girlfriend a witch? If so, why didn't she teleport?"

"No. Her mother was mortal, and she never knew her father. But she had no powers to speak of."

"It wouldn't have mattered," Lo added. "Anyone near us that day had their powers subdued. Had she been a witch, and she was within touching distance, she couldn't have teleported."

"But she fell down a mountain. At some point, she'd have been far enough away to save herself," Castor countered. He paused, seeming to consider all the information. "Can we talk to her mother? I'd like to get a sense of who Abigail was." He leaned forward when Wilder frowned. "At the very least, if I've ever encountered the mother or your girlfriend, I may be able to travel back to that time. Possibly warn one or both."

"Do you remember every face you've seen?" Ebba asked, eyes wide with wonder.

"Yes. Every interaction, too. It's a curse."

"What if we speak to Death?" Lo suggested. "She's your son's mother, right? She might be inclined to help us locate Abbie on the other side."

"She's not dead!" Wilder snapped. All eyes focused on him. "I'd feel it. Here." He pressed his hand to his chest. "She's not dead."

"May I see her picture?" Castor asked gently.

"Oh, wait! I have one!" Ebba raced to the mantle and returned with a framed photo. "Here."

Castor looked ill.

"Her mother," he ground out, expression tightening. "What's her name?"

"Beth Monroe," Wilder said, watching him closely. "Why?"

Castor repositioned the frame for them to see. "The blonde is Abigail, I presume."

Laszlo's jaw dropped. How had he never realized Castor was an older, male version of Abbie? He glanced at Ebba, who plunked down in her seat and covered her mouth. Their gazes met, then turned to Wilder.

"You guessed?" Lo asked his brother.

"I came here to ask Ebba's wolf to see what she could find. When he opened the door, I knew," Wilder said, his attention never wavering from Castor's grim face. "You and Beth had an affair, didn't you?"

"I'd have thought the picture was enough evidence for you. You're asking for a DNA match?"

"What does that mean for her?" Lo asked. "Wouldn't she have similar abilities to yours?"

"I don't know. One would think she'd be powerful, but that's not how magic works. Sometimes it's diluted. There are those with witch DNA whose powers never develop." Castor rubbed the back of his neck as he studied the image. "I can't believe Beth never told me."

"How could she? Weren't you in hiding for years?" Ebba asked. She clasped Castor's free hand, giving it a squeeze.

Lo's heart swelled in his chest. She was nothing if not kind, and her innate need to comfort those in need was what he loved most about her.

"Yes. I suppose you're right." Castor exhaled a heavy sigh. "How old is she? Abbie."

Wilder sipped his coffee and swallowed hard. "She would be forty-one next week."

"Older than Quentin," Castor mused. His lids slammed shut. "Christ! I need to tell my son he had a sister."

"Has," Wilder stressed. "Has a sister."

The Traveler's ice-blue eyes were filled with regret as he stared back at him. "If she's alive, I'll find her, Thorne. Get some rest. We leave tomorrow morning for the mountain." He stood and hugged Ebba. "You won't be needed on this trip, love. I've got it covered."

EPILOGUE

"Have you heard from Castor or Wilder?"

Dropping the crystal on the map, Laszlo straightened and turned to welcome Ebba with their standard hug and kiss.

"No, Sweet. Still no news."

Two months had passed with no word from either man. They'd gone up the mountain the day after Spencer's tribunal and never returned. No amount of scrying or spellwork revealed their whereabouts, and Lo feared the worst.

Ebba's concern mirrored his. "We should go. I've been watching the forecast, and we're still within the safe-weather window."

A flush climbed his neck, and her eyes narrowed.

"You already went up there, didn't you?" she asked. Her voice lacked condemnation, and Lo felt comfortable revealing the truth.

"Yes." He carried her grocery bags to the kitchen counter and began unloading them. "Alastair, Damian, and I went two days ago. Kyrella helped."

Mid-process of putting cans in the pantry, she spun to face him and scowled. "Why didn't you ask me before the shift?"

"I wasn't trying to hide anything from you, Sweet. You'd already agreed to help when Wilder initially asked. Three nights ago, Francesca's traveling globe lit up, and Quentin went to Alastair."

Her expression cleared of ire, replaced by curiosity. "Francesca? Alastair's granddaughter?"

Lo nodded.

"She's a Traveler, too?"

"According to Quentin, yes. The night my spirit returned from the past, Castor told me father and daughter had changed a timeline. Apparently, Frankie—that's what Quentin and Holly call her—used an object entrusted to her by Athena to save her dad."

"A mysterious glowing globe." Ebba snorted and returned to putting away groceries. "Those things keep popping up."

"It would seem so." Laszlo hugged her from behind and dropped a kiss on her exposed neck. "Did you get my cereal?"

"As if I'd forget. You eat that shit morning, noon, and night. And before you asked, I got the family-sized box."

He laughed and turned her to face him. "Have I told you how much I love living with you?"

"Yes, and stop trying to change the subject. I want to know what led you to take Ky up the mountain."

"Quentin can't touch the globe. For some mystical reason, it only works for Frankie. But like her, he can peer into it. He saw Castor and Wilder head into a portal, and it appeared to be located at the base of the mountain."

"Ohmygod, Lo! That's huge!" She frowned as she watched him. "Isn't it?"

"It would be if we could find it. But we couldn't. Not even a signature, which is fucking weird. Damian should've been able to sense that, at least." Feeling defeated, he grabbed the box of cereal from the bag and poured a bowl. "I'm worried, Sweet. If Castor and Wilder were able, they'd be back by now. Both Damian and Al agree."

Ebba handed him the milk jug. "Don't lose faith. Castor seems self-serving, but he's street smart and fast when it comes to thinking on his feet."

He glanced up sharply. "That's exactly what Damian said."

"Yeah, I'm just repeating what Kyrella relayed to me."

"Wait! When did she say that?"

"When I left for the grocery store. She told me all about your trip." Ebba bit his earlobe. "Jerk."

Laszlo drew her onto his lap. "I'm sorry. I should've said something before now."

"I understand why you didn't." Wrapping her arms around his neck, she buried her face against his throat. "I'm sorry about Wilder, Lo."

"Yeah. I keep praying to the Goddess that he's with Abbie." He swallowed hard. "I don't know what I'd do if that happened to you, Ebba."

She drew back and smiled tenderly. "You'd do whatever it takes. You did, if you recall."

Leaning in, he kissed her, and her eager response filled his heart with joy. Following on the heels of his happiness were sadness and guilt. Did he deserve to feel this way when his brother was suffering?

Ebba gripped his face between her hands. "Tomorrow, we'll try again, okay? We'll search every day until we find them and bring them home. Abbie included."

"I don't deserve you," he whispered roughly.

"Meh. Maybe not, but you're stuck with me."

She surprised a laugh out of him.

"No, Sweet. I meant that you're too good for me. Not the other way around."

"I knew what you meant. Either way, you're stuck with me."

He nipped her lip. "And I'm a happier man for it."

"You always know the perfect thing to say."

***

TWO MONTHS EARLIER

WILDER'S HEART WAS IN HIS THROAT AS HE STARED AT THE pulsing blue wall centered on the rock. "What the fuck is that?"

"A portal." Castor's tone was as grim as his expression. "Fuck, I hate portals."

"They're bad?"

"You watch movies, boyo. Ever see where they led to anything good?"

The urge to laugh was weirdly strong, but Wilder suppressed it. In the short time he'd come to know Abbie's father, he understood where her sarcastic humor and unstoppable drive originated.

"She's alive, sir," he told Castor. "I feel it."

"I'm counting on that feeling to help us find her." The older man focused his determined, ice-blue eyes on Wilder. "And no matter what happens on the other side of that door, you find her and get her out of there. Got it?"

"You're not sounding too optimistic about your chances."

"I'm a survivor, boyo, so don't worry about me. But my goal is for you and my daughter to return here in one piece."

"That's good because that's my goal, too," Wilder assured him.

A wry smile curled Castor's lips as he drew back his long white-blond hair and tied it in a ponytail. "Be prepared for anything and utilize your magic if you have to."

Wilder nodded, facing the pulsing portal with determination. "I'll do whatever it takes. Abbie's coming home."

"Don't let go of my hand until I tell you, Thorne. Traveling is an art form, and if you get lost in time, no one is going to save you."

"Noted."

"Let's go."

Thanks for taking the time to read CAPTIVATING MAGIC. I hope you enjoyed it, and I'd really love it if you'd leave a review.

The next story in The Thorne Witches® series will be DISCOVERED MAGIC, featuring—*you guessed it*—Wilder and Abigail.

CLICK HERE to reserve your copy!

BOOKS BY T.M. CROMER

Get your printable list [here](#)!

PARANORMAL ROMANCE

The Thorne Witches® Series:
SUMMER MAGIC
AUTUMN MAGIC
WINTER MAGIC
SPRING MAGIC
REKINDLED MAGIC
LONG LOST MAGIC
FOREVER MAGIC
ESSENTIAL MAGIC
MOONLIT MAGIC
ENCHANTED MAGIC
CELESTIAL MAGIC
EVERLASTING MAGIC
CAPTIVATING MAGIC
DISCOVERED MAGIC

The Thorne Witches: Happily Ever Afters Series:
ENDURING MAGIC
BOUNDLESS MAGIC

The Unlucky Charms Series:
PINTS & POTIONS

WHISKEY & WITCHES

BEER & BROOMSTICKS

COCKTAILS & CAULDRONS

WINE & WARLOCKS

HIGHBALLS & HEXES

The Sentinels of Magic Series:

THE AETHER

THE DEATH DEALER

THE SEER

THE TRAVELER

The Angels of Legend Series:

LUCIFER

CONTEMPORARY & ROMANTIC SUSPENSE

The Stonebrooke Series:

BURNING RESOLUTION

HIDDEN RESOLUTION

The Holt Family Series:

GOODBYE TO YOU

THIS TIME YOU

INCLUDING YOU

A LIFE WITH YOU

The Fiore Vineyard Series:

PICTURE THIS

RETURN HOME

ONE WISH

ABOUT THE AUTHOR

T.M. Cromer is a multi award-winning, bestselling author, who loves to craft wildly entertaining stories designed to keep you glued to your seat, turning the pages to find out what the hell happens next. She specializes in kickass heroines and the men who adore them.

Genres she writes include paranormal romance and romantic suspense.

Want to stay up to date on what's happening in the world of T.M. Cromer? Subscribe to her newsletter or text JOIN to 1-877-795-1526 to receive release news and promo alerts.

You can also join her VIP reader group on Facebook to chat with her, participate in polls, or just keep current on what's happening. Become a member today!

FOLLOW T.M. CROMER:

facebook.com/tmcromer
instagram.com/tmcromer
tiktok.com/@tmcromer
pinterest.com/tmcromer
amazon.com/stores/T.M.-Cromer/author/B011QK3WXY